THE BLOODY MAIDEN

First Printing, January 2021

ISBN 978-1-913716-08-0 (Hardback)

ISBN 978-1-913716-10-3 (eBook)

ISBN 978-1-913716-09-7 (Paperback)

Cover Design & Map Artwork By: ArtbyKhuggs

Illustrations By: James Mitchell

Published by Ink & Fable Publishing, Ltd.

For Lincoln ~
My first and forever, my greatest accomplishment.

And Seamus ~
For inspiring me to write it in the first place.
I wouldn't be here without your influence and inspiration
as a teacher.

THE
BLOODY
MAIDEN

WRITTEN BY
S.M. MITCHELL

INK & FABLE PUBLISHING

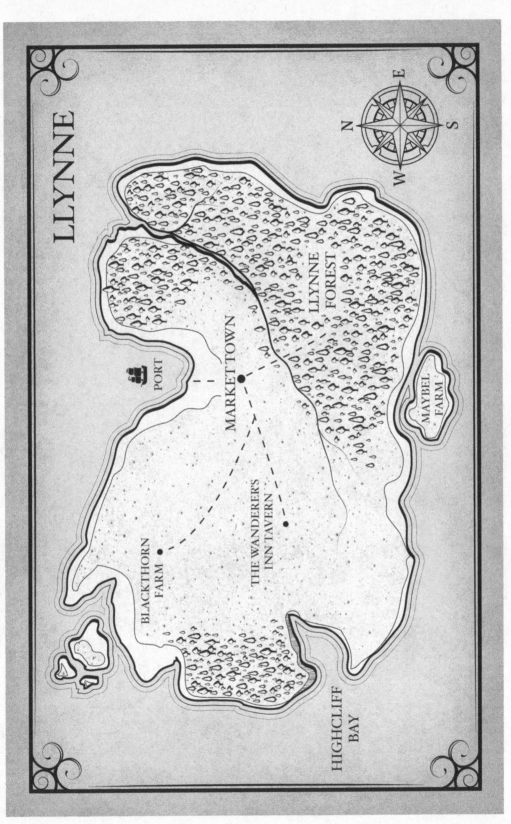

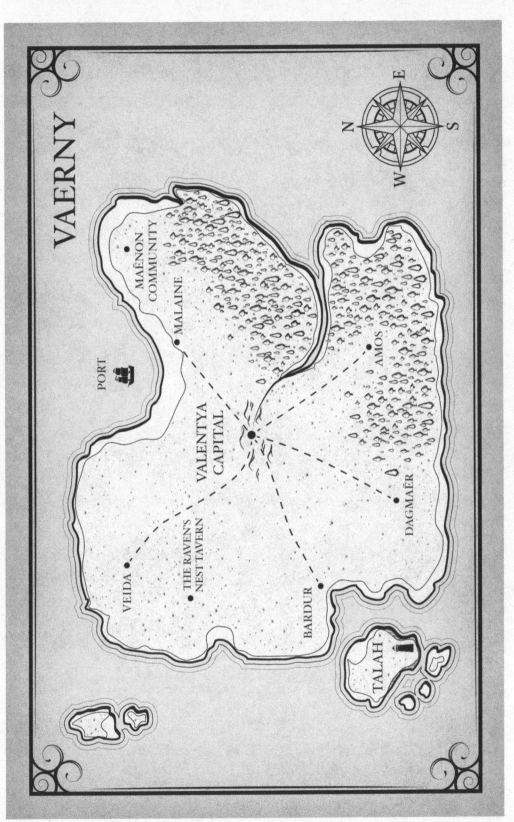

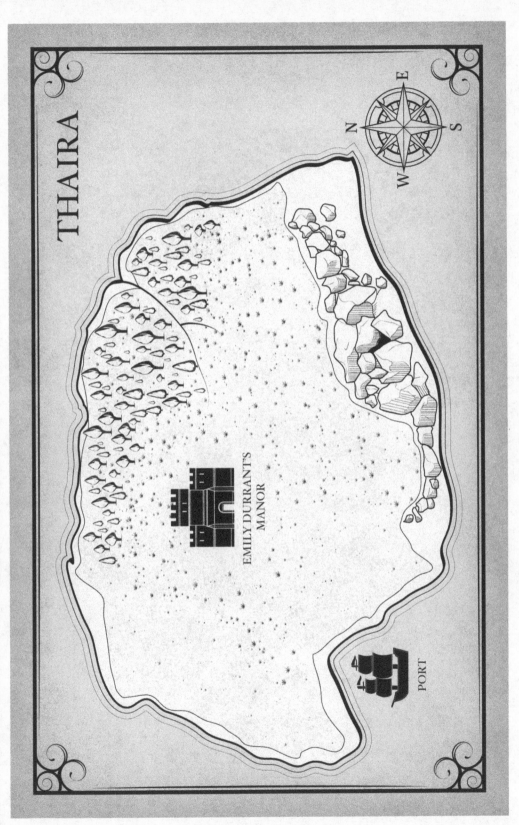

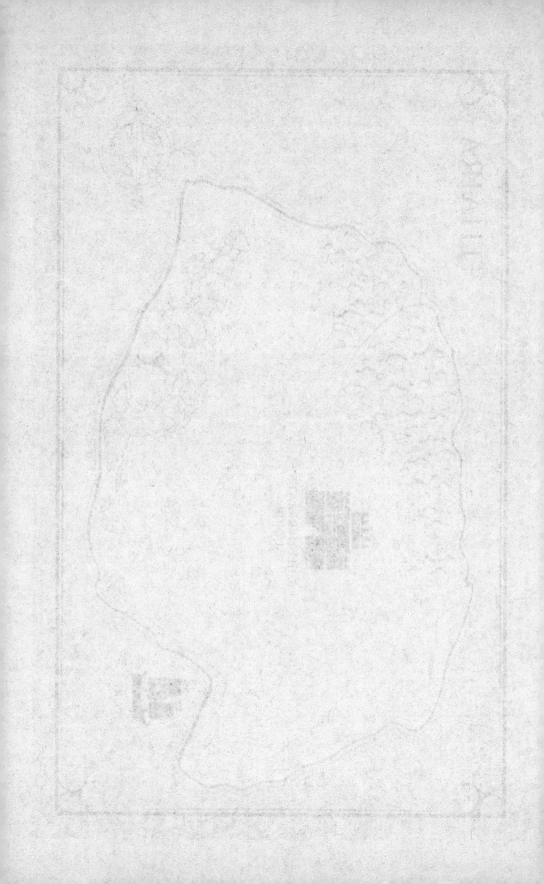

1

THE WANDERER'S INN

"**B**ring yourself and another bottle over here, darling," the man slurred as his drink sloshed over his arm.

Prudence bit back a sigh and grabbed another bottle of rum from behind the bar, jolting as Mrs. Langley threw another drunkard out the door, her voice guttural and rough. The sodden mud splashed onto his clothes as he hit the ground.

Mrs. Langley was a plump, stumpy woman with a short fuse. Her clothes stretched around her sides and Prudence could smell the vomit and alcohol seeping from the old woman's pores as she squeezed around her. She reminded Prudence of a sow.

Prudence held her breath as the old woman snapped. "Hurry up girl, stop dawdling!" Mrs. Langley scowled at her, her eyebrows lowered so far that Prudence was surprised that her face didn't stay that way. "Standing around like that won't get any work done. If ya can't crack on down here, then maybe I should send you upstairs with the rest of the whores!"

Prudence hurried back out to the table and slammed five drinks down, scurrying away before any wastrels had a chance to grab her—as they so frequently did. She swept the mangled mess of black hair out of her eyes as she caught sight of Eleanora stood by the bar, assessing the room like a wolf watching its prey. Prudence wandered over to join her.

The other girls fanned out from the stairway to swarm the room like vultures. Many of them spoke to Elea on passing, greeting one another as they got to work. They took one look at Prudence beside her and eyed her carefully.

"Don't let them get to you, Pru." Elea smiled, dimples showing at the corners of her mouth. "The men want you; you could earn more." Eleanora's face, naturally warm in tone, housed a hundred freckles. They were like little constellations dotting her cheeks. Her brown eyes had always made Prudence uneasy. They seemed to look deep inside her and know exactly what she was thinking, even if Prudence didn't know herself.

Prudence rolled her eyes. "I'd rather die. No offense." She knew Eleanora had no other means of living but she would never consider it—she had more dignity than that. She pitied Elea, and so Pru's resolve to rescue her from their life grew stronger every day.

And Prudence... Prudence just wanted *more*. There must be more to life than what she had. Slaving away for a place to sleep was not living. It was merely surviving... and barely at that. The endless days of abhorrent men leering at her, Mrs. Langley accosting her, and the pitiful amount of food she received, had led to Prudence becoming wistful of any escape. By whatever means necessary.

The cliffs surrounding the bay were high enough, and it was only a short walk from the tavern. A wide stretch of heathland led out towards an enclosed bay, so clear that you could almost see the bottom. Occasionally, on walks when the sun was out, Prudence had stepped right up to the edge and peered over, thinking that if somebody had just *pushed her,* she would be away from all of this by now.

Some days, Prudence imagined strangling Mrs. Langley until she turned purple. Prudence pictured the expression on Mrs. Langley's face when she, for once, was not the one in control, the panic on her wretched old face, wrinkles so deep that they looked like they had been carved with a knife.

The slam of a hand on the bar next to her distracted Prudence from her indulgent thoughts of murder and back to the present. The man scowled at her.

"Are you deaf? I said I want another drink," he spat. His face was covered in dirt and grime and the stench of animal shit assaulted Prudence's senses.

"You useless harlot! Get on with it!" he hissed in her face. A loud crack rendered the rest of the room silent as they turned to stare at the man, now with a red hand mark across his cheek, and to Prudence who stood stock-still, a flare of rage still coursing through her.

She had hit him. He had deserved it, but she had hit him. This would be bad, Mrs. Langley would be furious.

She drew her hand back and shoved it into the pocket of her apron. *Bollocks.* She stared at the floor as Mrs. Langley stomped around the corner to see what the fuss was about.

"The stupid bitch hit me!" he pointed a grubby fat finger at Prudence, his face now completely red with anger. Prudence could see the fury and humiliation in his eyes. She knew that he couldn't believe someone so low would disrespect him, so low and a woman at that.

Mrs. Langley hauled Prudence by the arm into the back room. As soon as they stepped through the sloping doorway, her hand flew round to meet Prudence's cheek once, twice, and thrice again.

"You foolish girl!" she screeched. "How dare you act in such a way? You are a serving girl, a wench, nothing more! You shall learn your place or so help me; I will throw you back out there to die in the gutter!"

A few tears slipped out of Prudence's bright blue eyes. The area around her eyes and nose stung and would no doubt be bruised, again. Her hands came up, instinctively, to protect her face from any more harm, quaking slightly from the shock of it all. Mrs. Langley tutted and pushed past her, back to the main room to appease the bullish man.

With the admonishments finally over and panic clouding her judgement, Prudence left the tavern and ran down towards the shore, her face reddened and sore from the landlady's beating. It was a regular occurrence; any slip up would result in a nasty blow to her face or body, either by Mrs. Langley's hands or something heavy that she had to hand at the time.

4

Rage pulsed in her veins until it almost overwhelmed her. Controlling her emotions had never been easy. She kicked herself for lashing out; huffing and grumbling as she threw rocks into the waves. Walking along the shoreline and up towards the cliffs, birds sang, and the evening had a beautiful orange glow shining out from the horizon. The last speck of light fighting back against the overbearing dark.

The waves beat against the cliff walls, and gulls called from their nests as the crisp air carried the scent of salt and seaweed. The bay down below glimmered as the light bounced off the rippling water like shoals of little fish swimming frantically in every direction.

Prudence plonked herself down, closed her eyes, and listened to the *whoosh* and *crash* of the waves colliding with the rock, as it moved back and forth in its little pen. Eventually, darkness fell over the little island like smog, but Prudence stayed where she was. Soon, the stars appeared and the moon came out, casting a white glow across the rugged landscape.

"Stupid, so stupid. You should know better," she groaned to herself. Every day it was the same menial life, the same tiresome people, the same hideous comments, yet it still enraged her.

The sound of the waves grew louder as the sea grew angry. Standing at the very edge, with her toes teetering off the cliff, Prudence looked out at the world below her and saw only hell. A cage she would have to live in until the day that she died. Life would never change; the people would never change. She was, and always would be, a serving girl in a small tavern, of no importance to anyone. This could all be over in one easy movement, she told herself.

Jump.

No longer would she have to endure the disgusting hands of grotesque men. No longer would she have to endure the beatings of a woman so bitter and spiteful. It could all be over.

Jump.

The life she had always dreamed of was so far out of reach, that Prudence could no longer feel it. It would be over quickly.

Jump.

She felt so hollow. The light inside her dimmed more each and every day. *Jump, jump, jump.* The thought pounded in her head, but Eleanora...

Eleanora deserved better, she needed better, and by the gods she would get it no matter what Prudence had to do. Prudence would find her escape, she assured herself, but it would be an escape she could share. She stepped away from the edge and collapsed on the ground, breathing heavily.

Feeling furious at her moment of weakness, she stood up and made her way back to the tavern. She needed to sleep, to rest her weary head and forget these foolish thoughts. Too often Prudence found herself filled with anger at the end of the day. And she had endless reasons to be angry at the world. Alcohol and opium helped clear her mind and help to push the anger into the dark corners of her mind, and they stayed there, at least until the next day.

"Pathetic," Prudence chastised herself, regretting her

brief insanity. How would Eleanora cope if she found her friend dead? It had been a selfish thought. A selfish thought that Prudence would try her best to ignore from now on.

This was not the life that she yearned for. But life would never be what she dreamt. Prudence's world was a mess of shattered pieces on the floor, puzzle pieces that would never fit together.

MRS. LANGLEY STOOD IN THE KITCHEN DOORWAY, LANTERN in hand, as she peered out towards the surrounding heath. Prudence could see the light flicker as it swung in the slight breeze that had picked up. She could see the rough, sagging face of Mrs. Langley through the sea mist that had descended upon them. She was looking for Prudence. It was late and she had run out without leave; no doubt there would be trouble waiting for her. Mrs. Langley finally caught sight of her in the dark and beckoned for Prudence to come inside.

The kitchen was damp inside and it stank of piss. Straw lay scattered over the stone slabs that Prudence had so diligently washed the day before. She frowned. George, the tavern cook, lay across sacks of grain in a drunken sleep, a bottle still clutched in his scabby paw. A volcanic snore erupted from his throat and he rolled over, shifting the sacks underneath him to the point of nearly bursting them under his weight. The bottle dropped from his grip with a clink and rolled across the floor to Prudence's feet.

Mrs. Langley dragged Prudence, nails dug into her

wrist, through the kitchen and up the stairs to her office. The silence was far more terrifying than if the old lady had screamed at her. She unhooked a huge ring of keys from her waistband and unlocked the door, stepping aside to let Prudence in. A mostly bare room, made more obvious with an oversized wooden desk placed in the centre. A quill, ink, and paper lay unused on its pockmarked surface. A cabinet sat in the corner with the topmost cupboard locked up tight, where the brutish landlady kept their wages.

"I'm docking yer pay." Mrs. Langley announced, her brow furrowed and lips pursed.

Prudence's head snapped up; eyes locked with Mrs. Langley in challenge. "Beg pardon?" She could feel the anger rise up inside her again like the bile in her throat. This was the last thing she needed after the day she had endured.

"I'm docking pay. The trouble you caused t'night lost me business." She narrowed her eyes at Prudence and chucked a bag of coins into her hands. It felt considerably lighter than usual. A week's worth of work, knocked down to a few hours pay, all for a little disturbance.

"I hardly think tha's fair!"

"If it happens again, you'll be back on the street faster than you can blink. Unless o' course you've reconsidered working for coin, *on yer back*."

Prudence caught Mrs. Langley's eye; she knew what Prudence thought on the matter. She'd sooner be kicked out than be one of her whores. The harlots were composed of anything but self-respect; sleeping with anyone able to pay the meagre two pieces it cost. Moans

8

and grunts could be heard from the rooms beside Mrs. Langley's office as Prudence left. She stomped past the many rooms used by the whores towards her bedroom.

Caroline stepped out of the room closest to Prudence, and wrapped a shawl around her bare chest, a handful of coins clutched in her spindly fingers. She slipped past Prudence and down the steps to the landlady's office, shooting a look of contempt in her direction. Like most of the girls, Caroline considered Prudence to be supercilious. The prostitutes avoided her like the plague, all except for Eleanora. Prudence sighed and opened the door to her minuscule room and let her tired body drop onto the bed to sleep.

A HARSH KNOCK AT THE DOOR MADE PRUDENCE LIFT HER head, still dazed from sleep, before her head once again hit the pillow, the world back in darkness. Prudence barely registered the sound of rushed footsteps coming closer until Mrs. Langley's voice rang out right next to her. Her face loomed into Prudence's vision, too close for comfort, and Prudence could not help but stare at the wart under her nose and the sweat that lined her forehead.

"Get up girl! Get yourself downstairs. We've a load coming in that requires storing," Mrs. Langley ripped the moth-eaten covers from the bed, letting the frigid air of the early morning brush Prudence's skin. "Make haste!" cried Mrs. Langley before bustling out of the room, a sack of coins in her plump fist—no doubt for the business downstairs.

Sitting up, Prudence's head rushed and she promptly vomited onto the floor. She would have to clean that up later. Prudence sat there for a moment, a fleck of bile still on her chin, until the spots left her eyes and she could see almost clearly again. The smell of the room, heavy with incense, filled her nostrils and made her retch again, but there was nothing left to come out.

Downstairs, the back door into the kitchen was propped open wide and Prudence lugged a hogshead barrel of tobacco through and into the pantry. The landlady didn't like to spend her money in the town when she might pay half for stolen goods. Though the business was risky, Mrs. Langley preferred to rely upon smugglers to provide her with the finest silks, tobacco, and sugar. The merchants often kept the best of the goods to sell on themselves, and this way, Mrs. Langley ensured that she obtained the finest that was on offer.

The men stood outside, their faces obscured in the dawn mist, with lamps by their sides, and a cart full of barrels and boxes. They worked off the coast of Llynne and throughout the Western Tides. Most of the stolen goods were shifted through corrupt merchants willing to sell on the illegal product. Prudence disliked being roped into dealing with these men. Mrs. Langley avoided the dealings as much as possible, though only for fear of being seen to be associating with them. She was forever thinking of self-preservation.

Despite the separation that Llynne had from its mainland Vaerny, the townspeople were still loyal to their governor and his ambition to rid the seas of piracy and smuggling. Khari, the man who spoke and dealt with buyers, handed the final barrel over to Prudence, who struggled under its weight. His thick dreadlocked hair was pulled back behind his head. With his hair away from his face, his features stood out even more than normal. Beautiful brown eyes, sharp cheekbones and full lips that often held a smirk.

"Tha's the last of 'em. And the paymen'?" Khari's Ta'ih accent was heavy and guttural.

Prudence grabbed the sack of coins and pearls off the worktop and handed it to the man. His dark skin brushed against hers, making Prudence look even more pale than usual. Prudence's skin was as close to ivory as it could possibly be. The pale skin, coupled with hair as black as crow feathers that came almost to her hips, made her look washed out. Almost ghost-like in the lack of colour. It made her stand out on their little island where most of the people had a ruddy complexion, worn from weather, and outdoor labour.

"That should be the right amount. By all means check, but the landlady is careful when it comes to lookin' after her money."

Avery, the other man, cast a glance at Prudence before opening the sack and counting his way through the pieces. He was, in contrast to his companion, a man that sent a chill down Prudence's spine. He never spoke, not in Prudence's presence at least, and his handsome features were concealed underneath a big white scar that ran from his forehead, over his eye, and down to his neck. The gash stood out large and jagged against his face and had turned pink at the edges. It had made him blind in his right eye and turned the pupil a repulsive milky-white. He nodded and slipped the sack into his jacket. Khari tied the rope back in place that was keeping the rest of their trade in the cart.

"Good doing business with ye, *keine*." He tipped his hat mockingly at Prudence before leaping onto the cart with the crates.

"Ye keep callin' me that. What does it mean?"

Khari turned to look at her and flashed a grin. "It means 'little girl'... 'cause you are." He laughed at Prudence's disgruntled face as Avery climbed onto the seat at the front and whipped the horse into a steady trot. They were gone by the time that the sun started to rise.

THE COINS JINGLED IN PRUDENCE'S POCKET AS SHE AND Eleanora walked the path from the tavern down to the market arm in arm. Aside from the two large farms and the tavern, Llynne's inhabitants lived clumped together in wonky houses that always seemed, to Prudence, too fragile to survive the strong winds that often plagued the island. But survive they did.

The town grew around their little port, which for the most part, contained only small fishing boats. Llynne was left to itself by the rest of the world, separated from the governing island by a trench that, as the stories told, went not only to the bottom of the ocean, but right into the centre of the earth itself.

They followed the winding path into and past the

wonky wooden houses. The smell of fish and livestock hit Prudence's nose and she held her breath. She would never get used to that smell. Out on the cliff the air was clear and fresh, whereas the town stank of people, animals, and filth. Every time she smelt it, she was reminded of her childhood.

Eleanora tugged her arm. "Come on Pru, Nell's waiting for us at her stall." She sped off dragging Prudence behind her as they reached the edge of the marketplace.

Prudence pulled her arm free. "I'll catch up with you Elea, I've got to run an errand... for Langley."

"All right. But don't be too long, Mrs. Connell has my dress ready to try and I want you to see it."

"I'll be there." She smiled at Eleanora before picking her way through the clustered homes until she got to one of the biggest houses in Llynne. Its wooden porch wrapped around almost the entire house. Mattie, a tall, blonde woman, sat on a rocking chair by the door, her hands gripping bundles of wool as she plunged them deep into a bucket of dye.

"Prudence, sweetheart, I haven't seen you in a long time. Thought you'd become a hermit."

Prudence scoffed. "I tried. Langley won't let me." She walked up the steps to Mattie. "I'm looking for a gift. It's Elea's birthday soon."

Mattie wiped the dye off her hands and gestured for Prudence to follow her into the house. Prudence cast her eyes around, it truly was a grand home. The wooden structure was solid and well-built, its interior beautiful. The stairs wrapped around the edge of the living room, leading to the bedroom. A fireplace sat in the far corner with a large crackling fire inside it, the smoke billowing up the chimney in waves. Mattie's goods lay on the dining table. Shawls, blankets, and other fabrics were piled high in all kinds of colours.

Mattie's late husband had been one of the few men on the island who traded with the outside world. His merchant life had taken him to many corners of the Western Tides but a storm had taken his life, and the lives of his crew, many years ago. Mattie had managed to scrape by ever since by selling her knitting. Prudence usually wouldn't spend so much money on garments, but Mattie's skill for dyeing the cloth such vibrant colours made them well-desired amongst the people of Llynne.

A deep blue caught Prudence's eye. "This is beautiful," she said, pulling the bright shawl from the pile and running the soft material between her fingers.

"Ah yes, woad makes for a great blue, especially on the goat's wool. Sheep's wool isn't white enough really. I'm verra pleased with that one, it came out beautifully."

"It would look wonderful against her hair." Prudence turned to Mattie. "How much do you want for it?" She could feel the weight of the coins in her pocket; a constant reminder of her only means of escape. She had been saving for so long it ached to part with it. That money was meant to get her and Eleanora off this spit of land once and for all... but using a small chunk for her friend's birthday was important too.

"Eight silver pieces, dear."

Prudence winced inwardly. Eight silver pieces—that was three weeks of wages. She fiddled with the coins in her pocket, feeling the rough metal brush against her skin. It was beautiful though... dark blue would suit Eleanora so well with her fiery hair. She pulled the coins from her pocket and handed eight to Mattie.

"She's going to love it."

Mattie smiled at Prudence and waved as she left the house. Prudence tucked the shawl inside her basket and headed deeper into Llynne towards Mrs. Connell's home. The cottage was tucked between the baker's house and the blacksmith's. Its crooked walls and sloping roof looked like it should have fallen down many years ago. She stepped through the tiny door into the one-room house.

Eleanora perched on a stool as Mrs. Connell's hunched frame crouched at her feet, stitching the hem of her dress. "Doesn't it look wonderful?" she squeaked delightedly.

Nell sat in the corner, her blonde locks pulled back away from her face, flowers entwined in the twists like a crown. "You look beautiful, my love. Doesn't she, Prudence?"

Prudence smiled and planted a kiss on Eleanora's forehead, "You're always radiant, my friend."

OVER THE COURSE OF THE AFTERNOON, CUSTOMERS ARRIVED in little groups and stragglers. By the evening, the room was packed full. Prudence was kept busy behind the bar, pouring drink after drink and collecting the coins that men threw at her.

Every now and then someone wanted food. Prudence was forced to wake George from his drunken stupor to cook their meals before serving them. George wasn't the greatest cook but he was considerably better than Prudence. Despite spending a lot of time in the tavern kitchen, she could only cook a small handful of things— and not well.

"I'll have another, missy," called a man to the side of her. Prudence glanced up and caught eyes with a dark-haired young man, significantly more sober than everybody else in the tavern. He grinned at Prudence, and she smiled back. Prudence poured him a drink and gave it to him.

"Henry."

"Thank you, darlin'."

Prudence smiled to herself and continued to work. She could feel the heat of his gaze on her from his stool at the counter. She did her best to ignore him as she served drinks and took dirty dishes back to the kitchen to be washed later.

Outside, on her only break of the evening, Prudence found herself watching her breath, like dragon smoke in the night air. It was cool out here, refreshing. Times like these made the tavern on top of the hill seem rather beautiful.

She pulled her knife from her dress pocket, turning it in her fingers as she stretched her muscles. Gripping the handle tightly in her palm she thrust the blade in a downward strike, mid-air. Back and forth the blade shone in the moonlight as Prudence sparred alone in the cold.

"Nice night tonight, isn't it?"

Prudence jumped despite herself. Henry cast a smile in her direction. She tried to put on a serious face. "Customers aren't meant to come back here, you know."

"Oh, who's gonna know?" He sidled up to her and offered her a swig from his flask. She took it and winced. The liquor hit the back of her throat like fire. His brown eyes watched her from under heavy brows, a sparkle of mischief in them. Prudence had known Henry for a number of years now. His family owned one of the only two farms on Llynne and he often came by the tavern to deliver goods.

Despite her initial distaste for the attention he gave her, she had succumbed in a low moment of loneliness some months ago, and ever since, their trysts had been frequent. It meant nothing more to Prudence than a pastime, and Henry it seemed, was content with being her distraction.

He had no desire for more from Prudence; their relationship was a deal of sorts. Prudence found relief in his company and Henry's needs remained satisfied without having to take a wife before he wished. It worked for both parties.

Prudence pursed her lips but she couldn't help smirking. "Any minute someone will be searching for me to complain about something. Never a dull moment being me, you know."

Henry chuckled and fiddled with the cigar in his hand before taking a drag. "So, when do you think you'll be done for the evening?" He put the cigar out on the kitchen door frame and put his arms either side of Prudence's head, pinning her against the wall.

Prudence scoffed. "At this rate? Tomorrow morning."

"Guess the only time you've got is now then?" His gaze moved down her legs and back up again.

Prudence caught his eye. "I guess so."

He smelt strongly of cigar smoke and straw from working at the farm. His breath against her ear made her shiver. Henry's attention didn't make her heart flutter like in the stories that Eleanora had always liked listening to, but it cleared her head of thoughts. At least for a short while.

BACK UPSTAIRS, ELEANORA'S ROOM STOOD NEXT TO Prudence's at the end of the corridor. Through the door she could hear giggling and loud chatting. She was glad, really, that Eleanora had lots of friends, but sometimes the sound of them so happy made her blood boil with envy. She had never had that.

Prudence opened the door and stepped inside to see a number of the whores sat on the bed with Eleanora, fiddling with the coins and trinkets that lay in front of them. The laughter stopped as if on cue. Their faces turned towards the movement at the door and cast their eyes on Prudence, immediately becoming hostile. Prizes were snatched up in shares from the bed and shoved into pockets and purses.

The girls clambered off the bed and went back to their chambers. They gave Prudence a wide berth, with noses turned up, as they strutted past her.

"Night El, happy birthday." Caroline smiled at

Eleanora before casting a wicked glare at Prudence. Other murmurs of well wishes could be heard from the hall. No doubt they would have been in much greater spirits on their friend's birthday had Prudence not turned up. They all loved Eleanora, but that love was always hidden beneath deep hatred in front of Prudence.

The hate was a rather mutual feeling. None of them thought Prudence should be allowed to stay on living at the inn when she wasn't willing to work by bedding men.

Once the room had been vacated by the harlots, Prudence grabbed a glass and bottle off the vanity table and poured herself a drink.

"Another year gone already, has it? Seems like ye only walked through that door yesterday, soaked from the rain, skinny as ever, hadn't eaten in weeks." She sat herself next to Eleanora and rested her head against her friend's.

"It would appear so. And still not much has changed, has it?" Eleanora glanced at Prudence out of the corner of her eye. "You are still in the place you've always been, scathing and complaining about the men, the landlady, the tavern, and the pay. You have never been content in the entirety that I've known you."

"I know El, am not the easiest of companions, am I? Still, I can make it up to ye someday. Here, I have something for ye, happy birthday Elea. I'm sorry I missed yer little gathering, I thought it best to steer clear. It's not as much as ye deserve but still, I think it will suit ye." Prudence handed Eleanora the package wrapped in cloth, which she opened eagerly; the happiness of a child painted once again on her face.

It was something that Prudence saw so little of—the

age she truly was. The innocence. Eleanora placed the blue wool over her head, wrapping the ends around her shoulders. The sheer blue contrasted wonderfully with Eleanora's wild red hair that, now untied, hung around her frame like a curtain of fire.

"Oh! It's beautiful Prudence, thank you." Prudence nodded and smiled. She liked to see Eleanora so carefree. She was happy in the moment where it was possible to forget how they came to be friends, how it was that she was able to still be here, what it was that she worked as.

"It must have cost you most of your savings, oh Prudence, you shouldn't've." Prudence shook her head and stroked her friend's cheek, fingering the sole curl that poked out from under the fabric.

"Don't ye worry yer pretty head. I can do with it what I will, it's mine after all." Prudence rose from beside Eleanora and kissed her cheek before departing from the room.

2

NIGHTMARES

As her shift ended, Prudence climbed the stairs back to her little bit of freedom. She had a bed and a window, a hook to hang her few dresses, and the table that she had converted into an altar. It wasn't much, but it was hers and hers alone. Prudence stared out to sea from her perch on the windowsill and dreamt of sailing away. Clouds gathered across the night sky and thunder rumbled in the distance as a storm started to roll in.

Prudence slipped into her nightgown and climbed into her uncomfortable bed. The sheets were old and moth-eaten, the straw mattress narrow and cold. The sound of the storm outside that banged against her window soon faded away into silence.

The sea was calm and peaceful in the darkness. The pale moonlight bounced off the water, lighting up Prudence's ivory skin as she stood at the water's edge. The night was quiet and comforting to Prudence—a relief from the regular rabble of people yelling at her. She wanted to stay like this forever, in this moment, quiet and alone where she could breathe. A haunting melody called to her from somewhere on the horizon.

She wanted to be out there looking in, rather than trapped here on the inside of this nightmarish life. She would do *anything*. She couldn't quite understand at this moment what was stopping her from leaving. Was there anything? A glow, man-made and warm, shone out in the distance. As it drew closer, more lights appeared clustered together—it was then that Prudence recognised the dark hull of a ship. The vessel looked beautiful under the starry sky as dots of light covered the deck like fireflies.

Prudence discerned the silhouettes of men moving around onboard. She could make out a cannon moving starboard, aiming towards the town, towards her. She turned towards the town, to run and warn somebody when at her feet, appeared a mass of red. She stopped.

Blood splattered bodies covered the beach. Her dress was stained with blood that dripped down her arms and clung to her hair. Her fingers clenched tightly around a silver blade, now coated in thick liquid.

Something pressed against Prudence's shoulders as she thrashed against them. She kicked and bucked against the weight that held her down. Drenched in sweat, Prudence jolted awake with the vision of blood still strong in her mind.

"Prudence, wake up! Stop, it's me. Wake up."

Prudence vaguely recognised the sound of Eleanora's voice hovering above her. She stopped thrashing and slowly opened her eyes. Eleanora let go and Prudence blinked at her blankly for a moment as she sat up.

"You were having a nightmare again, Pru. You were screaming. I managed to convince Mrs. Langley that I could get you to stop before she came in here."

Instinctively, Prudence glanced down at her hands—clean and delicate. They were normal, besides the shaking. Taking a few deep breaths, she climbed out of bed and moved to the window. A storm beat down on the cobbles below. Clouds covered the whole sky and waves crashed down on the sand, not at all calm like the start of her dream. It was just a dream, nothing more... but the churning in Prudence's stomach continued and she couldn't shake the feeling that it was something more. Laying back down, she tried to fall asleep again, but the ship loomed into view every time she shut her eyes.

The blood and bodies rushed through Prudence's mind along with her crimson dress and hands. But the dagger was different. The dagger—it was *hers*—kept under the bar downstairs for the more raucous clientele. She remembered the cold iron gripped in her palm and the feeling of, not regret, but relief. It was the feeling of freedom. Her conscious brain knew it was wrong. It was unthinkable. But her gut was telling her something else... it was going to happen.

Eleanora eyed the pipe on the little table next to Prudence's bed, still smelling strongly of opium and tobacco.

"I couldn't sleep, I just had a little." Prudence avoided Elea's judgemental gaze, feeling like a child being berated for making a mess. It wasn't as if she were addicted to it, not like those men she used to see living on the dock when she was young. She just used it when she needed to.

It was a comfort, an escape after spending her day being bossed around by the likes of Mrs. Langley.

"I'm worried about you. You seem to be getting worse, Pru. This is the third time this week. What on earth do you keep dreaming about?" Eleanora asked.

"I wish ye wouldn't look at me like that, El. I'm not a child. In fact, I'm the older of us two, if anyone's closer to a child, it's you."

"Mature." Eleanora rolled her eyes and began absentmindedly tidying Prudence's room.

Prudence snorted and climbed out of bed, ignoring the woozy feeling she got from standing too quickly. She stripped off the dress that she had fallen asleep in and swapped it for her other one, before washing her face in the basin and tugging on her leather boots.

"Put that down and come have some breakfast with me, El. We can sneak the good stuff before George wakes up."

Eleanora cast a glance at Prudence, her hands on her hips. "You're not listening to me! This is not normal Prudence; I'm worried about you. There's plenty of good in this world if you look hard enough, you just choose not to. You're so focused on the bad, it's killing you!" she sighed, "The girls think you're going crazy."

"Trust those stupid bitches," muttered Prudence, a firm scowl now on her face. Any mention of the other girls working at the tavern put Prudence in a foul mood. She scraped her hair back into a rough knot. She winced as she yanked a handful of hairs too hard. "Son of a—"

"—You need to get a handle on this Pru, I don't know what else to do for you, except call the doctor."

Prudence's head shot up. "No! No need for a doctor here. I'm fine Elea, really. I'll... I'll do better. I promise."

Eleanora frowned at her for a few moments before sighing. "This is the last time I'll listen to that promise, understood?"

Prudence grinned and linked her arm through her friend's. "Understood. Now come on, I'm starving."

THE WANDERER'S INN STOOD TALL AT THE END OF THE dusty track that led almost all the way up to Highcliff Bay. Looking down the heath towards the little town, the inn was isolated from all other life, braced against the wind and rain that so often frequented Llynne. Eleanora and Prudence trudged up to the back door, their arms laden with baskets piled high with food for George to cook later.

The door creaked as Eleanora shoved her way into the cramped kitchen with Prudence following behind. The baskets barely fit through the door, they were so stuffed. George was nowhere to be found and Mrs. Langley was most likely shut up in her office, asleep over her pile of coins. The women dumped the supplies onto the counter before climbing the stairs to get aprons; the animals outside would need mucking out and feeding before the tavern opened, and Eleanora liked to help Prudence when she could. It was often the only time they got to spend together.

From the hallway, they could hear the moans and banging coming from a few of the girls' bedrooms. Whilst the tavern didn't normally open until mid-morning, some of the villagers were known to pay for the whole night. It had made sleeping difficult when she first moved into the tavern, but after all this time it was easy to tune out. One of the doors slammed open and shut behind a dishevelled Nancy. Her dress was rumpled and ripped in places, and her makeup was smudged across her face.

"Fine!" she screeched through the door at what could only be a man who had paid for her company. "Have her instead!" And then she caught sight of Prudence stood in the corridor, watching with a slight smirk on her face. Eleanora groaned inwardly. Not again.

"What are you looking at?" Nancy hurled the words at Prudence, spitting them out like poison. Her face was a perfect picture of loathing and humiliation. "Do you find this amusing? Ignorant servant." Nancy scoffed at Prudence. Prudence raised an eyebrow and Eleanora mentally prepared herself for the inevitable fight.

"I beg yer pardon?" Prudence growled, her hands on her hips, her chin jutting out defiantly.

"Pru meant nothin' by it Nancy. Come on Pru we have to—"

"—You heard me, wench. You're nothing but a useless barmaid... one that's not good enough to bed." Nancy marched up to Prudence, taking out her aggression on the perfect person. The way her dress had torn made her large breasts spill out even more than normal. She reached out and shoved Prudence hard in the shoulder. Nancy let out a cry as Prudence's heel dug into her foot. *Shit.* It infuriated Eleanora that her two friends couldn't abide one another. She considered, not for the first time, how amazing it was that they had not killed each other already.

"You mind yer manners, whore. I will not be walked over like the rest of ye." Prudence hissed at Nancy, whose nostrils flared and eyes bulged. "You women, too weak to look after yourselves, preferring to sell yourself off to anyone willing to pay. And from what I can see, not many men are keen to pay for you, *Nancy*."

Eleanora bit back the temptation to remind Prudence that she was one of those whores. "Do we really need to have this same fight again? Just leave each other alo—"

Nancy's hand flew round and collided with Prudence's cheek. The snap rang through the corridor, leaving a sizable red mark across Prudence's face. Eleanora covered her gasping mouth with her hand. This would be bad. Doors opened along the corridor and the many prostitutes stuck their heads out to see what was going on. Prudence's eyes narrowed.

"Pru, come on, it's not worth it." Eleanora took Prudence's arm and attempted to pull her towards her bedroom.

Prudence yanked her arm free. "You vulgar whore! How dare you?" she growled at Nancy and shoved the woman onto the floor. Nancy landed heavily with an *oomph*. She cradled her wrist in pain and suddenly kicked her feet out, sweeping Prudence's legs from underneath her and knocking her to the floor. Eleanora tried to wedge herself between the two of them and pull them apart as Nancy's fist thrust forward and hit Prudence square in the face, cutting her lip. The onlookers made noises of surprise and encouragement. Prudence pulled herself up and landed a solid punch on Nancy's face. She hit her again and again, until Nancy's face blossomed into a red that would no doubt swell into an impressive bruise by tomorrow.

"Pathetic." Prudence spat before she stood up and strode to her room. Eleanora rushed after her.

"Are you quite insane? Nancy will never forget this. She'll hold that grudge for life." Eleanora seated herself on the single chair in the corner and looked at Prudence, concern etched on her face. "What possessed you?"

"She's insufferable." Prudence grabbed a jacket from her bedside table and once it was on, she slipped down the stairs and out the back door to see to the animals.

Eleanora resisted the urge to follow her and instead headed back to her own room, next door. A naked Nell lay asleep in the bed, her blonde hair sticking out at the top of the sheets and her arm hanging off the edge. Eleanora sank down onto the bed beside her, trying not to wake her.

"You sound happy," came a sarcastic mumble from the pillows.

Eleanora glanced behind her and smiled. "Sorry, I didn't mean to wake you."

"I wasn't asleep, not with that racket outside. Besides I've got to get going soon, mam will be wondering where I am. What was going on?" Nell lifted her head to look at Eleanora's face. "Let me guess, Prudence again?"

"And Nancy this time. I know they hate each other but the fighting is exhausting. Mrs. Langley's gonna be furious when she sees Nancy's face."

"I know how much you love Pru, but you have to admit El, she's not exactly..."

"I know."

"Stable."

"I just don't know how to help her. I know the girls grate on her but she doesn't help with stupid comments."

Nell wrapped her arms around Eleanora's waist and placed her head on her lap. "Has it ever occurred to you, that it's not your responsibility to fix her?"

AT THE END OF THE DAY, PRUDENCE DECIDED TO HEAD OUT to the beach for a swim—it wouldn't be possible for much longer; winter was growing closer every day. She loved the beauty of autumn, but the chilly winds that were so common on Llynne were not her favourite.

Prudence loved to swim out in the dark waters when the rest of her world was far off in the distance. A far-off sight that could no longer reach her. The water was warm tonight, despite the bitter winter that was on its way. It was strange, but rather pleasing all the same. Warm water was not something that Prudence was used to swimming in. It washed over her hands and chest, reaching up her neck almost to her chin. It felt nice to the touch and Prudence tilted her head back to feel the water lapping at her hair, to soak it under the ripples that brushed the surface.

The water rose to her face, glazing her cheeks and eyes. Prudence raised a hand to wipe it away when she noticed red. It trickled down her fingers and Prudence checked for a head injury. There was nothing.

She glanced down at the water around her... but it was all the same. A dark crimson instead of salt water. It grew thick and sticky when she touched it, as she tried her best to swim back to shore. Her panic made her swim faster with every stroke. It went into her mouth, slipping down her throat, and making her gag at the foul taste.

The blood became more solid as she moved—it clung to every inch of her and dragged her down. Sucking her down into the bloody ocean, no matter how hard she tried to escape. The shoreline was getting further and further away the more that she swam. The island soon became a dot on the horizon as Prudence sunk into the deep expanse of red. She coughed out the blood that was desperately trying to fill her lungs, but more just took its place.

She tried to call out to someone, anyone to help her. There was no one. The island was no longer in sight. Everywhere around Prudence was a mass of blood. Her arms flailed above her head as she was sucked beneath the depths of the waves. She searched frantically for the surface through the murky water and just made out the shape of the red foamy waves above her.

The ocean pushed against her, crushing her lungs until she could no longer breathe. Spots of bright colour floated in front of her eyes, making her feel dizzy. Prudence shut her eyes. This had been what she had wanted. She had wanted to die.

Maybe it was finally time. No more fighting. There was no hope. No reason anymore. It felt like she had been under the water for an eternity; time had no power here as the minutes, or hours, stretched on. The world finally went dark as Prudence went unconscious and finally succumbed to the will of the sea.

Prudence could feel something hard pushing against her chest as she coughed out the water in her lungs. She could feel wet, coarse sand beneath her cheeks and frowned. Pru opened her eyes to see Eleanora leaning over her with tear-stained cheeks and her red hair a tangled mess around her little face. Prudence attempted to smile but the effort was too much. She lay there, exhausted.

Safe in her little room, Prudence allowed Eleanora to lay blankets over her and tuck them up to her chin. She too was soaking wet, despite Prudence's attempts to get Eleanora to go and dry off. Her only concern was for Prudence, who looked ashen and cold.

"I can't leave ye now. You might get into even more trouble." Eleanora smiled lightly at Prudence and laid down with her under the warmth of the blankets.

"Why did you do it?" Eleanora sighed and looked at her friend with pain in her eyes. "Why would you try to hurt yourself like that? Prudence, you nearly died!" Tears escaped Eleanora's eyes and she brushed them away quickly with her sleeve.

It took Prudence a long moment before her brain caught up with what Eleanora had said. Elea pounding on her chest had left it sore and achy. Her lungs felt like they were on fire, burnt dry from the inside out. Speaking felt like so much effort. Eleanora was still hovering over her like a mother bird, yet it was as if Pru was deep inside

31

her own mind, disconnected from the part of her that could respond to her friend.

"I... I'm sorry, Elea." Prudence closed her mouth slowly. She didn't know what else to say. Or even if there *was* anything to say. Prudence had been suffering, and in the moment, she had let it win. She hadn't wanted to face the world any longer. It had been so easy to submit to the fury of the waves. To open her mouth and let it come crashing into her lungs until she couldn't breathe. She had accepted fate, and fate had spat her back out into the world.

It didn't want her yet. Fate had more in store for Prudence, it didn't care about what she wanted. If it did, she'd have died along with her father as a child. Eleanora pursed her lips but refrained from saying anything.

"I need to leave Elea. I can't be here anymore. It's killing me." Prudence confessed before she could stop herself. Eleanora bolted upright and stared at Prudence.

"Leave? You can't leave. I—I need you, Pru. You're all I've got. You're like family. Our life is here, where would you even go?"

Prudence sighed. "It was just a thought. Don't worry, go to sleep."

DAYS LATER, BY SOME GENEROUS TWIST OF FATE, PRUDENCE found herself with some hours free. She had managed to get all of her chores finished in the early hours and miraculously Mrs. Langley had been too wrapped up in herself to chastise Prudence for once. And so she had slipped away before anyone could notice. Wrapped in her coat, as the weather grew ever colder, she made her way past the town and towards the forest.

The track was long but Prudence enjoyed herself. Time outdoors in the fresh air without anyone to bother her—it was near perfect. She headed south-east, taking the longer track so that she wouldn't have to go through the middle of town. The walk was only a few hours.

The river that provided Llynne with its only water source, save for the wells, glistened in the sunlight ahead of her. It wasn't too deep. There was a bridge further down where the track from town headed towards the forest, but Prudence had no issue hitching up her skirts and wading through the cold, clear water. Fish swam away at the sight of her, leaving the water empty except for the weeds. She tried to ignore the slimy feeling of them as she made her way to the other side and climbed out onto the dry heath.

The trees of Llynne Forest rose up at the horizon, stark against the flat heathland before it. After some time, Prudence reached the end of the track as it led into the trees. The track had been formed over centuries as people went to forage in the woods, sticking to the same trusted route to avoid getting lost in the darkness.

It was muscle memory for Prudence; she had walked this path many times through the winding trees. Always to the same spot. The further into the woods she walked, the more the light was cut off by the thick canopy. It was as if the forest was separate from the outside world. Once inside, the sun could not be seen and the forest was eerily quiet.

Although the townspeople took advantage of the bounty within the forest, it was rare to come across anyone. Most people didn't like the feeling of being completely and utterly alone in the dark, but to Prudence, it was a kind of freedom. She could forget about the world to which she was usually confined and she could really be herself.

Deeper into the woods, Prudence left the downtrodden path taken by the townsfolk and set off through the brambles and bushes until she came to a little grove. The town had carved out a space at the edge of the forest where they lay their dead to rest. But Prudence had never been one for tradition—she also hadn't been welcome there after her mother had disowned her—so she had made a kind of altar to her father in the woods. She had taken a couple of items with her when she left home that had been his, and decorated the grave with flowers.

She knelt down in front of the makeshift grave. "I brought ye some whiskey, Da." She grabbed the bottle that she had stolen from the tavern out of her bag and placed it on the headstone. "I know it's not yer favourite, but Mrs. Langley was out of brandy this time." Prudence brushed away the dirt and dried leaves that had settled on his grave with her hand. "I'm sorry I haven't been to see ye in a while. Things have been hectic. Mrs. Langley doesn't give me much free time, I swear as the years have gone by, she only hates me more." She chuckled softly. "Would've loved to have seen ye give her a piece of yer mind. She wouldn't know what hit her."

The altar was rough, just a large rock for the

headstone. Prudence had planted some flowers at its base so that when winter thawed, crocuses and daffodils bloomed. She had carved his name in the stone with a blunt knife, and the words *loving father*.

After some time alone with her father, Prudence stood and brushed off her knees.

"Bye, Da." She slung her bag back over her shoulder and began picking her way through the undergrowth back towards the path. She froze. The hair on the back of her neck stood up as she turned towards the sound of a branch breaking behind her. Nothing. There was nothing there.

"So jumpy. Don't be stupid," she told herself. She shook her head, but she couldn't get rid of the feeling that she was being watched from the shadows. She glanced around again but saw nothing besides the mass of trees and foliage. Not even any fauna in sight.

Prudence sighed and carried on her way. Though she didn't get far. Halting at the edge of the dirt track, she locked onto the red eyes staring right at her. A yell hound. *Shit.* She breathed out slowly and backed up a step. Prudence knew not to panic. If it *were* here for her, panicking and running would only make it kill her faster. If it wasn't... then she would be ok. It moved out of the cover of trees and Prudence couldn't help but stare. It was the size of a pony, with bright, bloodthirsty, red eyes, and matted black fur.

Yell hounds were terrifying beasts. She had heard tales of them ravaging people, ripping them to shreds and feasting on their innards. But for the most part, yell hounds were an omen of death. Not necessarily your death... but someone would die. Despite the shiver of fear that ran down her spine, she forced her feet to move forward. If it were going to kill her, it probably would have done so by now.

Prudence gripped the handle of her bag so tight that her knuckles had turned white. She just needed to get onto the path and walk until she had passed it. If it didn't follow her, she'd be fine.

She forced another step forward. It watched with an intense gaze but didn't make another move. So far, so good. Another few quick steps. Still nothing.

"Oh gods, just get it over with." She sucked in and walked on, much faster than a normal walk, yet not quite a run for fear of it chasing her. Prudence made her way down the winding path and as soon as she could spot daylight coming through a gap in the trees, she broke into a run.

As soon as she was clear of the trees, Prudence stopped and bent over, out of breath. The sheer terror of having her throat torn out made her heart beat so fast that it felt like it might burst from her chest. She turned back towards the forest for a final look. Prudence could just make out the gleam of red eyes watching her. It hadn't chased her, so what was it doing? Was it trying to communicate with her? She shuddered.

No kind of communication from a yell hound would be good news. She had never seen one herself, but she distinctly remembered her father telling her bedtime stories about them as a child. They had scared her so much that she hadn't been able to sleep for a week. She didn't know much, but she did know that if you saw a yell hound... somebody ended up dead.

THE MOON SHONE COLD AND PURE AGAINST THE SAND AS Prudence walked towards the shoreline, the night air raising the hair along her arms. She removed her dress and left it lying in the surf before diving into the icy sea. The water felt like pins against her flesh as she swam to fight the cold.

Once she could no longer feel the ocean floor between her toes, she swam more easily, her legs beating against the blue, keeping her suspended. Being in the water gave Prudence an otherworldly feeling; it made her body feel like it was floating through the night sky amongst the stars.

The waves shimmered with an eerie glow, frigid and incredible, as Prudence swam further and further away, until she lost all sight of the town that she called home. Many nights were spent here, alone with the ocean. Her thoughts became clearer and she could almost taste the freedom that was just out of her reach. The world felt simpler here. Away from the hustle and bustle of town, the air seemed lighter, the atmosphere no longer suffocating. No longer could Prudence feel tendrils of anxiety gripping her neck, tightening whenever they got the chance.

From here, the small island looked almost quaint. A tiny bit of rock in the south of the Western Tides, hidden from most eyes. There it stood, covered in moorland and swampy marshes, and a thick wood to the south-east. She looked towards Llynne almost tenderly, a feeling that rarely touched her, especially when thinking about the sorry life that she lived. The water was freezing this close to winter, and she could no longer feel her feet. She waded as long as she could hold out, before finally returning to shore.

Prudence lay on the sand, her body heaving from the effort of swimming so far. The sand was comforting and cradled her sides as she sunk into it. If she could just lie here and forget about the duties that waited for her back in the tavern. Alas, the night was growing colder by the minute and if Prudence stayed where she was, she'd be dead by morning. Grabbing her dress, Prudence threw it over her damp body and trudged along the beach towards the marshy heathland and her home.

The tavern was still open, although the crowd was thinning out now in the early hours of the morning. Men and women were returning to their homes and families. Prudence collapsed onto her bed with the relieved feeling that she had finished working for the night. Her vision was soon clouded and the world fell away beneath her as she slipped into her only escape. The opium made the room smell and the air heavy and close. It would last her until daylight—it would make working harder, but it made sleep possible.

That night, Prudence dreamt of great battles and fearless men. She dreamt of freeing herself of her bonds and slashing away at the people who pushed her down. The blood would flow a crimson red, down streets of corpses where judgement was made. Prudence could feel the fire inside her that screamed for war, feel the blood that seeped through her clothes and over her hands. Her hands were coated in blood. Blood that would not wash; a permanent reminder of her actions.

Prudence bolted upright in her cot and wiped her face with a hand. It left a wet feeling across Prudence's forehead and she glanced at her hand, seeing it covered in blood. The tang of copper was so strong that it made her weak. From her seat on the bed, Prudence caught a glimpse of the body lying on the floor. Facing away from her, it lay still. It was a girl. A girl with fiery red hair that hung down in waves over her shoulders. A small girl with dainty hands that rested at her sides. Prudence leapt out of bed and hurled herself at the corpse, turning her over. The bloodied face of Eleanora stared back at her with dead eyes.

Prudence awoke with a shock. Her whole body quivered and she could not help the squeak that escaped her lips. She glanced at the floor instinctively. It was bare. There was nothing on her floor, certainly not a lifeless body. Prudence dashed out of her room and opened Eleanora's door. Elea was safe in her bed, like always.

Prudence sighed and ran a hand through her knotted hair. This was getting out of hand. Perhaps she was becoming insane. Growing more and more delirious as the days went by. She was a danger to Eleanora. Quivering, she shuffled wearily back to her bed and tried her best to go back to sleep, but every time that Prudence shut her eyes, all she saw was Eleanora, lifeless on the floor.

PRUDENCE STARTED THE DAY BEFORE THE SUN EVEN ROSE over the horizon. The rest of the world lay asleep while Prudence dashed about working herself to exhaustion. It was the only way to keep the bad dreams away. Whenever Prudence found herself alone and still, those heart-breaking sights found their way into her mind. They found her weakness and made her vulnerable. Prudence avoided Eleanora as much as she possibly could that day, busying herself anywhere that Elea wasn't. She couldn't face her after the dreams she had suffered the night before.

What would she say to her? Prudence could not face the humiliation and shame of admitting to Eleanora what had happened. She could not face the idea of telling Eleanora that she had dreamed her dead, and by her hand no less. Prudence would have to see Eleanora eventually, but until she had worked out what was going on in her mind, she would hide out in the kitchen, or outdoors with the animals.

George was slumped in a chair in the corner of the kitchen when Prudence came back inside. His large middle spread out over the edges of the chair, making the legs and seat warp with his weight. In his hand was yet another bottle of something, being gripped mercilessly by his chubby fingers.

"Ello' sweet'eart, how are ya?" George burped at Prudence.

"Oh, you know. Same as always, bitter and miserable, George," Prudence grumbled at him as she cleaned out the larder. Despite his uselessness, Prudence rather liked George. He wasn't sour like the rest of the people here. He may be drunk almost twenty-four hours a day and smell like rancid meat—but all in all he was fairly pleasant to Prudence, never rude or disgusting. Some days he was even nice to talk to. He knew how Prudence felt, living in The Wanderer's Inn, and sometimes he was a comforting ear for her to rant to.

Prudence liked it when he listened and gave her consoling words to help her feel a tiny smidge better. George struggled to rise from his chair, partly from the alcohol and partly from his weight. He plonked the bottle on the side and strode over to help Prudence with the sacks of food and grain.

"Gonna be a miserable day today. Black outside already." He groaned under the weight of a large sack full of dried meats and shoved it onto the worktop.

"Tha's heavy that is. Why do we need so much of it? Not like many people come 'ere to eat anyways." George muttered, a small scowl on his face at being interrupted from his lounging. George was never a fan of doing anything. Besides the short time he spent of an evening cooking, George was happy to sit and eat and drink, or sleep. There was nothing much else for him to do out in the middle of nowhere, and he was far too lazy to go into town.

Prudence shook her head. "Perhaps it is to do with your cooking. I know that most people aren't too big a fan of stale bread and meat stew every night." Prudence caught the look George gave her and she burst out laughing. He knew that his cooking was terrible.

Everyone knew it. What Prudence didn't know was why Mrs. Langley kept him around. Regardless of the answer, Prudence was glad she did. He made her laugh. They worked in silence for a while, and got food ready for the customers later on, cleaned out the store room, and put all the supplies back in once they had done.

Prudence washed a few tankards in a bucket of cold water outside the kitchen door. She swished them around in the water and sang to herself as she did. The sight of a bloody leg appearing in the corner of her eye made Prudence drop the glass and it shattered on the stone. Prudence looked up to see the incredibly pale and bloody body of Eleanora stood over her. Her skin had turned pale and green as if she had been dead for a while. Her eyes were void of all colour, the whites of her eyes now completely eclipsing the pupils. Prudence stifled a scream and shut her eyes in fear.

Nothing touched her or made a sound, it felt as if no one was near her at all, and eventually Prudence opened her eyes to see that she was indeed alone. All she could see around her was the wild heath, no people, no life. She sat there shaking for a few moments, trying to compose herself. She must be seeing things. Imagining things after the terrible night she had had. The morning stretched on as Prudence found all sorts of jobs to do around the tavern in an attempt to make herself forget what she had seen. The chores were tiresome and quickly she grew bored of the tasks she had been doing.

Evening came around quickly and as the sun began to lower itself in the sky, bathing Llynne in a warm orange glow, townsfolk quickly filled the tavern hall. Prudence picked up the tray, laden with tankards and bottles, and worked her way through the tables. The men who had ordered were already far too drunk, but as long as they paid, Mrs. Langley kept them buying. Prudence plonked the tray down, sighed and cleaned up the mess they had made.

"Lookie what we got here boys," one man grinned, staring at Prudence bent over and cleaning. He slapped her arse and guffawed with his friends. Prudence jerked upright, her stare enough to burn a hole through his skull. She bit her tongue and growled, stepping back. She didn't want another incident like before. But the men were so vile!

Huffing and complaining to herself, she stomped away, collecting empty drinks from tables and wiping up spills. The men in the back continued to be rowdy and their laughter irritated Pru, making her mood worse with every breath.

Prudence filled glasses and placed them on the table in front of her. These men were surprisingly quiet considering the din coming from every other corner of the room. The tavern was filled with noisy sea shanties as fishermen and farmers drank themselves into a stupor. Looking at the faces of the men in front of her, Prudence realised that they weren't regulars. Her heart fluttered in excitement.

"You boys visiting?" She enquired, curiosity taking over.

"Aye miss," one of the men met her eye, putting his drink down, "just passing through," he drawled. His voice was gruff, as if the words grated like sandpaper in his throat.

"Sounds nice." Prudence smiled half-heartedly and headed back to work before Mrs. Langley could notice her absence. She weaved her way through the many men that filled the tavern, tray in one hand and cloth in the other; it was a familiar dance. The man continued to stare at her from the furthest table until their eyes met and Prudence looked away.

She continued to daydream as she went about the tavern. Daydreams of running away somewhere exciting, sailing to somewhere new. How she'd love to take Eleanora and escape this place. Alas, that would never happen. Prudence's fate was sealed. She would die here. She would never leave this place. She would be as old and haggard as her landlady before she found an escape.

"Looking for someone to cheer up that miserable expression, love?" The man she had spoken to earlier smirked, running his gaze over her figure. Prudence scoffed. She was used to men like him. Chucking the cloth on the counter, she frowned at him.

"Not likely... love," she rolled her eyes and continued to clean the bar. The man grinned.

"Get us a drink then, woman." He sat down on the nearest stool, dropping a few coins onto the bar. Prudence placed a drink in front of him as he continued to talk.

"You're very dull, you know. Would have thought a girl like you would be up for some fun." He gulped his rum. Prudence was almost amused.

A girl like her. She smirked despite herself. It was then that Prudence noticed the scar on his right cheek. It stood out white against his tanned face and she wondered how he had gotten it.

It began just below his right eye and stretched from his nose across almost his whole cheek. Despite it though, there was no denying that he was a handsome man. His mane of blond hair was tied up in a knot at the back of his head and his beard was thick and bushy. He was a broad-shouldered man, not scrawny like Henry had always been. He reminded her of how her mother had described her father, *he's not going to get blown over in a strong wind*.

"You might want to loosen that corset love, might help you be less uptight."

Prudence glowered at him. She would not let herself get wound up by another imprudent man. The man chuckled and waltzed back towards his men, who were drinking their steady way towards unconsciousness. He was a tall man of big build, and yet, he managed to weave his way through the chairs so elegantly.

Her eyes remained on him as he returned to his table and Pru couldn't help but catch part of their conversation as she cleaned the bar next to them.

"Captain, we are to leave on the morrow?" An older, wrinkled man looked up at him, as he returned from the bar. The captain nodded and sat himself back down amongst his crew.

"Aye bosun, stay the night, we set sail for Vaerny at dawn." The Isle of Vaerny had a decent population, plenty of women, plenty to drink, and plenty of plunder. Prudence wasn't surprised to hear that their destination was Llynne's governing island. Around here, it was the perfect spot for piracy.

"Vaerny does have soldiers though men, as opposed to this quaint little town, so we shall have to keep a sharp eye out. It seems the governor has almost lost his reach over here." The glint in his eye suggested that he quite liked the idea of a lawless place. The captain chuckled and swallowed some more rum before wiping his chin with a rather dirty sleeve.

"But it'll be a plentiful picking ground. Vaerny will have many treasures." An old man interjected gleefully. Prudence assumed he must be a man of some importance to the crew; despite being so much older than the rest of the men, they listened to him intently. He had a kind face, Prudence thought, a face that made her momentarily think of her father.

It was strange to think that such a kind face belonged to a vicious pirate; especially a man of his age. The gods must look out for him to live the life that he does and to have survived this long. Prudence never pictured herself getting to be that old. Gods! As a child she didn't even imagine getting to the age of twenty-two, yet here she stood. Fate, it seemed, had a funny sense of humour.

Prudence ended her shift late in the evening and left her apron on the kitchen table, bumping into Mrs. Langley on her way out. Her foul expression warned Prudence not to speak.

"Where do you think yer going, wench?" She glared up at Prudence, her neck craning up to look at her.

Prudence frowned. "I 'av finished working, *miss*," Prudence spat the last word out like it was poison, biting her tongue as she stared at the impish woman. She silently begged the grouchy landlady not to take that away from her. Prudence's fingers twitched at her sides as she envisioned gripping her tightly around her stumpy little neck.

Prudence would squeeze and Mrs. Langley's eyes would bulge out, her face purple, and she'd scratch at the hands clutching her windpipe. Prudence wouldn't hesitate though. She'd crush it until she could no longer suck in air. She shook her head to rid herself of the fantasy, waiting for the landlady's retort. But it didn't come. Mrs. Langley nodded stiffly, a scowl etched onto her face. Prudence sighed gratefully and walked quicker and quicker until she was almost running, leaving the kitchen before Mrs. Langley changed her mind.

At the edge of the tavern hall, the men from earlier continued to drink and lark, leering at the harlots that circled the bar like vultures. A hand grabbed at her arm. The man who had touched Prudence earlier grinned a toothless grin in her direction. His face was scarred and dirty. Prudence reeled backwards, the stench of his breath overpowering. She tugged and clawed at his hand, trying her best to break free.

A loud *thunk* startled Prudence as a fist came from above and collided with the man's face. Prudence leapt back, whipping her arm free. The captain thrust his fist into the drunkard's face again, pummelling him, blow after blow. He pulled away and looked down at her. "Are you all right, lass?"

3

TASTE OF FREEDOM

Prudence gulped as words escaped her for the moment, but she nodded at him gratefully. The drunk man's party leapt to his aid at once, attacking the captain, weapons drawn. The crew joined the fray, fighting for their captain and wounding many. Knives and swords clashed and metal rang in the air. Prudence dashed back to the bar, leapt over it, and grabbed her knife.

The entire tavern erupted in a cacophony of fighting cries. People fought and punched each other, intoxicated by the drink; many of them didn't even know what they were fighting for. A man was flung over the bar and landed next to Prudence, who was crouching out of sight. The man groaned and upon noticing Prudence, attempted to reach out to grab her, touch her.

The knife slashed into his palm. He cried out as Prudence leapt to her feet, full of nervous energy and pushed into the throng of men that surrounded the bar.

Prudence was pulled into the chaos and shoved around until she felt like she couldn't breathe. She watched, astounded, as blood flew across the room from knives and swords slicing through flesh and knuckles connected with jaws in a sickening crunch.

Prudence pushed at the people surrounding her. The lack of air was suffocating. The cries of men and women from all around rang throughout the tavern. Bodies flew and weapons slashed as people fought their kin, their neighbours, their friends. The tavern was a tidal wave of bodies, a sea of crimson and flesh.

Prudence fought her way through the chaos towards the centre of the room. The red mist of anger fogged her vision. Adrenaline pumped through her veins. Blood pounded in her ears. It was enthralling and Prudence didn't even try to fight it. She welcomed it. The question of fight or flight consumed her, but not for long. Prudence knew the answer. She wanted to fight. She wanted to taste it, that primal urge to tear into flesh, to feel the *riiiippp* of muscle as it yields to steel. The atmosphere was completely intoxicating and Prudence was swept along with it. The primal chant of *fight, fight, fight* buzzed inside her, charged by the violence in the air.

A chair leg collided with the back of her skull, knocking her forward. The man in front of her swung it back, getting ready to hit another person, and smashed it into the back of Prudence's head. He was too focused on his goal to notice her. A coppery taste filled her mouth as teeth tore through her tongue. She whimpered. Prudence grabbed a sword from the person beside her, snatching the blade from its sheath, and spun to face him.

The brute with the chair leg gargled and blood poured from his mouth as the blade sliced through his ribcage. His body slumped forward in a lifeless heap. Prudence tried to tug the sword out but it wouldn't budge. It was jammed between the man's ribs, trapped under the weight of his large frame. There was no way that Pru could lift him up. The sword was stuck. She looked around frantically for another weapon, feeling the panic rise in her chest.

Mrs. Langley's voice howled over the racket. Prudence could see her a few feet away, screaming and swinging a knife around wildly. Sweat clung to her forehead and her clothes were torn. She'd injured her hip—Prudence could tell by her limp. She watched for a moment that seemed to stretch on forever, twisting her hands round and round the cord of her dress. The old woman had had enough, she didn't stand a chance now, not in this brawl. Prudence untangled the cord from her waist and wound it tight around her hands. She crept up behind old Langley and slipped the cord over her neck with ease. The landlady didn't notice a thing until her eyes bulged out of their sockets. Her hands leapt to her throat and she clawed frantically at the cord.

Mrs. Langley's face swelled, her cheeks turning purple. Prudence tightened her grip and pulled the cord harder, crushing it into the old woman's windpipe. She gulped like a fish out of water and tried desperately to breathe in some air. Prudence wrestled against the woman as she flailed and thrashed in her grip. After a few minutes, Mrs. Langley's body slumped backwards. Her dead weight almost knocked Prudence over. Prudence dropped the cord and let it fall to the ground along with Mrs. Langley's large, lifeless body.

Prudence's eyes scanned the crowd, searching for Eleanora. She shoved people aside, desperate to find her friend. Elea was sweet and delicate, Prudence grimaced to think of what might happen to her. The young girl had cornered herself behind the bar along with a few of the other prostitutes. Men advanced on all sides, some with blood on the brain, some with other things in mind.

Prudence leapt over the chairs and tables that blocked her path, shoving people out of the way as she moved. The blood pounded in her ears.

Eleanora let out a scream of sheer panic as a man tugged at her skirt. Hands grabbed at her blouse, popping the buttons and ripping the seams. He gripped her ankles and pinned them to the floor. Eleanora struggled under his weight but she couldn't break free. While the bigger man held her down, his friend undid the tie of his own trousers and forced Eleanora's skirts up around her hips.

Prudence slammed her foot into the bigger man's side and sent him stumbling as he lost his grip on Eleanora. Prudence slashed at his face, the dagger cutting his cheek. His breath reeked of alcohol as he snarled at Prudence and grabbed a fistful of her dress. Prudence could feel the putrid heat of his breath as his face loomed close to hers. He had been one of the crew sitting with the captain she had met earlier. His hands gripped Prudence's shoulders tightly, fingernails digging into her skin.

Prudence gripped her dagger and thrust it forward into the man's gut. Tearing upwards, the dagger carved through the bulk of flesh. The *crunch* and *pop* noises made Prudence feel sick. Her hands shook as the dagger opened the man's belly. He groaned and slipped to the floor as his intestines spilled out from the opening in his stomach. Prudence thrust her hand into the wound and yanked, ripping the last of the guts out.

The man slid from Prudence's grasp and she promptly vomited. Her arms ached with the effort it had taken to use the dagger. It lay on the floor coated in bright red blood and chunks of flesh.

Eleanora sat whimpering in the corner and stared at Prudence with undisguised fear in her eyes. Prudence stepped towards her and pulled her upright.

"We need to get away from here, Elea," the words came out garbled and Prudence retched again; the taste of blood lingered in her mouth. Eleanora stared blankly ahead, her face white and her cheeks hollow. Prudence grabbed her arm and dragged her wooden form through the mass of bodies that filled the tavern.

Prudence hastily climbed a few stairs, dragging a catatonic Eleanora behind her. They would wait it out here. It was a few miles to the town from The Wanderer's Inn. In the middle of night, it would be too dark to see. Marshes and swamps were everywhere and it would be dangerous. They would wait.

THE CARNAGE PILED UP AROUND THEM. BODIES HAD FALLEN in all directions and there was blood everywhere. Prudence and the captain glanced at each other. His crew were—for the most part—alive, despite being battered and bloody. The tavern fell into an eerie silence as the scene around them sunk in. What had started as an act of valour on the captain's part, had swiftly turned into a massacre.

Prudence sighed. She grabbed a drink from behind the bar and took a big gulp. She felt numb; the sight of what she had done was yet to affect her. Seeing the pale body of Mrs. Langley gave Prudence no feelings of guilt. Eleanora, perched on the edge of a chair by the bottom of the stairwell, was still shaking from fear. She stared at Prudence, bewildered.

The captain and his men slid into seats close to the bar. "Pass us a drink, lass?" he asked, his face gaunt and exhausted. Prudence grabbed some drinks for the men and placed them on the table. She owed him that much. Prudence hopped onto the bar to get a bit of distance between her and the blood-smeared floor. Such a mess would need to be cleaned up eventually—the blood would most likely stain. Then again, who would be here to complain? She stared blankly at the mess all around them, her mind reeling at the chaos that had spiralled from a single punch. Prudence's gaze landed on Eleanora and she frowned.

"Elea." She hopped down to crouch in front of her young friend and smiled gently. "It's all right, no one is going to hurt you." She grasped her hand softly, pulling her up. Eleanora let Prudence walk her towards the men and sit her down. She'd turned ghostly pale and shook almost violently. She stared at Prudence, her gaze never wavering. Prudence didn't feel guilty for her actions, but the way that Eleanora glared at her through the tears in her eyes made her feel like she had betrayed her friend.

She handed Eleanora some water and moved away, unable to stand the accusatory stare. She had done what was necessary. She had defended her friend from an attacker. She had defended herself! The years she had spent as a slave to that ghastly woman, how she received beating after beating—turning black and blue so regularly that people might have mistaken it for her actual skin colour—all of that could easily justify what she had done.

Tightening that cord around her neck had felt good. Liberating. As Prudence watched the colour drain from the old woman's face, just like Langley had drained the life out of Pru, a sick feeling of pleasure bubbled up in her stomach. Prudence had wanted her to die, and she did.

The men sitting around the table were by now yelling and laughing together, clearly drunk out of their minds. It's never a dull moment with pirates around. Prudence watched them from her perch at the bar. Most of them had survived the brawl, of course one of the dead pirates was the man that had gone for Eleanora. The men drank and laughed, joking with each other, clearly without a thought for the violence they had just taken part in. A slurred sea shanty erupted from someone's mouth and soon everyone joined in.

"A maiden fair out in the square, a maiden fair was she..." the men grinned, raising their tankards one by one and swaying along.

"Each day she toiled for meagre spoils and longer for life at sea, at sea, at sea..." Pru sang to herself quietly and smiled. The memory of singing this as a young child with her father was a happy one. However, what had followed was definitely not.

> A maiden fair with raven hair
> A maiden fair to see
> To sail the coast she yearned for most
> She wanted to be free
>
> At sea! At sea!
> She longed for life at sea
>
> A maiden fair without a care
> A maiden filled with glee
> A sailor's kiss, a life of bliss
> If only she'd agree

The words sang in Prudence's head and took her back to a life so long ago that it may as well have been a dream.

The feeling of eyes watching her brought Prudence out of her trance. The crew grinned at her as Prudence realised that she had been singing aloud. She blushed, embarrassed, and swallowed the last of her drink. Prudence had always been tone-deaf, but it didn't stop her after a drink or two. The hazy rush of alcohol swam in her head and grinning to herself, Prudence hopped down from the counter and joined the crew at their table.

The men cheered and raised their drinks in the air once more as they gulped bottle after bottle. The buzz of alcohol was a warm embrace after the chill that had swept over her as she surveyed the carnage. Prudence drank more and more, drowning in the seemingly never-ending bottles.

Together, Prudence and the crew drank, and celebrated, and sang, and drank some more; the party went on for hours. Prudence hiccupped and giggled.

"Captain, I want to join your crew. I know you're short a man." The words slurred together, her mind blurred and fuzzy. Prudence wanted to be a pirate, able to roam the oceans, wherever she pleased, to take what she wanted and have whatever her heart desired—freedom, most of all. Even in her drunken state, she knew that the longing inside of her begged to be let loose, to escape this life. Prudence had nothing left here.

The captain smirked at her, clearly able to hold his drink better than she could. He slung his arm around her shoulders and glanced down at her.

"What have you got in mind, lass?" he winked. Prudence rolled her eyes and shoved him off.

"I think you'll find, *Captain,* that our ideas differ greatly." She frowned at him. "I want to leave. Eleanora needs to leave." She gestured to her friend. "We have to get out of here but we have nowhere to go." Prudence stared at him earnestly, sobering up as the matter became serious. She couldn't stay in Llynne any longer, it wasn't her home anymore; she didn't have one. Prudence needed to look after Eleanora and she couldn't do that stuck here, especially after what had happened tonight.

The town would be in outrage, so many of their men and young women dead. Not that the women in the tavern really mattered to the townsfolk, they were harlots; unwanted within the town. The only place that since gave them refuge was Mrs. Langley's brothel—and she hadn't been picky with her employees.

A barrage of complaints erupted from the men. "Ye dumb bitch, who do ye think you are, speaking to our captain as such?"

"Cap'n ye can't really be considering this! It's preposterous!"

"I don't remember asking for yer opinion." Prudence snarled back.

The captain sighed, his eyebrows knitting together as he considered it. Women weren't usually found on ships, it was bad luck, of course. But Prudence knew he had seen how she sliced through those people, her expression matching his own, not quite glee... but free. Free to do as she pleased, whenever she pleased. The glint in her eye as she used her knife, how easily she held the blade as she stabbed and cut into flesh. She could do well; she knew she could.

"All right missy, listen here. You're very much welcome aboard my vessel and amongst my crew, but I will not give a free ride." His tone was stern but his gaze soft as he looked at her, so at home in such a ruthless situation. He had only hit the man because he had grabbed her.

"Captain, ye can't be serious!" A dark-haired older man interjected.

Prudence grinned at her captain, a silent thank you in her eyes. She grabbed another bottle from the counter and handed it to the men, a smile plastered across her face. She needed to speak with Eleanora. She had found them an escape they could share. A place they could go together, somewhere where she could look after her friend.

Eleanora deserved to be safe and loved. She was still a child in a lot of ways. Graceful at the age of sixteen, Eleanora had had a tough life, missing out on a big part of her childhood when she was abandoned. When she arrived at The Wanderer's Inn, Prudence had recognised the look in her eyes; it was mirrored in her own. A light that was slowly extinguishing for lack of nurture. But no more. From now on Prudence would be able to protect her and give her the life that she deserved. She smiled at her friend.

"Elea, get your things. We can leave. We can escape this awful place... it'll be gone from our lives!" Prudence grinned at Eleanora, exhilarated with their new plan. They could escape together. Eleanora would be free and be by her side. She failed to notice the sadness in her friend's eyes for what it was. She had shown a side that Eleanora had never witnessed before. Prudence turned back to the men for a drink. This was it. This was her escape. She could be free.

The feeling of ecstasy swelled inside her until it almost overflowed. This was what she had been waiting for. It didn't come in the way that she had expected, but even Prudence couldn't deny that it was better than jumping from that cliff. She would be no good to anyone floating in the bay, neck broken upon impact.

No, this was how it was meant to be. This was meant to happen. The ship from her dreams had sailed into reality and had brought her freedom. For that she would be endlessly grateful. Prudence joined in the celebration with the crew and drank, danced, and sang gleefully amongst the mess, feeling for once, at peace with the world. The tavern became alive once more, the crew were merry and Prudence smiled for the first time in a long while. She sat herself down next to the captain with an exhausted grin, her face flushed and bright. Prudence drank with the men and fell into a state of drunken happiness, a feeling that could only come from rum.

The dark liquid sloshed down his arm as he slammed down the glass. Captain Cain William Morris grinned drunkenly down at the barmaid under his arm.

"You'll do all right, lass," he winked. She grabbed his drink and took a swig.

"You have no idea." She glanced up at him. The yearning to escape was becoming more and more desperate each day. Pru wanted to do something unexpected, just because she felt like it. This opportunity was not likely to repeat itself.

CAPTAIN MORRIS OPENED HIS CABIN DOOR FOR THE GIRLS and followed them inside.

"You'll be joining the crew then, aye?" he looked up from his desk, strewn with maps and charts, to the two girls standing by the door.

Eleanora was reluctant, it had all been Prudence's idea anyway, she wasn't spontaneous, or adventurous, or brave. Prudence was meant to be here. The whole experience had brought the colour back to her cheeks and the light back into her eyes. Adventure and thievery were in

Prudence's soul. She craved it, thrived on it even. Prudence grinned at the captain.

"Aye Captain, if one would be so kind as to have us under your command, sir." She glanced up at him through dark lashes.

He chuckled at her. "Aye lass! Would be an honour to have you."

Prudence rummaged around in her dress pocket and pulled out a fistful of gold and silver coins. She dumped them on the captain's desk. "Captain, I know it may not be my place but I canna allow Elea or meself to share quarters with the rest of the crew. I hope this is sufficient payment for us to sleep elsewhere?"

Cain glanced briefly at the coins and scooped them up, counting them roughly. "I suppose I could assist with your request." He chucked the coins into a box and steered the women out of his cabin and down the steps towards the main deck. He opened the door and gestured inside. By the look of them, these quarters hadn't been used in a long time and there was only one cot in the corner. Prudence and Eleanora would have to share, but that would be fine. "You can both sleep in here. We never had the need for a war room," he shrugged.

Prudence looked at their new captain, puzzled.

"This used to be a ship of the royal fleet," he grinned at her mischievously.

"Thank you. Truly."

He nodded curtly before striding out, back to his charts and drink, shutting the door behind him.

Prudence sat Eleanora down on the cot and searched round the small cabin for a blanket to warm her up.

"How're ye feeling?" she smiled gently at Elea who still seemed rather pale and quiet. Unaccustomed to violence, Elea had gone into shock after Prudence killed the man targeting her. Prudence remembered the blood. A little of the blood was crusted under her fingernails even now.

The knife she had stuck in his gut had spilt blood and intestines everywhere.

Not that she minded; she had done it for Elea. As for Langley, the bitch had had it coming. She had beaten Prudence for the last time. When the fight had broken out and most of the customers were already slaughtered by the captain's men, Prudence found herself wanting to join in, the adrenaline had surged through her, urging her to fight, to win. Prudence held no regrets. As far as she was concerned, the landlady had committed far worse crimes than she.

Eleanora stared up at Prudence who hovered over her with a moth-eaten blanket she had found. "How could you?" she whispered, her eyes boring into Prudence, "*Why* would you?" Prudence knew that Eleanora had always fretted about Prudence's 'troubled mind', but thinking about it now, Eleanora had never seen the darkest parts of her. Prudence sighed and sat down next to Eleanora on the little cot bed.

"He wanted to hurt you, Elea. I couldn't let that happen." Prudence felt guilty all of a sudden. What she had considered to be the best thing for the both of them, might not be what Eleanora wanted. She realised that she had never asked Elea for her permission throughout any of this. She took her friend's hand.

"I'm sorry El, but what did you expect me to do? Leave

you to that pig?" Eleanora scowled at her. "I saved us from that awful place. I'm not going to apologise for it." She kissed Eleanora's head before leaving the cabin. Perhaps some space would do her good. Eleanora might not understand right now, but she had witnessed the same atrocities that Pru had, maybe she would feel differently once she'd had time to think.

Prudence knew in her heart and her head that they were both better off away from The Wanderer's Inn and the likes of Mrs. Langley. Eleanora deserved a better life than the one she had been living and Prudence was determined to give it to her. Whatever the cost.

The night crept on as Eleanora slept soundly in the small cot. Prudence laid a blanket over her sleeping friend and snuck out the door, making sure not to wake her. Elea had been through a lot, she needed to rest. Most of the crew were asleep below deck, but the few that remained on duty sat on upturned barrels around a crate, drinking and betting the few coins they had left. Every now and then the men would shout up to the crow's nest to check that there were no other ships around. Prudence watched the men in the dark, casting shadows in the faint lamp light.

Mr. Norton, the Quarter Master, was at the helm, guiding *The Bloody Maiden* through the dark. He seemed like a nice man, older than most of the crew; the age where one might think of him as a father. He had spoken softly to the women when they climbed aboard.

The coordinates were set for their destination; Vaerny. Mr. Norton would make sure that *The Maiden* travelled safely through the night, and after a few days, they would arrive. Prudence climbed the steps up to the helm and stood beside him.

"Tis a beautiful night, miss," he smiled, keeping his eyes on the water. Prudence sighed and looked up at the stars.

"That it is." The sky seemed to be an endless expanse of black from her place on the deck, an entity that stretched on for eternity and would still be here long after they were all gone. The stars winked against the cloudless sky, they seemed even bigger out on the water. Away from the light of man, the ship was bathed in a pale glow. Pru's face fell, thinking that perhaps this whole idea had been a mistake, maybe she didn't belong here. Eleanora's words had pierced her more than anything else. She didn't want Elea to think ill of her, she was the only family that Prudence had. Mr. Norton glanced down at her.

"Why so sad missy? You've run away to become a pirate, whatever would your parents think?" he chuckled, trying to make her laugh.

Prudence frowned at the image of her old life in her head and the faces of her parents swum in her mind. Her mother's long brown hair that hung limp down to her hips; her father's eyes that twinkled whenever he smiled at her. Images that looked nothing like her last memories of her parents.

"They wouldn't know." Prudence stated and turned her back on the Quarter Master. She sauntered towards the back of the ship, away from the busy crew. She was out of earshot before Mr. Norton could open his mouth.

Mr. Brady, the Boatswain, slouched against the side, supposedly on watch as he drank out of a flask and stared out to sea. Prudence glanced at him before sitting on the side, her feet dangling out over the water.

"You don't belong here, miss." Mr. Brady gulped down more rum. "Women, don't belong out at sea. Terrible things will come of this, you mark my words. There's a reason most find themselves down in the depths with the sirens to eat their flesh. They're the devil's work," he spat.

Prudence stared at him. "I beg yer pardon?"

"You don't belong here. You're bad luck, you hear me? Bad luck for the ship. Bad luck for us. Bad luck for our Cap'n. If you know what's best for ye, you'll leave once we reach land." The Boatswain turned his scowl in the direction of the waves, away from Prudence. He was a short man, hunched slightly in the shoulders with a pot belly from too much liquor. His hair was greying in patches and he had a look of bitterness on his face, the kind that made Prudence think of longing. The type of longing that Prudence knew was reserved for a woman.

Mr. Brady continued to sit and stare out to sea as if Prudence did not exist, which only maddened her further. Her cheeks grew hot and her jaw ached with the pressure of gritting her teeth.

He was an ignorant man—an insufferable one at that. Prudence clenched her fists and stepped towards him, but she held herself back. She should not be fighting with the crew, not when she had only just been accepted. Mr. Brady would get his comeuppance, Prudence would make sure of it. Just not yet. She relaxed her grip and stepped away from the man, choosing instead to sit on the edge and dangle her feet over the water. She would have to make more of an effort to be one of them.

CAPTAIN MORRIS SAT AT HIS DESK WITH CHARTS surrounding him and a bottle of rum in his hand. He sighed and glanced at the cabin door. The deck, he could hear, was quiet, save for the men on watch playing cards. No point in staying the night, Cain had decided, not after the incident in the tavern. The whole town would most likely know by dawn; once the women realised that their men hadn't returned to their beds.

No, better to leave straight away. The passage to Vaerny would be just over a week, as long as the wind was with them. There would be plenty of time to rest once they had arrived in Vaerny's port. No one would be looking for them this far south yet.

Cain and his crew had sailed for many months in search of somewhere new to raid. Previously, he had been sailing around Aelin Isle—their capital, the King's country. But the crew had been found and soldiers had searched for them for many nights before they finally set sail, out of their reach.

Despite how tired he felt, the little time he had to himself was reserved for finishing the adventure left on his side table. The faded blue cover of the book was faced up, the pages splayed, just waiting for Cain to pick it up again when he returned. The pages were worn and ripped in some places, yellowing at the corners. Cain's face was inches from the words, his nose almost touching the paper as his eyes devoured the lines.

His head was filled with tales of faraway lands, where dragons roamed the skies and people were free to live as they wished. The stories that Cain collected were an escape from his life of running. It was the life he chose. It was a life he loved, but it wasn't always what he wanted. One day he would be free to settle somewhere and could do something with his life that was different from what he had always known. Something peaceful.

After a chapter or two, he put his book down and went out on deck to help his men. Gabe stood at the helm, his eye on the horizon, with one hand on the wheel and the other on his flask. He was considerably younger than any Sailing Master that Cain had ever met but he was a damn good pirate.

Cain had found Gabe trawling the docks for work down in Pirn a number of years ago with his older brother, Danny. He had worked hard as a cabin boy and a powder monkey despite the less than pleasant tasks. When Mr. Dunstan had died of a fever, Cain thought it only fair to give the lad a chance to prove what he had learnt. He'd been Sailing Master ever since.

He slapped Gabe affectionately on the shoulder. "Do you think we'll see a good wind on our voyage, Master Gabriel?"

Gabe cast a glance over his shoulder at Cain and grinned. "Aye Cap'n if Artos be with us, we'll reach Vaerny soon enough." He hesitated, weighing up the benefits of voicing his thoughts. "I, er—I see we've got some new crew mates then?"

Cain nodded. "The red head may not be worth our time but the other just might be. Yet to see a lass handle a blade as well as 'er back there. Fights as well as most men. Could come in our favour having a woman around.

People won't look twice at a young lass wandering about, not like they would us."

The captain wasn't as inclined to believe the superstitious nonsense that some of the crew did. Bad luck was just that... luck, or lack thereof. Maybe women *were* bad luck but as far as Cain was concerned, with their lifestyle, bad luck was bound to follow them either way.

A hand slapped Gabe's shoulder as the face of Mr Rundstrom loomed into view. "The captain must 'av lost 'is head during the brawl Master Gabriel, only explanation for bringing a wench aboard... and two at that." A hearty laugh burst from his lips, loud like the beat of a drum.

Cain scowled at him. "Are you certain that your head remains intact, speaking to your captain in such a way?" He shoved the blond, broad-shouldered man in the chest and rolled his eyes.

"Ah 'tis true. The captain is besotted! 'Twas that dark-haired one that did it. Only way to explain it." Mr. Norton chuckled and grinned at Cain wickedly.

"You've all forgotten your place and I'll see you all flogged come the dawn," Cain joked and shook his head. He couldn't blame them. Maybe he had lost his mind somewhere along their travels, but there was something in her eyes that spoke to him. Something that said they were kindred spirits, specks of the same star hurtling through time, somehow passing right by each other.

4

SIREN SONG

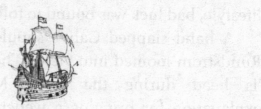

The wind tore at their cheeks as Cain watched Prudence tighten the halyard and Mr. Lowell began to climb the ladder. It swayed back and forth under his weight as he scaled higher up the rigging. She could see how easy it would be to fall in bad weather. Cain took the hemp rope from her hands.

"Almost got it, just need to loop it round like this..." he tucked the end underneath, through the loop, and pulled it tight. "There. You learn quick though I'll give ye that, lass. Won't be long until you're a skilled hand."

"Thank ye. Spent my childhood around fishermen but a few simple ropes are nothin' compared to all this." Prudence turned from her task and looked at the captain. "Since yer here, Captain, I thought I might just ask..." she tugged at her sleeve and glanced at the floor.

"Spit it out, young'un!" Mr. Norton laughed and clapped Cain on the shoulder. "The Cap'n don't bite... much."

"I want to learn the sword," Prudence blurted out and glanced at Cain.

Mr. Kenny appeared at Cain's side and a laugh erupted from his chest. "Don't be daft, girl. Why would a woman need to know the sword?"

"I held my own in that fight back there, and I intend to continue to do so." She glowered at the two of them.

Cain brushed a blond strand of hair out of his face. "Well—"

"—Well maybe so... but you have to admit it blue eyes, women aren't warriors." Garrick touched Prudence's arm but she shook him off. Cain smirked.

"Get yer hand off me. Ye've clearly never heard of the Great Goddess. Women can make fearsome warriors—some even mightier than men! Tethida is fierce and deadly, and ye underestimate me like the God of Death underestimated her."

A couple of the men snorted indignantly at her but Cain cocked his head, interested. He gestured for Prudence to continue.

She nodded slightly and hopped onto a crate. The men around them continued to work while they listened, some reluctantly, to the enthralling story.

"When the world rose up out o' the sea thousands of years ago, Vaegar, God of Death took a wife named Tethida. Tethida was strong, beautiful, and some say even smarter than Vaegar himself, for she knew how to control death in a way that no one else could. They birthed Light and Darkness and together they ruled the land, the sea, and the sky. But Tethida was more than just a wife and Goddess. Tethida was a warrior..."

Charlie sniggered and Garrick clipped him round the back of the head. Prudence gave them a sharp withering look and they fell silent once more, listening intently to her tale.

"She would follow her husband, God of Death, into battle, shrieking like a banshee. A golden helm upon a head of hair as black as the farthest corners o' the universe; stardust smeared across her ochre cheeks; sword raised; and eyes the colour of sodden earth, glinting with a fierce bloodlust. Killer of Men. Mother of Gods. And desired by all immortals.

But Vaegar was a prideful and gluttonous god. When mortals began worshippin' Tethida, it filled him with an inescapable fury. He banished Tethida to the uninhabited island of Tisnear, where he hoped she would fade from the minds of mortals."

Like tales told in the flames of a roaring fire, Cain could see it play out before him. The Great Goddess, Tethida, riding her colossal war horse into battle, her powerful arm wielding a shining silver sword, cutting down anyone that got in her way.

"Did ye not wonder why we do not get many visitors to our little island? Llynne used to have a twin. The Great Goddess herself was banished to Tisnear, our neighbourin' island. Banished and utterly alone, save for small wildlife. Now mortals may have short memories, but humans as a species 'av a kind of history that gets passed down in the bones of their children, like instinct. They did not forget Tethida even as the gods of old began to drift from their conscious mind."

"Vaegar sent the few mortal men that were still loyal

to him to kill Tethida, but the men were returned to him in pieces. So Vaegar sent his hounds to kill Teethed but she slaughtered them easily, for she had raised them from pups. Finally, Vaegar himself went to Tisnear. The island shook an' thund'rous booms came from its shores as god battled goddess. They fought until the sea itself opened up an' swallowed the island whole, leaving nothin' but the trench in its wake."

Cain watched Prudence's lips curl up into a wicked grin as she saw that the men were entranced with her. Cain couldn't help but smile; she took so much glee in the violence of it all.

"What happened to the goddess then, blue eyes? Did she die? Did the God o' Death die?" Garrick asked.

Prudence grinned. "The God of Death did not die," she paused, "for ye must be alive in order to die. But he could not find any sign of Tethida. Now, Vaguer remains on his throne of bones, forgotten in the minds of humans as the new gods arrived and took his place. Yet, the spirits of his dead hounds stalk the earth searching for the wife of Death, still. Yell hounds with eyes the colour of the blood Tethida spilled."

"I've heard of yell hounds! Terrible beasts." Charlie seemed to shudder at the thought of blood red eyes and foaming mouths.

"I've seen one." Prudence stuck her chin in the air, a sense of pride about her as the men nudged each other, silently impressed. "Ye need not run from 'em though. Unless yer time on this earth has come to an end, they will leave ye be, searching for their old mistress, thirsty for revenge. And if it has... ye won't make it more than ten paces anyway." She basked in the atmosphere that surrounded them, clearly pleased with herself. A haunting, dangerous air that conjured images of war, bloodshed, and ruin swam into their minds.

"So, *Captain*, would ye teach me the sword?"

"Aye, lass. I'll give it a go. Let's see what you're made of."

THE NEXT DAY THE SUN WAS HIGH IN THE SKY AS PRUDENCE tried to prepare herself for her first lesson. Mr. Norton nudged Prudence's shoulder. "Yer not going to be able to fight in that thing," he gestured to her dress, "let's get you some different clothes."

She followed Mr. Norton as he led her below deck, past the sleeping quarters of the crew. Below deck was somewhat dark, the light of day didn't penetrate the wooden planks above their heads, their only light coming from oil lamps whose warm glow only stretched out in a small ring of yellow.

It smelt damp and musty. The number of sweaty, dirty men that slept there all together kept the space unbelievably warm and rank. Mr. Norton rummaged around in a chest in the corner. He grunted slightly as he stood and stretched his back. "These bones aren't what they used to be." He tossed a handful of clothes at Prudence. "This'll do ye much better, girl."

He headed back towards the ladder to give her some privacy to change. The britches fit snugly over her hips. They were much easier to move in than a skirt, so freeing.

She pulled the shirt over her head. It was large, the sleeves tapered off with an inch of frill at her wrists. Prudence looked down at herself and grinned. Men's clothes were much more comfortable; there was no restriction across her chest. She pulled her boots back on and tied the laces tight. She didn't want anything getting in the way in her first lesson. She went up to the main deck to see that the captain was standing waiting for her, a training sword in each hand.

"You will have to train daily with myself or another of the crew and work on building up some upper arm strength. When I tell you to do something, you do it." Cain paced up and down the deck in front of Prudence, as he lectured her. "There aren't many rules with the cutlass. It's rather simple and improvised. Now, first..." he placed the wooden cutlass in her palm and curled her fingers over the hilt. "Your thumb should line up along the blade edge." His thumb brushed over her fingers lightly.

Prudence watched his hands as he tightened his grip on his training sword and released. "Like this?"

"You're gripping too tight, lass. Loose grip allows you to change position easily. The sword needs to become part of your arm, not just something you hold. Where your arm goes, the sword goes too. You need to let the cuts and jabs move through you as well as for you. Now, footing. The steps are very basic. Step forward, advance." Cain placed his hands on her shoulders and moved her backwards. "Step back, retreat. Got it?"

Prudence's eyes locked with Cain's. She nodded.

He circled her. "Now, when you need to move to the side, your back leg crosses over your front." He knocked her side with his wooden sword. "Straight posture." He stepped closer and lifted her chin with a finger. "Chin up, lass." Prudence caught his gaze and they watched each other momentarily.

They spent all afternoon in the middle of the deck as *The Bloody Maiden* cut through the gentle sea, with Cain showing Prudence how to hold herself, where to step, how tight to grip the wooden sword that he had had Ephraim make especially. All the while Prudence listened to every instruction, her gaze intense as she watched him, taking in as much as she could.

The moves seemed simple enough, but remembering them while a sword came at her, even just a wooden one, was more difficult. Prudence was well-practised with a knife but swords were a different matter altogether. The positioning, the way she had to stand, the distance between her and her attacker, it all felt strange to her. No doubt she would make sense of it with time, but it was an infuriating wait. She had been using her blade since childhood, now she felt like a child again learning something new.

THEY HAD BEEN AT SEA FOR FIVE DAYS. PRUDENCE STOOD AT the helm at Captain Morris' side as Mr. Norton steered the galleon across the wide, open water that separated Llynne from the rest of the world. It would be a few miles until they reached Tethys Trench, but already the water looked darker, and the lack of life made them feel completely alone.

Captain Morris clapped Norton on the shoulder and gave him his leave. The man had been at the helm all night, now it was the captain's turn to steer. The men worked hard, swabbing the deck to make it spick and span. They took turns watching from the crow's nest and pulling on the mainsail to change course. Prudence found herself helping Mr. Duarte, the ship's cook, as she'd at least had some experience assisting George back at the tavern.

The Maiden cut through the water with speed, eating up the miles beneath her with ease. She was a magnificent vessel, perfectly slender as she cut through the ocean like a knife, pressing on and gaining ground with every breath. The men were jovial as they worked, excited at the prospect of new ground to pillage. They sang as they went and Prudence could not help but join in.

> A month at sea has done and passed us by
> Nothin' but the sea and endless sky
> But, my lads, we must keep watch ahead
> A sleepy sailor is as good as dead!
>
> Heave, ho, don't let go!
> Heave, ho, ebb and flow
> Heave, ho, don't you know?
> The devil's down below!
>
> Raid and plunder, that's the life for me
> Give me nothin' but a life at sea!
> A ship is only worth its weakest hand

Do yer part, or we'll be eatin' sand.

Their singing was joyful and pleasant to hear out in the middle of the ocean, away from the rest of the world. But as they neared Tethys Trench the world seemed to grow darker and cold. Oblivious to the change in atmosphere, the crew carried on, singing away as they built up a sweat despite the harsh winds. Creatures began to come up to the ship, fascinated by the men's song.

One of the beast's fins broke through the surface of the water, their olive scales glistened against the sunlight. Prudence caught a glimpse of pale skin through the waves. An ivory white that looked too ghostly to be human. The skin was gaunt and almost purple in places it was so waxen. One creature bumped against the side of the ship and let out a small cry that sounded much like a gull. It ducked its head quickly below the water and away from the ship, as if it were scared of what was above the surface.

The crying song that the creatures made sent chills up Prudence's spine. She felt her eyes glaze over and Prudence's head was consumed by their mysterious song and the longing that it made her feel. It spread through her body like wildfire, exploding inside her chest. The melody was intoxicating and Prudence could hear nothing else. One of the crew, so entranced by the music, climbed over the side and dropped down into the freezing depths. The mermaids set on him in an instant, they tore hungrily at his flesh and scrapped over the pieces.

Prudence couldn't help but stare, eyes wide with shock and her hand clamped over her mouth. The beasts seemed to swarm around *The Maiden* becoming more alive by the minute. They cried and groped at the ship, trying to get hold of someone, anyone. The water buzzed with energy as the mermaids called for more of their own, all of them coming up to the surface and rocking the ship where she was. They made the water beneath them tremble with waves and the crew backed away from the sides in terror. They clung to one another to stay away from the man-eaters that called for their flesh. Prudence bit down on her lip to stop a whimper from escaping.

"Captain! Orders?" Mr. Norton yelled at Captain Morris with a look of despair. There was not much that could be done except try and steer the ship away from the monsters.

"Hard to port Mr. Norton! More speed men, we need more speed!" The crew rushed to their posts to make way and get as far away from this nightmare as possible. Within moments the rocking stopped and the waters were once again calm. The crew carried on rushing around but Prudence stopped. Were they gone?

Prudence caught a glimpse of one or two below the water's surface but most of them were gone from sight. A haunting melody drifted into Prudence's ears and she couldn't help but listen. The sound swam around her and seeped into her head, dancing like tinkling bells in her mind. She giggled. The sound was nice. It made her happy. The sirens bobbed in the water with only their eyes visible. They hummed their soft song and murmured the words, getting louder as they did so. Every crew member was stuck to the spot, entranced by the beautiful music that wormed its way into their brains. Some of them leant over the side of the ship to get a closer look at the mermaids.

"Pretty fishy. Look at the pretty fishy," one of the crew chuckled, "so pretty." His hand stretched out over the ocean in an attempt to reach them. Others began to lean over the sides and climb up the rigging, trying to get closer to the beasts that crooned to them. Prudence laughed softly and swayed her hips as she listened to the lilting tune. No one paid attention to the *splosh* as one of the crew members leant too far over the side and flopped into the sea. His laughter turned to piercing screams as the sirens tore into his limbs, but no one cared; the song was too hypnotising. He was dragged under and drowned.

Eleanora stepped out of the girl's cabin and smiled at Prudence. "Isn't it beautiful?" She smiled to herself and grabbed Prudence by the arms. "The pretty music! I like it! Where does it come from?" Prudence pulled Eleanora to the side to take a look. The women felt as if they were floating, a sense of glee washed over them as they leant over the side trying their best to catch what was down there.

"Look! I see one! There, oh I want it." Prudence pouted. Her conscious mind elsewhere, all she could think about was their beautiful harmony. As the crew fawned over the mystical beasts, *The Bloody Maiden* drifted far off course and deeper over the trench. Neither the crew nor Captain Morris noticed the crags of rock that lay ahead waiting for them. The beasts pushed and drove the ship towards the rocks where more of their singing sisters waited. The ship groaned as her sides dragged against stone, the last remnants of Tisnear.

Captain Morris fell as *The Maiden* bashed against the stone, banging his head on a lamp. The fall hurt and made his eyebrow bleed. The pain broke through the lilting voices of the beasts and he could hear the screams as his men were being ripped to shreds and drowned. Their song no longer held control over his mind and Captain Morris dashed to the helm at the sight of the danger that lay ahead. He couldn't let them crash, they'd be devoured within minutes, and his beautiful *Maiden* would lay wrecked on the seafloor.

Cain pulled the wheel hard to the right, as far as it would go. The rudder and ship turned, too slowly and not sharp enough. The ship's keel dragged on the jagged rocks beneath them and tore a hole in her side. The crew snapped out of their trance just in time to notice the water rushing into the hold. Men rushed down below deck with anything they could get their hands on to plug the hole.

"Get the shot plugs and mallet!" Ephraim yelled to his assistant, Thomas, who nodded and sprinted away to the carpenter's bench for the tools. Ephraim grabbed a rope and hauled it to the top deck. Prudence followed, desperate to help.

"What can I do?"

He tied the end of the rope around his waist and threw the other end at her. "Don't let go of that. I've gotta go over the side to plug this hole, if the waves get rough then I'll need you to haul me in, got it?" Prudence clutched the rope in her hands and nodded nervously. She looked around for another pair of hands, certain that she wouldn't be able to hold Ephraim's weight if it came to it. Garrick was throwing tools down the hatch for the men. "Garrick! Come help me."

He leapt to his feet and was at once by Prudence's side. Thomas appeared a moment later with shot plugs and a mallet which he handed to Ephraim. He steadied the plank as Ephraim climbed over the side and onto the wood with the tools. "Lower me slowly, got it?"

Thomas nodded and gripped the rope holding the plank and carefully released it inch by inch. Ephraim's face disappeared down the side of *The Maiden* and as he reached the gap, he yelled to the men inside to remove the padding they were holding in the hole. Soon, Prudence could hear the banging as he pounded a shot plug into the hole.

"Don't worry." Garrick flashed a reassuring grin at her. "We've been in worse scrapes. She'll be fine, she's strong." He patted the side of the ship affectionately.

After a while, the banging stopped and Ephraim yelled to be brought back up. Thomas hoisted him up slowly and with a huff, Ephraim pulled himself back onto the deck. He charged up the stairs to Captain Morris.

"She'll hold until we get to Vaerny—provided there ain't any more problems—but it'll need to be fixed soon, Captain."

Captain Morris nodded and motioned to Gabe to take over the wheel. "Thank you, Ephraim. Gabe keep her on course. No detours, we need to reach Vaerny as quickly as possible." The captain stepped away from the busy deck and into his cabin.

THE SHIP AND ITS CREW MANAGED TO GET BACK TO SOME kind of normal within the next few days when Cain insisted on a final lesson before they anchored in Vaerny's port.

"So, if I put my sword here," he lifted his wooden sword over his head and brought it down just over Prudence's shoulder, "then you will block it like this." Cain guided Pru's training sword slightly to the left, protecting her upper body from the downward blow. "Almost. You were just off. And now," Cain says, tilting Pru forward, "you lean in to add weight and strength. Are you ready?"

Prudence gripped her practice cutlass tighter and before she could respond, Captain Morris had swung his sword round to meet her side. He swung hard, the wood hitting Prudence's side with force. She winced as the blow stung. The few crew members who were watching their lesson sniggered, making her face burn red. She raised her cutlass high above her head and brought it down at the captain who blocked it easily with his own. The two parried slowly together over the length of deck swinging at one another. They soon developed a rhythm. As the afternoon sped by before their eyes, Prudence began to grasp the advice that Cain had given her. Their training swords clashed more quickly, each hitting the other harder with every blow.

"You block this swing, with your sword like this..." Cain guided her wooden sword into place, helping her to visualise the moves.

Their swords clashed when Cain gave a gentle swing but the blows often resulted in a minor strike to Prudence's ribs or shoulder and she would growl in both pain and anger.

Cain smirked. "You've got to keep your cool, lass. Get angry and you'll get sloppy. You're not going to beat anyone while you're in a huff." He knocked his sword against hers so hard that it almost flew from her grip. He raised his sword again and brought it crashing down against her own. Prudence growled again. Anger bubbled to the surface with every embarrassing hit.

She pushed forward trying to force Cain backwards across the deck, but he didn't budge an inch. She hurled her wooden sword in the direction of Cain's head but he ducked, narrowly avoiding the blow.

"You've got to watch yourself, lass. With a real sword... could've cut your head off by now." He knocked his sword gently against her head, a laugh erupting from his chest. The few onlookers cackling behind Prudence only infuriated her more. She glowered at Gabe, making him blush red, and gritted her teeth.

She threw herself forward, her training sword flying through the air, aimed directly at Cain. She would get a hit in somewhere, if it was the last thing she did. The humiliation burned on her cheeks as more of the crew gathered round, the amusement clear on their faces.

Cain's sword clashed against Prudence's multiple times before she found an opening. She swung the training blade over her head, cracking it down on top of Cain's skull. His hand pressed against the blow, an almost impressed look on his face. She dropped the sword and it clattered against the deck.

"I think that's enough for now." He smiled briefly at her, before turning on his heel and walking away. "It was a lucky shot," he called over his shoulder at her, despite the smile creeping onto his face.

Prudence puffed her chest out, a minuscule feeling of pride swelling in her bosom at the achievement. Perhaps this new life was the right path for her. Despite the pushback from some of the crew, she felt comfortable on these decks, at home surrounded by dirty, rough criminals.

The smell of the salty sea air left her lungs feeling fresh and clear. The wind blowing through her hair as they crested waves gave her a feeling of freedom that she'd never known back home. No, not home. That had never been her home, she realised that now. This was where she was meant to be. A simple, long life where nothing ever happened was no life at all. But this, this was truly living.

She locked eyes with Mr. Norton who had been watching her from the wheel. He winked at her. "You did well, miss. Soon you'll be fighting as good as any man on this ship. Shit, maybe even better."

"You really think so?" she asked, a grin breaking out across her face. She couldn't help but feel attached to the old Quarter Master despite the short time they had known one another. He had the kind of personality that radiated love. Prudence imagined that he was the kind of man who would make a perfect grandfather to someone.

"Aye, missy. You've got a spark in you that I don't often

see. And I've seen more than my fair share of people in my time. You'll be fitting right in, in no time." He patted her shoulder. "You ever need someone to spar with you just let me know, all right? I may not be a spry as I was in my youth, but damn it I still know my way around a sword or two."

Prudence smiled at him. "Thank ye, really. I'll keep that in mind, Mr. Norton." She squeezed his hand affectionately.

"If ye can cope with almost getting eaten by those fishwives the other day, then learning to swing a cutlass will be no trouble." He chuckled lightly and frowned. "'Tis a horrible fate."

She had never seen such things before, had never known that that was why the fishermen on Llynne stuck close to its shores. She had never realised that that was why the outside world never bothered her small island; out of fear of being torn apart by ferocious beasts. "To be drowned and eaten? Yes, truly I cannot imagine something more terrible." She pursed her lips and fiddled with her fingers. Mr. Norton shook his head and turned to her.

"No, my dear. Not us, them."

"What do you mean?" she frowned.

The old man sighed and sat back on his stool. "They were women once. Like yerself. On ships like this one, pirate ships, merchant ships, ships of the fleet. But ye see, a lot of men think women aboard are considerably unlucky. Witches, some men call 'em. Wicked women who bring bad luck onto sailors and their vessels, it's ridiculous o' course. But that's what some men think.

Think that women will curse 'em and cause 'em to crash and drown. Bollocks I say, but that's what happens. Anyway, these women, overpowered by bastard men, were bound by the hands and feet with rope, and tossed over the side to drown before they could cause any damage."

"Oh my goodness, that's awful. How terrifyin'. What happened to these women?" Mr. Brady drifted into Prudence's mind. It wasn't so surprising that it happened though.

"Well according to some legends, they change into the very beasts that attacked us earlier. As the story goes, some old witch was charged this awful fate and before they could condemn her to the depths, she cursed herself. Cursed any woman that was tied up and drowned to change into these creatures and get their revenge on sailors by drowning 'em. Not many people believe it, they think they're just creatures that live down below, but I know that's the truth."

Prudence nodded intrigued by the whole thing. "How do ye know?"

"I just feel it in my gut to be true, missy." Prudence nodded vaguely, deep in thought. It was truly amazing to think about.

They stood in comfortable silence next to one another with Mr. Norton's hand on the wheel as Ephraim, the ship's carpenter, threw knives at the wooden door below them, notching the wood with every flick.

Prudence watched him, fascinated. He never spoke much, at least not around Prudence. His shaved head practically gleamed in the sunshine and the slightest glimmer of sweat coated his brow. Despite his silent demeanour, he seemed very popular with the rest of the crew.

Prudence descended the stairs towards him. "I suppose I have ye to thank for the training swords. There's probably not much need for them here normally."

Ephraim nodded curtly but didn't speak. He threw the knife in his hand at the door once again, the tip of the blade burying itself deep into the wood. "You shouldn't stand so close ya know. Might catch ya by mistake." He plucked the blade from the door and wiggled it between his fingers. He spun on his heel, letting the blade fly loose from his grip, making Prudence jump.

She stepped back slightly. "Yer really good at that.'

"Should hope so, been doing it since I was ten."

"Ten?!"

He smirked at her. "Gotta learn fast in this life, girly. Never know when something might stab you in the back. Best to be prepared."

Prudence opened her mouth to speak but found no words available. Ephraim's revelation hit her like a slap in the face. She had been so focused on the good of getting away from Llynne, she hadn't thought much about the dangers. She supposed she should take Ephraim's advice. Learn now... and fast.

NOT LONG AFTER PRUDENCE HAD GOTTEN TO SLEEP IN THE cot she shared with Eleanora, she was woken by the sound of shouting on the deck. The ship was rocking so violently, it was hard to stand. Out on deck, the rain hammered down hard and lightning flashed overhead. The men tugged on the ropes, trying desperately to lower the sails before they could be destroyed by the weather. Only the mainsail would remain up. Water was flooding the deck, making the wood slick underfoot. Prudence steadied herself against the railing as she made her way over to the helm and to Captain Morris.

"She's gonna struggle to keep it together in this storm!" The captain shouted over the noise. "We have to get to port!" Prudence knew that *The Maiden* was nearing port by now and grabbed the captain's spyglass from his belt. It was difficult to see through the storm; the rain was slashing down and the sky was as black as squid ink.

"It's no use, I can't see anything!" she hollered over the crashing of the waves all around them. *The Maiden* groaned and veered wildly against the strong wind. She could just about make out the shape of Mr. Norton and Mr. Brady yelling at the crew as they ran from their posts to minimise the damage.

Lightning flashed a wide sheet of white across the sky, illuminating the ship for a fraction of a second. In the sudden brilliance, Prudence spotted Mr. Lowell climbing the rigging as it flailed wildly. "Should he really be up there? What if he falls?"

Cain cast a brief glance at the crew member above them. "Haven't got much choice lass, we need those sails down before they're all destroyed. Mr. Lowell has steady legs, you'd be better off worrying about the lightning." He clung tight to the wheel as the ship lurched once again.

"Help the men tie things down. We can't afford to lose our supplies!"

Prudence nodded and helped Charlie, a sandy-haired young man around her age, secure the barrels on deck, tying them to whatever she could. The smaller crates on deck were passed down through the hatches before being shut tight. The windows below deck were covered with panels and the opening ports were secured shut.

Eleanora found Prudence below deck, sodden with rain. The young girl's red hair, loose from sleep, was now plastered to her face. "What do we do?" she asked, shivering in a shift and jacket, and wiped her nose against her sleeve.

Prudence grabbed Eleanora by the collar and hauled her further down below. "You are going to stay right here, got it?" She pointed Elea toward the main bulk of the ship's supplies. "Tie these down, ok?"

Eleanora nodded, then paused. "You're not going back out there, are you? It's insane!"

Prudence shoved a bundle of rope into her hands. "I'll be fine. The men need help." She gave her friend the brightest of smiles before climbing the ladder and disappearing out of the hatch.

On deck, Prudence staggered across the soaked floorboards as they crashed through the waves. She found Cain kneeling at the stern fumbling about with a wooden device that Prudence had never seen before. "What are you doing?!" she cried, but he hadn't heard her over the cacophony of the storm. She placed a hand on his shoulder and knelt next to him. "Do you need help?" she yelled close to his ear.

Cain turned to face her. "I need to get this drogue over! It's the only thing that's going to help her stay steady in this wind!" He stood and lifted the wooden contraption onto his shoulder. With a grunt of effort, Prudence helped the captain throw it over the back of the ship and watched as it bobbed in the aggressive waters below for a moment before getting caught in a wave. Cain made sure that the drogue was secure, wiping endless fat rain droplets from his face as he smiled. "That'll keep us from tipping!"

Prudence nodded but the sight of the wooden drogue sliding over the waves didn't do much to quell the nerves inside her. Such a little thing to put all of their trust into with a giant storm raging overhead.

After some time, Prudence could just about see lights bobbing in the distance and yelled to Captain Morris that they were headed for land. Finding port wasn't as easy however, and Prudence couldn't tell what part of the island they were heading towards—whether it was the port or a cliff face. The storm pushed and pulled at *The Bloody Maiden*, dragging her this way and that as she got closer to the island of Vaerny. The rain soaked the crew and tossed them about the deck as the ship battled the bumpy waves.

"I can't make it out, Captain!" Prudence had to scream over the roar of the ocean and the shouting of the crew. The captain grabbed the spyglass from Prudence and took a look. The ship swayed harshly in the storm and Cain realised that he couldn't work out where the port was with what little he could see.

"She can't take much more of this!" He yelled and steered hard to starboard. Prudence hoped that they would find anchorage soon. The storm raged for only a few hours, though it felt like years. It wreaked havoc on the ship's rigging and injured a few of the men, the mainsail was ripped in the mayhem and needed stitching before they could use it again. Thankfully, the island was now only a mile or so away. And port, it seemed, was to the left of them, at the edge of the island.

The Maiden was damaged and made slow progress with only the foresail and topsail in use, but eventually she sailed into Vaerny's port and berthed away from the few others already there.

5

MAN'S WORK

Prudence skipped down the small pathway that led into the centre of town. Without Eleanora by her side, it felt strange somehow, like she was missing half of herself. In spite of the hollow feeling in her chest though, it was incredible to see the little town. Quite similar in size to that of Llynne, Malaine was a quaint fishing town nestled at the edge of Vaerny.

Only a few minutes' walk from the port, Malaine was the island's main source of all manner of fish, molluscs, shrimp, oysters, and crab. As such, the market was overflowing with food from the sea, overwhelming the surrounding area with a stink that only comes from being so close to the water. Salt hung heavy in the air, fish were being gutted on the pontoon, and seaweed was drying in the sun. The smell reminded Pru of Llynne.

The entrance to the fishing town was a narrow path that went from the shoreline, up the sand dunes, and over a few yards of heathland before arriving at the edge of the bustling town. It reeked of all kinds of fish and an overload of spices and salts that assaulted Prudence's nose as she walked. There were people everywhere, hurrying about from their boats in the harbour.

Their wooden houses lining the streets were so crowded together that there was no space between the buildings and the town market. The market was nothing more than a bundle of wooden shacks propped up in the midst of the chaos. Every stall was piled high with goods as people bartered for what they needed.

Women hung clothes on washing lines outside their homes and brought out buckets of oats for the goats they kept grazing outside, tied to stakes that were fixed in the earth. Cats swarmed around a small thatch-roofed shop that smelt strongly of fish and assorted meats. Prudence watched as a man came out with a plate full of fish heads and tails, which the cats leapt on hungrily. Children ran about the streets playing a game of bulldog, chasing one another down alleyways and Prudence could hear them yell 'oh' and 'not me!' as they were caught. She chuckled to herself. It was lovely to see so many people. She hadn't seen this many since Llynne's busy marketplace.

The path was dusty beneath Prudence's feet, it rose in clouds and clung to her skin as her boots scuffed the ground. It was warm in Malaine, the sun shone strongly, despite it being late autumn—an extremely different environment from the storm that Prudence and the crew had witnessed the night before. The townspeople seemed happy, rather content with their busy lives, and everyone welcomed the crew brightly when they bought goods or chatted to the people. Captain Morris caught up to

Prudence who had walked quite a way further than the rest of the crew, and passed her a handful of coins.

"Anything you fancy purchasing, lass?" He grinned.

Prudence glanced at the coins curiously. "Where did you get these from then?" They felt warm in her hand and she clutched them tightly, not wanting to lose them. Cain smiled at her knowingly and glanced at the people around them.

"They're everywhere if you know where to look." He winked and moved away from her, back to his crew who were laughing and mucking about in the street, browsing what the market had to offer. Prudence looked at the coins and smiled. She was sure she could find something beautiful to buy with these. There were shops and wooden stalls down almost every street in the centre of Malaine and Prudence explored them excitedly, looking for things that she'd like. Prudence followed her nose down a small alleyway until she came to a bakery with delicious smells wafting out the door.

She pushed open the door and the bell rang loudly, announcing her entrance. A riot of sickly-sweet smells assaulted her senses as she stepped inside. The woman in the little shop smiled at her as she walked in and smiled even wider when she spied the coins hidden inside Prudence's sweaty palm. Prudence browsed the buns and pastries that the woman had made with a new intense hunger. This smelled better than anything she had ever eaten before. At home, she was too used to stale and burnt things. On the ship, it had hardly been better. Here, there were sweet breads and sticky buns that made her mouth water.

Prudence bought herself some warm biscuits that tasted like cinnamon. She ate one hungrily and saved the rest for another time, savouring the sweet taste on her tongue. She had only tasted the exotic spice a few times before. Avery and Khari had once delivered a small sack to Mrs. Langley at The Wanderer's Inn. She wondered how the baker had gotten a hold of the spice, perhaps there were smugglers working through Malaine. Perhaps *The Maiden* and her crew could take advantage of the business.

For most of the morning Prudence wandered around the new town, meeting people and looking at everything they had to sell. She found some beautiful pieces of jewellery on a stall near port, sold by a pretty young girl with stunning silver hair. She was a sweet girl, about the same age as Eleanora, and she chatted away happily to Prudence. She reminded Pru of her friend, so sweet and innocent, like she lived in a different world to the one around them. As she was about to leave, Prudence noticed the brooch that the girl wore; another Maenon witch. Prudence smiled at the girl.

"Thank you for these."

The girl nodded. "Not at all, miss. It was nice to meet you." Prudence turned and headed down to the shoreline. The island wasn't just considerably different from Llynne —it was *extraordinary*. The port was man-made, with walls and wooden jetties leading out onto the water for the smaller boats to be moored. There were worn paths and dirt roads leading from the towns to the city at the heart of the island. Merchants travelled to and from the island regularly, trading with townsfolk and the governor.

It was a beautiful island. Prudence could see *The Bloody Maiden*, the size of a dinghy from this distance, towards the far side of the harbour, away from the other ships. She watched as children played on the jetty. Little ones running up and down the wobbly planks trying to catch one another. Some of them tripped and fell on their bottom— one little girl lost her balance and toppled over the side into the harbour. The child bobbed up instantly and took a deep breath in, her brown hair plastered to her face as she held onto the other children's arms as they pulled her up.

Prudence watched her giggle and try to make the other children wet. She smiled to herself. They were cute, squealing with excitement if they got too near the wet little girl. It was nice to see them playing freely, unconcerned with the adult worries of life. It was a stark contrast to the childhood that Prudence had experienced. At least theirs seemed like a happy one.

Along the bank where Prudence had walked was a dusty track that led off into the distance. From this high up, Prudence could make out the shape of a little town, miles from where she was. Perhaps she would go there whilst they were here. It would be nice to see more of the island than just this tiny fishing town. Maybe Captain Morris would join her? Prudence highly doubted that Eleanora would want to spend time with her, but maybe Cain would.

After a while, Prudence found her way back to Captain Morris and his crew. Eleanora, it seemed, had decided to remain on the ship. Prudence's heart sank slightly, she thought that Elea might change her mind. The captain smiled at her indulgently when he noticed that she had returned.

"Have you been enjoying yourself?" he asked her.

Prudence nodded and lifted her cloth bag full of purchases. "Aye, there is some beautiful stuff 'ere. Are we to return to the ship now?" She wished to go back and see Eleanora, and try to make Elea forgive her. They had not spent this much time apart for many years, and Prudence felt lost without her friend by her side. It was abnormal for them to be against one another; the girls had almost never argued in the entire time that they'd known one another, despite their many differences.

"We thought tha' we might check-in some place around 'ere, woman." Mr. Brady grinned at the thought. Prudence could see it on his face, he wished to spend the whole night looting men and spending the coin on whores.

Prudence shook her head. "Wouldn't it be safer to stay away from people? What reason have we for being here that they won't get suspicious of? A large group of rowdy men are going to stick out in a quiet place like this. I don't care what ye do but I'm going back to the ship." Prudence crossed her arms indignantly. Captain Morris sighed and glanced at the crew.

"The lass is right; we've got to lay low. Men, we return to the ship. Any man who wants to stay behind is welcome, but if he gets caught, we'll not be coming back for him." Cain stared pointedly at Mr. Brady, who had difficulty controlling himself at the best of times. He might not like it, but he wasn't stupid—he didn't want to be sent to the noose any more than the rest of them did. Mr. Brady huffed and sulked his way back to the ship with the rest of the crew, not wanting to disobey his captain.

On board *The Maiden*, some of the crew went below deck. Mr. Duarte began to cook up food for dinner whilst the men stashed whatever they had managed to steal whilst on the island. Prudence went to check on Eleanora, only to find her asleep on the cot. She couldn't begin to guess what her friend had been up to all day... but something had worn her out. She didn't want to disturb her, but impatience won over as Pru was desperate to give Eleanora what she had bought her. She couldn't stand Eleanora thinking ill of her any longer, she had to fix it. She shook Elea gently and sat on the edge of the bed. Eleanora stirred, opening her eyes slowly and seeing Prudence.

"You're back," she muttered, still sleepy, "I thought you'd be staying in the town."

"I didn't think we'd blend in so well. We'll head back there tomorrow, I imagine." Prudence nodded to herself. Eleanora looked like she had gotten some sleep at least. The bags under her eyes were less prominent than before and the colour in her cheeks had returned. She rolled over to face away from Prudence and shut her eyes again.

"I uh, I got you something," Prudence grabbed her cloth bag from the floor and put it between them. "It's not much but... I thought you'd like it. Green always suited you." She reached into the bag and held out the jade necklace for Eleanora to take. Eleanora turned reluctantly to face her.

"It's not stolen, is it?"

Prudence sighed. "I bought it."

Eleanora hesitated, her hand poised in mid-air before taking it. "It's beautiful, thank you."

Prudence smiled curtly. "You're welcome."

Eleanora fell silent after their short exchange, placed the jewels around her neck and stared at the ceiling. It was clear to Prudence that they had finished conversing for now. She didn't want to push her luck. For now, she was just grateful that Elea was speaking to her at all. She stood and left the room, not wanting to prolong the awkward silence that filled the space between them. It would be best to leave her be. She would come around eventually. One day they would be best friends again, closer than blood sisters, always by one another's side and always happy together.

Most of the crew were still in their quarters eating whatever the cook had scrounged up for the day. A few of the men were on deck playing cards and throwing knives at the ship's side. Prudence eyed the pile of coins and jewels that lay on the table next to them. It was a hefty loot for just one person. Perhaps they had put all of their lots together? They had collected some magnificent prizes, that much was plain to see. Prudence glided down the stairs and ran her hand along the collection, the coins clinked under her touch.

"Oi missy, how's about we let you touch that prize if you let us touch something else." Mr. Reed clapped his hands together and licked his lips. Prudence scoffed.

"I mean it 'ardly seems fair you havin' a whore stashed up there all for yourself. Come on... share."

Prudence's face darkened and she stepped up to the man. "I think ye'll find that's a dangerous thing to say to me. Step down." Her fingers twitched to grab a blade and shove it into his stomach. She gritted her teeth so hard that it caused a painful throbbing in the centre of her forehead. Mr. Reed was a fool to think that Prudence would tolerate disrespect. A few of the men heard her stirring and came over to watch the scene unfold.

"Manny's right, wench. That's all women are good for anyway, isn't it? Whoring their lives away and obeying their men." Mr. Brady smirked at Prudence and tried to grab her arm. She slapped his hand away and scowled at him.

"Yer a pig." Prudence glared at the men. They were revolting. She moved back towards the stairs and placed a guarding hand over the rail, barring them from hers and Elea's room. "Any of ye go near her an' I'll kill you myself." The men roared with laughter and snorted at her.

"Oh, yeah. How do you plan to do that, *milady*? A little whore like yerself against us?" Manny smirked at her before erupting into laughter again, encouraging the other men with him. Prudence took the chance whilst he wasn't looking and grabbed the stool closest to her and brought it crashing down over his head, knocking him to the floor. The stool broke into pieces and she snatched up the sharpest one, gripping it so hard that her knuckles turned white. She faced the rest of the crowd.

"Now... who would like to say that again? Hmm?" Prudence kicked Manny, still on the floor rubbing his head, as she stepped past him. "I can give as good as any of you *men*. If any of ye so much as try to go near her...

you'll be sorry." The men chuckled but walked away from her all the same. It was clear that they wouldn't be able to get rid of her as easily as they had thought, especially not with the captain on her side.

Prudence sighed and glanced down at Manny on the floor. The idiot would most likely have a lump on his head on the morrow. He deserved it. Eleanora was out of the question.

The sun had sunk so low in the sky, it was almost entirely hidden by the waves when Prudence found Captain Morris on deck, staring at the island. It looked beautiful in the light of dusk, with only a faint orange glow. Everything was quiet. Peaceful.

"Do you ever wonder if there is anything more beautiful than this in the world?" Prudence breathed out and leant on the side.

Cain turned and looked at her. "I'm not sure anything could be." He cleared his throat and tugged at his shirt sleeve. "Would it be in your interests to accompany me to shore, lass?"

Prudence smiled. "O' course, Captain, but what would we be doing?"

The captain chuckled and tapped his nose. "You'll see."

"IT's BEEN YEARS SINCE I DID THIS, I'M NOT SURE I remember how. I'm sure I've lost the touch."

Cain nudged Prudence forward. "You can do this, it's easy. Walk past and bump into him." Prudence nodded and stepped forward into the middle of the street. The man ahead of them had many coins in his pocket. Prudence's eye held a gleam of familiarity and Cain knew that she must be thinking back to her childhood.

The man turned away from the stall he had been perusing and headed unknowingly towards them. Prudence moved ever so slightly away from Cain and towards the unsuspecting man. He barely noticed her as he walked past stalls of spices and silks, meat and mead. Cain watched with his arms crossed over his chest and a smirk on his face as she bumped into the man's shoulder. The collision sent his sack flying and sent all the goods rolling on the floor. Prudence bent down at the exact moment that he scrambled around to pick up his belongings.

"I'm so sorry, sir, I didn't see where I was goin' please, let me." She tucked a piece of hair behind her ear as she handed him back his things. Cain bit back a chuckle. She was charming, there was no denying it. He was surprised the man wasn't completely entranced by her.

"Am so sorry to have inconvenienced ye like this," she leant towards him as she spoke and slipped her hand into his pocket, hand clasping the coins. Her hands moved to round her back as she smiled sweetly. "Av a good night, mister."

The man frowned and scowled at her before hurrying away, his mood considerably worsened by the inconvenience. Prudence skipped back to Captain Morris, flinging her arms around his neck and giggled, pleased with herself.

"Did you see that? I did it! I can't believe I did it!" She

showed him the coins gripped in her hand, there was plenty there, enough for a hefty meal or a place to stay. Prudence had done well.

Cain grinned at her and slung an arm over her shoulder. "You did good, lass." The two meandered down the street with the sound of coins clinking in their pockets and took their time spending it on trinkets, dark rum, gin, and all manner of delights that were rarely available on *The Bloody Maiden*.

They spent a lazy evening sat in the far corner of the local inn, boots resting on the table edge as they drank, ate, and played cards. Every now and then an old patron would scowl and moan at the noise they were making. Prudence had a laugh that was less than dignified and her loud guffaws were often accompanied by a loud snort. That only entertained Cain all the more and made him try even harder to amuse her. And as the night wore on and the brisk air of autumn gave way to a wintery cold, he removed his worn burgundy coat and draped it over Prudence's shivering shoulders.

They entertained themselves for hours, finding all manner of stalls in which to buy things with their stolen loot, until eventually, it had all been spent. They wandered around the little fishing town for a while, taking in the sights that came alive in the darkness. Oil lamps and lanterns gave the world a warm glow as men and women traipsed the streets, their voices loud and merry despite the chill in the air.

Eventually, the pair came across a group of men, clearly intoxicated, heading down a side alley. The men seemed to be distracted, arguing amongst themselves.

Cain eyed one man's possessions from their spot at the end of the alley. The men had not yet seen them, but they seemed different from the rest of the townsfolk; an air of danger surrounded them.

"Cain. Forget them, we can find money elsewhere. Let's leave before any trouble starts." Prudence tugged at his arm but he shook her off.

"I'm hurt that you doubt me." He placed a hand over his heart mockingly. "This'll be easy, lass." The bag that the men had at their feet was open slightly and Cain and Pru could see the silver poking out, taunting them. The men argued and shoved one another, too busy in their own business to pay attention to a drunk couple. Cain sauntered past with Prunier by his side and grabbed the sack from its place on the floor. Just as the captain grinned to himself, the men noticed the missing loot.

"Hey!" he screamed, causing the other two to turn around. "He's stealing our stuff!" The men glared at Cain and Prudence as the biggest of them pulled a knife from his belt.

Prudence grabbed Cain's shirt and pulled him round the corner. The pair broke out in a run, trying in their drunken state not to trip over the uneven cobbles. The men followed hot on their tail but Pru saw them struggling as they ran through the streets. The biggest one puffed and panted like a mare ready to give birth, his short legs staggering to keep up with his friends. Cain looked around. There were plenty of places to hide, but with the men so close behind, there was no hope of losing them so quickly.

He pulled Prudence down alleyways and through

stalls that had been set up for selling that morning. Prudence was quick on her feet and darted round the stands with relative ease behind Cain. His head whipped back and forth, flitting between checking on her and looking ahead to keep running. Luckily, the men were not doing so well as they all struggled to push past the hordes of people out in the market. They were disorganised, shoving one another to get through the small gaps, fumbling as they all pushed at once.

The men were just far enough behind that Cain and Pru could probably find somewhere to hide. If they were lucky.

From their spot in the little courtyard, Cain could see three streets leading away from their pursuers. He grabbed Prudence's hand and the two stumbled down the closest street, looking for somewhere to blend in. He could hear her breathing become heavier and Cain suspected that she was running out of steam. He knew that he'd guessed correctly as Prudence doubled over, clutching her side. "Come on, lass, we have to keep moving. We'll be able to stop soon."

The captain grabbed her hand and dragged her forward, they didn't have time to stop out in the open. As he turned to look behind, he bumped into the biggest of the men. *Shit.* He grinned at Cain and lifted the knife closer to Cain's face. They could hear the others somewhere in the distance. It wouldn't be long before they caught up.

"I do believe that the bag yer holding is mine. Clearly there's been a mistake." The clenched fist and dangerous glint in his eye made it clear that this was not up for discussion. The man was considerably taller than Cain, but he was also rather skinny, and no match for Cain's stocky build. Cain punched the man square in the jaw, sending him sprawling to the floor. As he fell, his knife caught Cain's side with a sharp sting. He grunted as it cut into him but pushed forward and hopped over the man on the floor, with Prudence at his heels.

The man clutched his face, groaning as the other two joined him. Cain and Prudence had already vanished from sight.

"Go get them!" He hollered. He tried to stand but his ankle had twisted and he gasped in pain. The other two continued their chase but they soon lost track of the pair and their stolen loot.

After a while of wandering down endless alleyways, they found a house that seemed empty. Cain picked up a rock from the path without preamble and hurled it through the window. Prudence winced at the noise, but no one seemed to hear it. Cain put an arm through the broken glass and wiggled the window frame until it popped open. The two climbed inside, careful to miss the broken glass.

The candles were all extinguished and it looked as if no one had used the fireplace for hours. Prudence froze at the sound of approaching footsteps and voices out on the street.

"I can't believe you lost them, fuck! Davey's gonna be pissed."

"Just shut up and help me. He doesn't have to find out if we can get to them first."

Eventually, the sounds faded and Prudence breathed a

sigh of relief. Cain glanced around at the cosy living room and ducked through an alcove. They might be here a while and his shirt was filthy.

"Where the fuck have you gone now?" He heard Prudence mutter and he chuckled. Amused, he listened to the way she marched, annoyed, from room to room.

He was looking for a bed chamber but couldn't help but glance at the leather-bound books that were lined up along every wall. He felt the impulsive need to scan the titles to see which he did not already own. It was a magnificent collection. It smelled just like his cabin. Rich, worn leather, the faint scent of smoke... it smelled like home. He had spent years cultivating his collection of escapist adventures.

It was a small room, with dust covering every surface, save for an old, worn chair in the corner of the room. The fabric was torn in places and a spring stuck out of the seat. It made Cain think of Captain Heil's office. He'd sat on a chair just like that, a snivelling ten-year-old, as the captain told him he'd be working as a cabin boy on *The King's Destroyer*.

Shaking himself out of long-hidden memories, he moved further into the house and found the bedroom. Cain removed his shirt, noticing the blood stains amongst the dirt, and rummaged through the chest at the foot of the bed for another.

"Where did ye get all o' those?" Prudence asked, making Cain jump. She couldn't draw her eyes away from the scars and tattoos that covered his chest.

Cain snorted. "Surprisingly, not where you'd think. Most of these were from *lawful* folks, not thieves or bandits, or whores like most people'd expect. We're not the only ones who should be locked up."

Prudence stayed silent, unsure how to respond. He could see that even though she wasn't sure what to say, she agreed with him. The people who were most corrupt hid behind stone walls and silk blouses. Power breeds corruption. How anyone could think that people who have nothing are the scum of the earth, when standing before them were the people of the law, was beyond him. It was no wonder that people who were strong enough to break free of lawful bounds decided to take their fate into their own hands.

Once they were sure that the crooks were truly gone, they left the house with the few provisions that they could carry.

PRUDENCE HEARD THE RING OF THE TOWN BELL ECHO through the streets as the clock hand hit the hour. The sun shone high overhead and beat down ferociously, making her eyes hurt, no doubt worsened by the liquor consumed earlier. She saw people rushing to the town square, and curious, she followed them. Captain Morris followed her but he kept his distance. He seemed reluctant to get too close to the townsfolk or the square. Hordes of people gathered in the small courtyard and Prudence was shoved towards the back of the crowd, unable to see much, even on her tiptoes. The crowd hushed suddenly and Prudence heard a commanding voice that everyone looked to as he spoke.

"This man, Charles Avery, has been found guilty on all accounts of thievery, piracy, and smuggling. He shall be hung from the neck, until dead." The crowd jeered and threw things at the man who was in chains on the platform. Prudence paled as the nerves rattled so fiercely in her stomach that she thought she might vomit. She turned to Cain.

"I know him! Cain, I know him, they can't hang him!" Prudence's voice came out squeaky and panicked. She was horrified but tried her best to hide it before someone noticed. Captain Morris shook his head at her. They could hang him and they *would* hang him, she could see it in his face. No need for a trial if it meant that the townsfolk got to see a hanging, and the governor would be burdened by one less pirate amongst his flock.

Prudence could not fathom the idea that a man she had traded with, on her small island where no one else dared to go, was about to be hung. She wondered for a moment what Mrs. Langley would think of her trader no longer being available. Prudence chuckled involuntarily and could not stop herself. Perhaps it was nervous laughter. It snuck its way out of her throat and would not stop. The people around her frowned and muttered as they tried to listen to the speaker on the platform again.

"On behalf of our Governor Atkey, I decree that this shall be his last waking hour." He turned to Avery. "Do you have anything to say before you die?"

The smuggler looked badly wounded, his face was bloody and his nose broken. His shirt bloomed flowers of dried blood across his middle and Pru guessed that he might have some broken ribs from the way he was straining to breathe. The executioner made sure that the noose was tight around his neck.

"Yer all wantin' to see criminals executed up here to make yerselves feel safer. To feel protected from the monsters that ye fear. But I am not that monster. 'Av no quarrel with any of yous. My quarrel is with them." He glared at the soldier to the right of him. "They have made me, and people like me, out to be those that you should fear. They mean to keep ye in line through that fear.

That fear is the only thing keepin' the likes o' them in charge. We are many. They are few. The day that ye forget the fear and see the freedom, is the day they lose everything. Those cunts—" He spat the word into the crowd as if left a terrible taste in his mouth, "will fall to a world of anarchy an' chaos that would free each and every one of ye, if ye weren't so shit scared to face 'em. The day will come when kings and gov'nors are trampled into the mud as they deserve. Death to the king and his dutiful soldiers for they have the blackest hearts of us all!" Avery's voice rose to a yell as he spouted curses and obscenities at the crowd as the soldiers tried to hold him still.

Captain Morris grabbed a hold of Prudence's shoulder and pulled her backwards, away from the crowd and the excitement.

"What are you doing?" he whispered sharply at her, "Do you want to bring attention to us here? There may be people travelling in and out of this island every day, but they'd soon realise that we look a little out of place if people stared at us too much!" Prudence sobered up quickly and looked at her feet.

"He's getting hung. A man I know." A man she was forced to interact with while Mrs. Langley did her business, was getting hung right in front of them. "Cain, what if that was us? What if that was Elea?" She couldn't hide the panic that rose suddenly in her voice, or the tears that threatened to escape her eyes. Captain Morris' gaze softened and he let go of her shoulder.

"It won't," he said quietly, unsure of his own answer. He didn't wish to lie to her, nor did he wish to flaunt death in her face. It would always be a risk. It would always be a possibility. But with that risk came life. Without that risk, Cain had no life and he doubted whether Prudence would have one either. At least the death they risked would be swift; hung or shot. Most folk weren't so lucky.

A creak came from deep in the crowd and a thud as the body dropped on the rope. The crowd made a loud gasp, followed by a cheer so loud that it filled the street around them. Prudence caught a glimpse of Avery's body writhing and struggling from the weight of the rope around his neck. The twitching lasted for a few agonising minutes before his body finally went limp. She gave him a curt nod before turning away.

The rest of the day seemed to pass slowly and quietly, as if Prudence was in a dream. It was a strange feeling to watch a man that she thought to be vile, hang, and actually feel sorry for him. Prudence had never liked him, but he was a string that connected her to her old life, something that now felt gone completely. She wasn't sure if that was good or bad. He wasn't a bad man, really. He was no different than her, deep down. He was doing what he felt was necessary to give him a life. Now that life was gone.

They returned to *The Bloody Maiden*, pockets clinking and bellies full, but Prudence's head felt like it was full of fog. Watching Avery hang had numbed her more than she would have guessed. It was a sobering reality to see yourself in someone else as they died. The day carried on being considerably dull; the crew did their work, played card games, and slept. Eleanora avoided Prudence as much as she could, but after a while, she had to put up with Prudence being in the cabin—there was nothing else to do.

Eleanora still ignored Prudence every chance she got. Prudence didn't bother to try and speak to her; she lacked the motivation. Why should she bother trying if her friend wanted only to avoid her? It was a pointless endeavour. They would speak civilly for a few minutes before everyone went quiet again, and Prudence would leave the room feeling exactly how she had before she went in.

So instead, she sat on deck, throwing knives at the wooden floor over and over again, completely bored with the day. She spent so long there that eventually it was as if her mind went into a trance. She could see the crew working in front of her, hear them speak to one another, smell the food that Mr. Duarte had cooked up down below... but it was all so muted and far away.

Eventually the day turned into night and the crew ventured off into the many taverns and brothels that Malaine had to offer. Once Eleanora was asleep, Prudence found herself filing through the trinkets that lined the shelves on the furthest wall, ones that Cain must have collected on his travels. It was strange imagining where Cain might have travelled to over the years. Prudence had never been anywhere. After browsing them for a while, she made her way out onto the deck. She lay down, limbs spread out and stayed like that, just watching the stars overhead.

A nudge to her side with a boot pulled her out of her semi-dozing state and she looked up at Cain hovering over her. "Wouldn't have guessed you were a snorer," he chuckled and offered a hand to help her up. "At least it's not loud snoring like Mr. Norton, keeping everyone awake."

Prudence rubbed her eyes and ran her fingers through her hair, mussed from half sleep. "What's going on?"

"You fell asleep."

Prudence nodded, she was beginning to remember how bored she had been and how the waves had made *shushing* noises that sounded so peaceful. The night air was warm so she'd thought, what if she just lay down for a moment before going to bed? At least she hadn't been there all night. Cain walked away from her as she got up and meandered over to the dinghy.

"Are you going?" Prudence wondered if Cain had decided that he too was bored and fancied a night with some whores to entertain him.

Cain nodded. "The night's young...ish. Plenty of people out and about, leaving their homes empty. Perfect time for a raid." It made sense to do it now when people were either asleep or too pissed to notice anything suspicious.

"I'm coming with ye then."

Cain looked back at her over his shoulder and sighed. "Come on then. Just make sure you keep up."

PRUDENCE GRINNED, THIS WOULD BE BETTER THAN wandering about the ship. This could be fun. She hopped over the side and down the rope net into the dinghy as it rocked gently on the small waves. Cain held a hand out to help her in.

"So where are we heading, Cap'n? Back to Malaine?"

Cain shook his head. "Nothing much there worth stealing, lass. I've got my eye on something bigger than a few coins."

He stayed silent for the rest of the row to shore and Prudence didn't feel inclined to end the silence. It was peaceful and Cain clearly had things on his mind.

Nearing shore, Malaine came into view with all of the little houses piled on top of each other, the cobbled steps making for a wobbly walk back home from the taverns for their patrons. Cain tied the dinghy up to the walkway before heading off down the planks, not bothering to wait for Prudence to catch up.

Passing all of the inner market stalls and taverns, Cain headed for a small farm on the edge of Malaine and knocked at the door. After a very long minute, an old man opened it, his frail arm shaking from the strain of holding it open. He had clearly been asleep. He was holding his thin robe tight around him, trying to keep out the cold.

"Yes?"

"How much do you want for the horses?" The old man glanced at Prudence before looking at Cain.

"You want my horses?" Cain nodded and the old man's leathery face turned into a scowl.

"Listen here son, I may be old but I'm still darned capable of running this farm, and in order to do that I need these 'ere horses. I'm sorry but they're not for sale." With a final frown, he shut the door in the captain's face. Cain huffed and clenched his fists.

Prudence touched his arm. "Why do we need horses?"

He straightened. "We don't. I'm sure we can get to Veida in a couple hours if we walk fast." Cain set off down the road and left Prudence running behind him to catch up.

"What's in Veida?"

Cain looked at her with a wicked grin. "Why, lords and ladies of course."

THEY REACHED VEIDA JUST AFTER MIDNIGHT AND WERE pleased to find that there were indeed areas, certain streets where the rich presided, that were quiet. Prudence watched Cain assess multiple homes, trying to decide which would be the right hit. It took several attempts before the captain found one that he was happy with. It looked like a lord's manor.

It boasted high walls with roses growing up the sides, now wilted from the cold around the front door. The old stone walls of the manor were chipped in places and weather worn but it did not detract from its grandeur or height. Standing before its wrought iron black gates Prudence felt as small as a child. The swirled metal that grew into sharp points above their heads made her think of prison bars.

Cain hopped over the gate and opened it for Prudence before scaling the latticework up to the bedroom window. Tucking his hand in his shirt sleeve, he broke the glass and climbed in, waving to Prudence once he was in.

The glass crunched underfoot as Prudence climbed through the window. It was a powerful person's house or at the very least someone highly respected. Luckily, the house was empty. They were alone. Prudence jumped as a hand grasped her shoulder.

"Shh," Cain whispered.

She scowled at him. It was his idea, sneaking into here. Prudence was plenty satisfied with the loot they had compiled back on the ship, but Captain Morris, it seemed, was never satisfied—not with gold and jewels at least. His breath stank of rum as he leaned into her face.

"Calm down, lass," he grinned his irritatingly charming smile. She knew it was bad, she knew it was wrong. But Prudence couldn't ignore the tremble that she felt when she was around him. He was free to do as he pleased. He could have anyone he wanted and he wanted *her*. Silverware and money were flung to the floor as Cain searched through drawers and shelves. Prudence watched him silently, taking him in. She hadn't been trouble growing up, she had tried to be good. She did what she was told by her mother and father, helped them as much as they needed. That had all been pointless though.

What was the harm in being bad when the rest of the world had screwed you over? This wasn't the life she had imagined from her windowsill, but this, *now*, was the life she wanted. Hopping down from her perch on the table, Prudence joined Cain scrambling through drawers and chests to find anything of value. A big trunk sat at the end of the bedchamber. Flinging it open, Prudence smiled to herself at the beautiful gowns and robes made for the lady of the house. A dark purple hue caught her eye from deep inside the trunk and she pulled it out to take a better look. The body was a deep plum colour with white ruffled edges and under sleeves. Ribbons stitched back on themselves to resemble flower blossoms adorned the seams. It suited her dark hair and fair complexion.

Was there any harm in trying it on? The lady it had been made for clearly hadn't used it for quite some time, and if she didn't know... it couldn't hurt her. She slipped into the adjoining room and pulled off her britches. After she'd struggled with the last hook, she smiled with herself, pleased, before stepping back into the large bed chamber.

Cain was busy talking to himself as he rummaged through the lord's belongings, but once his eye caught sight of Prudence, he was for once, stunned into silence.

"Do you dance, lass?" His eyes glinted in the moonlight and a hint of a devilish smile played on his lips. Prudence shook her head nervously but took his hand regardless. At the warmth of his touch, her heart went from a slight flutter to an unmistakable pounding inside her chest. In all the years that she had spent imagining escaping her life on Llynne, she would never have imagined a man like Cain being the answer. His hand gently grasped her waist as he led her around the room, guiding her, their heads filling with intense crescendos and magnificent symphonies as they moved in time together.

6

THE DEMELZA

P rudence had been training with Cain and the crew
for days. The weight of the wooden training sword
and the way she gripped it tightly had given her pus-filled
blisters across her palms.

"Is that all you can do? I can do this all day, lass. No
one is finer with a sword than I," Cain crowed.

Prudence growled in retaliation and thrust her
training sword at Cain, who side-stepped it easily.

"Come on, sweetheart. This is getting pathetic now.
My grandmother could do better than this, and she's
dead." He pushed forward, forcing her across the deck
towards the side. "You're not good enough." Their swords
clashed hard, stinging her hand. "You're never going to be
good enough." Prudence tried to hold her ground despite
the angry tears threatening to spill down her cheeks. She
refused to let any man see her cry. "You're going to end up
dead." He thrust forward, making Prudence stumble.

Captain Morris sniggered and swung his training

cutlass low at Prudence's ankles. She jumped out of the way and slammed into Cain's arm with her wooden blade.

"You sir, think too highly o' yerself. And you are wrong." She thrust her sword forward and hit Cain straight in the chest. That would bruise his flesh, certainly. Prudence chucked her sword on the floor at his feet.

"We're done for now." With a smug grin, she stalked off to her cabin. The cuts on her arms from the rough, splintered wood stung but they didn't hurt nearly as much as her wounded pride.

Eleanora was sitting on the cot with a book in her hand when Prudence walked in.

"I'm not done ignoring you, Prudence, I'm still mad at you for bringing me here." Eleanora stuck her nose in the air indignantly before turning to look at her friend. "Oh gods, more fighting? As if you didn't do enough back in Llynne. Those bruises... you need water." She put her book down and grabbed a rag off the side. "Why are you doing this to yourself?"

Prudence snorted. "Because the man's an arrogant sadist." At her friend's unconvinced smirk, she continued, "and I'm not learning quickly enough." She took the rag and placed it, damp and cold, over the worst of her bruises and sat on the bed. Prudence showed her injuries to Eleanora who shook her head and tutted at her friend's stupidity.

"You have no sense, do you? Deliberately doing this sort of thing. It seemed to me like you two were getting along quite nicely before this."

Prudence scoffed. "He's the devil."

"And you're the devil's conquest, it would seem." Prudence glanced at her friend, unsure of what to say. Eleanora nodded and rose from her seat.

"You need to be careful, Pru. This isn't a game, and these aren't boys. They're criminals."

Prudence scoffed. "No worse than the men you used to service. These men just happen to be honest about it. No one's completely innocent, not in this life."

Eleanora shook her head. "You're not understanding me Prudence! You think I don't see you? I see what you're like here. I see something in your face that I've never seen before. It's dangerous. Yes, the men I worked for weren't delightful, but it was business. It was for coin. It was to live. But you? You're getting invested, I can tell, this is personal for you, and that's far more risky than anything I've ever done." She rubbed her face with her hands and sighed. "I just don't want you getting hurt."

Prudence reached out and grabbed Eleanora's hand. "I know, love, I know. I'll be careful, I promise. I'm going to make a better life for us, El. Do you trust me?"

The unease was clear on her face but after some hesitation, Eleanora nodded. "I do." She gripped her friend's hand in return. "I do trust you, Pru." She settled down next to Prudence on the cot and rested her head on her shoulder. The girls sat together, their minds far away from the present peace of their cabin. Lost in memories of their long-ago formed friendship and how it had gotten to where they are now.

They had been through multiple lifetimes worth of

pain. But as long as they remained together, Prudence felt certain that they would be all right.

CAIN SLAMMED HIS CHARTS DOWN ON THE TABLE IN FRONT of the crew. "*The Demelza* is one of the biggest traders in the Western Tides. She'll be setting course for her long route to Aelin Isle in three days. We need to cross her when she meets open water, away from any help she might receive from Vaerny soldiers." He tapped the spot with the divider he'd been fiddling with. This was the biggest haul they'd had in months, nabbing it would ensure that the men had enough pay to keep them satisfied for a while. This haul would maintain the atmosphere aboard and keep everyone happy—provided they succeeded.

"We need to get ourselves sorted. We cannot afford to miss an opportunity like this. In five days' time we need to be there, right on course, no misfires." Cain caught eyes with every one of the crew, making sure they all understood. "I want supplies all stocked up, I need weapons cleaned, the ship needs some scrubbing. No one has time to lay about right now."

"Ever the dictator, Captain." Mr. Brady chuckled and leant back against the side. Captain Morris glanced at him, unsmiling.

"This is no laughing matter, Mr. Brady. *Everybody* needs to be at their best, everything must be planned so that we don't make mistakes. Understand?" Mr. Brady nodded and muttered a 'yes, sir' before shuffling off to take stock of the supplies down in the hold. Everything had to be set if they were to secure this catch. People everywhere were on the lookout for them, it had to be timed down to the hour.

Days passed and the crew found themselves busier than they had been for a long time. New supplies of food and drink were bought cheap from the market and piled high until there was no room left for any more. *The Maiden* was careened off a patch of shore far away from the prying eyes of town, and the men scrubbed her until she glistened. Prudence had been helping Mr. Norton heave crates up the gangplank and onto the deck. It was heavy work; most of the crates were filled with gunpowder and food.

She wiped the sweat on her brow away from her eyes with a grimy sleeve. Mr. Norton passed her a flask and she drank deep, the liquor running down her throat and filling her empty belly with warmth. It helped, momentarily.

They continued their work as the sun crawled across the grey sky, its movement often blocked by the clouds that seemed ever present. The weather had obviously been informed of the end of autumn, as it seemed to respond in kind with darker days where the sun hid whenever it got the chance. Prudence's sides were beginning to ache so she paused in her work to stretch and breathe in the sea air.

Charlie, from up above their heads, cursed as a rope slipped out of his hand. Prudence watched as the rope fell from high up in the rigging following a large crate on its plummet to the deck. "Move!" she yelled. The crate crashed and split on impact, contents flying across the deck and knocking Gabe to the floor.

The contents of the crate were spewed across the deck like fish out of a net. She saw Mr. Brady hauling Gabe to his feet as he yelled up to a nervous Charlie, who climbed slowly down.

Mr. Brady had already fetched the cat o' nine tails by the time Charlie's feet hit the wooden deck. "You need to learn not to be so clumsy, boy! Ten lashes should help teach ye that lesson."

Prudence gasped. Her eyes grew wide with horror as Mr. Brady nodded to two of the crew who grabbed Charlie and held him in place. They pulled his shirt up over his head to reveal his tanned and smooth back. This wasn't right. He'd only dropped it; it hadn't been intentional.

She noticed Cain emerge from below deck and ran to his side. "Surely you won't allow this?"

Cain's grim expression did nothing to assuage her fears. He cleared his throat and cast a sorry glance at her. "'Tis a punishment, lass. If I were a lenient captain, how long do you think I'd continue to be captain? It's only ten lashes—the boy'll learn not to let it happen again. He needs to learn. Or next time, someone could end up dead."

He turned away from her and spoke to Mr. Brady but his voice carried so that every crew member could hear. "Continue, Bosun."

Prudence tried not to wince as the whip came down on his back and she heard Charlie whimper, but it was difficult. Every crack echoed inside her head and the blood that dripped off him left her feeling ill. He was just a kid. This shouldn't be happening.

She counted along with the lashes and once the final whip had been cracked, the men dropped the bleeding Charlie onto the deck and headed back to their tasks. He stayed there on the floor, just panting. He was covered in an unsightly mixture of blood and sweat.

At that moment, Prudence could not understand the captain's logic of preventative punishment. She knew first-hand that fear was a strong motivation for loyalty, she had experienced just that in The Wanderer's Inn. But right now, Prudence didn't feel fear, nor loyalty. She just felt angry.

As the days passed, the attack on *The Demelza* grew ever nearer. Prudence spent her time practising the sword. With every hour she grew stronger, more precise. The door of their cabin had been carved every which way, much like the dresser.

The day before the attack, Prudence returned to her cabin to find Eleanora holding a bag in her hand. Prudence's gaze landed on the bag and stared for a moment or two before looking up at her friend.

"You're leaving?" Her voice wavered slightly but she sniffed once and shook it off. She told herself that she'd no longer allow Eleanora to influence every choice. They were not one person. They were separate, more so with each passing day. Prudence was coming to realise that hard fact. Perhaps away from the confines of a small island where they didn't have to see one another, they would naturally part ways.

"I cannot stay here knowing what you intend to do,

Prudence." She pursed her lips and Prudence could hear the self-righteous judgment dripping from her words. She snorted.

"Where will you go? Do you need money?"

"I shan't take stolen money, Pru. I'm not you. You do as ye wish, but I'm not a criminal and I don't intend to become one. I didn't choose this life, remember?" The silence between them seemed to stretch for miles. "I'll sell my things. I still have that scarf you gave me, and me locket. That'll sell."

Prudence tapped her foot on the floor, thinking anxiously.

"So, this is it, is it? Am I to never see ye again? You'll go to shore and find some place to stay, we'll head the other way and that will be it? This is where we end?" She bit her cheek crossly as she felt her nose twitch and her eyes swim. Eleanora and Prudence looked at one another for a moment that felt like an eternity, before Eleanora passed Prudence and left the cabin.

Hours later, Prudence heard a knock at the door and leapt to her feet, imagining wildly that Eleanora was waiting outside for her, that she'd changed her mind. Pru opened the door and came face to face with Cain. She sighed.

"Well, I thought you'd at least be slightly pleased to see me," he chuckled and shut the door behind him, "my mistake. I see your friend left. You know lass, it's probably best for her. She'd only be in the way here; she'd be at risk."

"So, what am I to do then, Captain? Watch her leave

and simply accept that I will most likely never see my only family ever again?" She stared at him indignantly.

"I cannot tell you what to do darlin'. I don't imagine anyone has ever been able to do that. But would you ever be satisfied stuck on this rock? Would you be willing to sacrifice all of this if that's what it took to get her back?"

Prudence knew that Cain had a point... but what would that make her? Someone who gives up family for a bit of excitement? Eleanora had always been her priority, her everything. To give up on her now would just be selfish. And oh, how lonely she would be without her friend. The only person who had ever given her comfort since she'd entered the harsh world that surrounded the inn. Without Eleanora, Prudence wasn't sure who she was. Life did not exist outside of Elea. Prudence had never given anything else room in her mind, everything else came second to her.

Without needing an answer to his question, Captain Morris clasped Prudence's arm supportively, before stepping out of the cabin back onto the main deck. Unsure of how to proceed, Prudence put off any difficult decisions by throwing herself into preparations for the raid. They only had until tomorrow to ensure that everything was prepared. The wind was keen but only strong enough to make the sails flap and billow on the deck. Its soft breeze made ripples in the water and made everything smell fresh and clean.

Prudence found herself helping Mr. Norton and a few others, loading barrels of salted meats into the hold, down below. Down there it reeked of meat, blood, and sweat. It was then, in that moment, that Prudence became aware of how used to the smell she had grown. She had settled into this new life like it had been waiting for her all along. As if this is what she had been made for.

Prudence's father had been a fisherman all his life. Though he never went far from home, he had loved the sea deeply and had thrust Prudence into that life and his passion from a young age. If Prudence had believed in fate, she might assume that it was her father at work, leading her towards this life. Whether it was her fate or not, Prudence lugged barrels and boxes from the deck and into the cargo hold, until the room could contain no more supplies.

By the time the sun went down everything was prepared for *The Maiden* to set sail. Mr. Reed was playing his fiddle, a simple calming melody. It was no surprise that men soon sat around him to listen in the dark, his face illuminated by the lantern swinging above his head.

"Pru?" Taken by surprise, Prudence spun around to see Eleanora climbing up the gangplank with a knife to her kidneys.

"What in the hell?" A familiar face came into view beside Eleanora's. Crew members stood and revealed weapons to the unwanted intrusion. Despite not caring for Eleanora, Prudence had found the crew to be loyal pack members, each very territorial about the ship. This was a breach of boundaries no doubt. And the crew weren't happy about it.

"Khari, what on earth do you think you're doing?" His chocolate brown eyes swivelled round to Prudence's face and Prudence was surprised to see fear in his eyes, not the usual greed and nonchalance. The last time they had laid eyes on one another was back at The Wanderer's Inn in the low light. She'd guessed that he was here on Vaerny when they'd seen Avery hang, but never in a million years did she expect to cross paths with him. Captain Morris placed a reassuring hand on Prudence's shoulder and stepped past her.

"And who do you think you are, making a scene like this on my ship?"

"Someone tryin' to get the hell off this rock as fast as is physically possible."

"And why would we help you, even with your, uh... threat." Cain stepped closer, his face a perfect emotionless mask.

"Because I know that bitch," he gestured to Prudence, "she ain't ever giving her up. Not for nothin'." Cain glanced briefly at Prudence and then addressed Eleanora.

"You left."

"I didn't think it was wise to argue that point with a knife in my side."

Cain nodded thoughtfully and locked eyes with Khari. "I'm Captain here and she doesn't mean a thing to me, why should I help you?"

Prudence tugged at the captain's arm. "Cain, what are ye doing? Ye can't leave her with him! He'll kill her!" Cain shook her off, his gaze never leaving Khari.

"I'm just as good a sailor as any of your men, probably better. Soon as we land somewhere, I can start a new life, I'll be out of your 'air."

Captain Morris pursed his lips. "You can sleep in the hold and I swear right now, you give me any trouble and I'll throw you over the side. Understood?" Khari nodded.

"Now let the poor girl go." The knife lowered from Eleanora's side and a grunt escaped her throat as Khari shoved her forward. Prudence helped Eleanora sit down and then advanced on Khari.

"Sleep with one eye open yer bastard, threaten her again and I'll gut ye like a fish," she hissed at him. He looked down at her and smirked.

"You haven't changed at all, have ye, *keine*?"

Later that night Prudence found herself unable to sleep and sat in the cold, listening to the quiet of the sea on deck. She thought about everything that had happened over these past few months and found herself to be extremely happy with her life as of that moment. It was strange to think how much had changed, and yet at the same time it felt like this had been her life all along.

The Demelza came into view on the horizon after four days of sailing. Cain heard Mr. Rundstrom yell down from the crow's nest and pulled out his spyglass to get a closer look.

The merchant ship was one of the finest trading ships that Cain had ever seen. Its ornate decoration made it seem grander than it actually was. He joined Gabe and Prudence at the helm as the men prepared *The Bloody Maiden* to approach the merchant ship slowly. Cain watched the approach cautiously through his spyglass with a furrowed expression.

"This is the tricky bit," Gabe muttered to Prudence.

She looked at him. "What do you mean?"

"Right now, *The Demelza* most likely assumes we are another merchant ship, but once we raise the black, it can go one of two ways," Cain answered, "Either they try to run or they surrender. Obviously, surrender is the preferable choice, but in these waters... a lot of merchants don't know better. Piracy isn't as prevalent here as it is in other parts of the realm. They think they can win. They don't want to give up their cargo and risk reprimands from their superiors."

Gabe nodded in agreement and pointed at the ship still some way ahead of them. "See? Right now, it doesn't seem like we're coming straight for them, we're just another merchant following the same route. But if they realise before we're close enough..." his hand shot out in front of his torso as he made a whistling sound. "Cannons in her stern. Damage her too much and it's hard to get hold of the cargo, not enough and she can scarper."

Prudence nodded. "I see." It was more tactical than she'd thought.

The Demelza was now only a league or two ahead of them. Cain grinned. "Are you ready for a hunt, boys?!"

The men raised their fists and weapons into the air directed at their captain as they roared in agreement.

Cain was reminded of wild animals. Ferocious wild animals filled with bloodlust and hunger for their prey. It was primal. Primal and right. He could feel the swell of bloodlust rumble inside his own gut, kindling a flame for battle.

The wild, violent freedom that he felt, like the anticipation of a coming storm, enveloped him in a turbulent embrace. Prudence, he could see, felt it too and she wanted to feel it again. The men began to pound on their weapons, grunting as he had seen wild hogs do before fighting another male for a mate.

Mr. Norton called over the din. "Raise the black!"

"Raise the black!"

"Raise the black!" A chorus of voices yelled over one another as the black flag climbed the flagpole. The skull with an axe embedded in its crown shined white and clear against the dark fabric.

They watched *The Demelza* eagerly, waiting to see if they would raise their white flag in surrender. Cain tightened the belt around his hips, making sure that the array of pistols and knives he carried into battle were fastened tight. It was nearly time.

The men aboard *The Demelza* could be seen, like little ants running around their hill, moving about the deck in a frantic manner. He squinted and raised his hand to his brow, temporarily blinded as the light from the sun shone brightly off the slight waves.

"What's going on?" Prudence pointed at the merchant ship and glanced at Cain nervously.

Cain reached for his telescope and frowned. "Shit." He turned to face the crew and yelled. "They're going to fight!"

"Fight? I thought you said they'd either flee or give up?"

Cain scowled and pulled his sword from its scabbard. "Seems like this merchant doesn't know what's good for him," he growled. *The Demelza* began to turn ahead of them, its bow swung around and Cain saw the glint of cannon ends shining on their side.

"They've got four guns, Cap'n!" Mr. Brady yelled.

"All crews! Guns at the ready!" Mr. Norton called as the men ran to their battle stations. Mr. Reed, the master gunner, yelled his commands to the men at the guns. Ephraim emerged from below deck, his face smeared with a white paint that contrasted with his dark complexion. It made him look feral—though that was the point. Cain caught sight of a number of the crew, Garrick, Thomas, Mr. Abbott and Mr. Scott, covered with Ephraim's paints as well. *His* crew. *His* men.

Shuu screamed a war cry with his machete high above his head and a wild look in his eye. Even Cain felt scared of the well-mannered man. *The Bloody Maiden* turned on the spot with such a great speed that Prudence had to grab a hold of the railing to stay upright beside him.

Cain watched, waiting with a calculating eye, his arm raised, hovering in the air. "Hold." It felt like everyone was momentarily frozen in time. He couldn't even hear anyone breathing. "Hold."

The Demelza and *The Bloody Maiden* finally came parallel to one another. "Hold." He heard Prudence hold a breath. "Now!"

As soon as Cain gave the word, the men lit the fuses. The *boom* of the cannons as they exploded ricocheted in their eardrums. All that could be heard was the splintering of wood and deafening screams as men were flung into the air, the deck beneath their feet obliterated into almost nothing.

The Bloody Maiden was almost twice the size of *The Demelza* and boasted many more guns. Her deck took a couple of hits but none caused permanent damage. The fight was finished within moments with the crew of *The Maiden* hooking *The Demelza's* deck and infiltrating the ship. The vanguard were the first to board, clearing a path from the deck down to the hold, dispatching *The Demelza's* captain in seconds. It didn't take long before the entire crew had crossed the wobbly planks between the ships and stood face to face with merchant sailors, ready to cut down whoever necessary.

NEVER BEFORE HAD PRUDENCE FELT SUCH A RUSH AS WHEN she shuffled along across the plank and onto *The Demelza*, with a pistol in her left hand and a dagger in her right. The ringing sound of metal filled her ears and the world was a blur of motion. The air hummed as people passed her by, swords clashing one another, knives and axes hitting their mark as a splash of red painted the floor around them. The blood pounded in her ears, blocking out the cries of men as they fell.

Prudence swung her arm upwards in a beautiful arc before bringing it down on the sailor closest to her. Before he turned around to see her and defend himself, Prudence's dagger landed with a wet slice of metal on flesh and a scream escaped his lips. The pistol fired a shot into his gut and Prudence pulled her dagger back as he slid to the floor at her feet.

She kicked another merchant to the floor before he could reach the gun that he'd been running towards. The butt of her pistol came down hard on the back of his head, knocking him out cold. Better to save the shots. She stepped over him and climbed down the ladder into the lower deck. She was suddenly grateful that Cain had provided her with britches. There was no way she could do this in skirts.

Below deck some of the men were already taking stock of the merchant ship's goods. This would make a decent haul. Prudence could see that the crates closest to her were stocked with tobacco and sugar. They must trade with the Southern Border, she thought.

She passed the crew who were beginning to move the cargo across to *The Maiden*. A creak sounded from the back corner. Prudence paused but heard nothing. Suddenly, a sailor came charging out of the shadows at her with a sword raised.

A squeak escaped her lips as she stepped out of his way. She shook herself off. Concentrate. She watched him, calculating his next move and raised her sword. She could do this. Cain had trained her well. The man was clearly no swordsman, his hand shook so violently that she thought he might drop the sword altogether.

Advancing, she herded the sailor towards the steps that led up to the main deck. The swords clashed against one another and although Prudence had the greater skill, the sailor was twice her size and held his ground well, relying on his strength.

With space between them the man took his opportunity to scrabble up the ladder and onto the carnage of the deck. Prudence made chase and stormed after him past sailors and pirates alike. There was a thud as the sailor slammed into the deck with an axe embedded in his head. Prudence looked up to see Gabe stood over him.

He pulled the axe from its place in his skull and wiped the blood and brain matter on his trousers before nodding at Prudence and returning to the fight. Prudence looked around her, lost for a moment in a sea of war.

Cain, she could see, was right in the thick of it. His muscular arms swung his sword and axe at so many opponents, cutting them down with ease. A wave of sympathy gushed over Prudence as she saw these men, these sailors for the first time.

They were not fighters. They probably had families back on land, waiting for them to return—not that they ever would. Their bodies will sink down into the crushing cold depths amongst the sea life, waiting to be fed on until they were nothing but bones. *We shall all meet the same fate one day.* It was a chilling thought. There shall be no shrine to remember any of them by. No memorial erected in their honour. Once they have all begun to rot in the ground we shall be forgotten.

Prudence glanced back in the direction of *The Maiden* for a moment, thinking of Elea in their cabin. She was safe there. Khari had only needed her as leverage. Now he fought alongside the crew against the merchant sailors as if he had been one of the crew forever. He stood tall over the other men at such a gigantic height that he even made Cain seem small. His dreadlocks were matted with sweat and blood from those that he fought.

The men all pushed their way towards the captain's quarters, forcing *The Demelza's* crew like cattle back into the room. The sailors that stood in their way did not do so for long. The men's blades were sharp and their guns were loaded, it didn't take more than a moment to slaughter them.

A shot erupted from behind her and Prudence turned wordlessly to see a sailor's hand shaking with fear, flintlock in hand, and a lead shot deep in Mr. Brady's chest. His eyes went wide as his shirt soaked up the pooling red and he dropped to the floor. A growl erupted from a member of the crew as he threw himself at the young sailor in a fit of rage. Prudence couldn't muster up any feeling of sympathy, or even any feeling at all. She always knew Mr. Brady would get an end deserving of his life. Now, it seems, he had.

Brought swiftly out of her thoughts by a shot that seemed to explode in her arm, Prudence looked down to see her sleeve torn to shreds. Wet sticky blood clung to her upper arm. The bullet had missed, just about. It was only a graze but it stung like fire. It was a pain that was only made worse by the salt in the air and the sweat on her body.

Captain Morris' crew went quickly through the men on *The Demelza*. Not long after they had reached her, the merchant crew lay sprawled across the deck, mangled bodies in positions that should not be possible. A number of Cain's crew had fallen in the fight. Mr. Marshall, Ted; Gabe's big brother, Danny; Mr. Scott, Mr. Brady.

The men wrapped their fallen comrades in cloth and tied down the bodies with rocks and other heavy items to make them sink. Cain stood solemnly at the side as the crew held the dead bodies on planks over the side.

"Today, we have gained a good haul. A haul that will

pay to last us a couple months once it's sold. But in doing so, we have lost men. Friends," he looked at Gabe, "Family. They did not die in vain. They died living as free men, free men who died allowing their family to succeed. They will not be forgotten."

He nodded and the few holding the planks tipped them up, allowing the bodies to slide overboard and splashing into the calm sea. The silence was deafening. In all her time with the crew, Prudence had never heard such silence. Even at night there were always a few on watch, laughing and joking with one another as they played cards or sang shanties. Now there was just silence.

Once the crew had mourned the loss of their brethren, Cain ordered the others to explore the rest of the ship and bring the remainder of the supplies onto the main deck to move them over to *The Bloody Maiden*. Before long, all of the loot was down in *The Maiden's* hold and the crew were back aboard.

Mr. Reed and Mr. Lowell trailed gunpowder over the deck of *The Demelza* before climbing back over to join the rest of the crew. Prudence watched, fascinated, as Mr. Lowell lit a match and threw it over onto the powdered deck. It was ablaze, the fire spread all over and up the sails. Prudence watched the fire rage and destroy as *The Maiden* hastily departed from the burning ship.

From a distance, Prudence heard a bang and saw the bulk of the ship splinter into pieces as the gunpowder left in the barrels down below exploded. The fire eventually died down into smaller flames as most of the wood sunk below the surface. Prudence looked at Cain at her side.

"What now, Captain?"

He smiled at her with a twinkle in his eye. "Off to Thaira, lass."

THAIRA WAS UNLIKE ANYTHING PRUDENCE HAD EVER SEEN before. It was a small rocky spit of land with plenty of beach, covered completely in tents and shacks for the thieves who resided there. The white sand seemed to stretch on endlessly. Prudence wondered how people could survive in such a place as this, with only sand and the slightest hint of heath in the distance. *The Maiden* docked a little ways off shore and Prudence found herself on the first long boat heading to the tiny scrap of land known as Thaira.

Smoke rose from various places where people had set up fires along the beach, whether they were for cooking food or for keeping warm, Prudence wasn't sure. The tents were roughly patched scraps of fabric that looked so worn, it was a wonder that they were still in one piece.

Captain Morris led the way through the huddles of people stretched out on the beach, towards a more permanent looking structure further up the island. A few of the crew came with them whilst the others stayed on the beach. They all carried big sacks of the things they had stolen from *The Demelza*. Prudence tried her best to imagine what this Madame Durrant she had heard so much about over the last few days, looked like. She imagined a fearsome lady with great power over her criminals. Someone with a stern frown who most likely ruled through fear.

Prudence wondered how the woman managed to make money from stolen goods. It would make sense that there were corrupt lords and governors around the Western Tides, she supposed. Perhaps she also traded with the other continents?

Many of the people stared at the group as they walked by, mainly at Prudence it seemed. Obviously, women were a rare commodity in Thaira. Most of the people were covered in dirt and grime, from living in tents on the dirty sand. The heat of the sun made everything smell like sweat, even with the nearing of winter. Soon they could see where the big house of Madame Durrant stood.

It was made of stone and cracked in some places. The sun had stained it a strange pink colour and there were big shutters over the windows for when it rained. There seemed to be a fair few people lurking about when the group went inside. Some of them looked fairly official with swords and pistols attached to their hips, whilst others looked more like beggars. Prudence assumed that these people were here to beg the Madame for money or work.

The man guarding the Madame's room went inside upon hearing Cain's name and returned moments later to guide the group inside. The woman who sat before them rose at the sight of the captain.

"Cain, my darling," she smiled warmly and opened her arms for a tight embrace. She was a tall woman, with an extremely thin figure; so thin in fact that Prudence could see her bony elbows through her dress. Cain smiled at her.

"Emily. It's nice to see you again. You look incredible."

She blossomed at the comment but shrugged him off cheerfully.

"Oh, you always were a charmer. So, tell me, what are you here for? I haven't seen you in a few years, young man." Cain chuckled and took a seat opposite Madame Durrant. Prudence and the rest of the group hovered by the door; clearly not a part of the business transaction. Madame Durrant seemed perfectly content to ignore them.

"I have some things I think you might be interested in, Emily." Captain Morris waved his hand towards the crew and they brought the bags forward before stepping back. The Madame peered over her large desk to peek at the bags and seemed pleased with what she saw.

"Well, darling, this seems to be quite the haul you've got yourself. I wonder if it is indeed *The Demelza*'s cargo that I've heard has gone missing?" Captain Morris chuckled and winked at her. They both knew the answer to that question. Madame Durrant pulled out some leather-bound pages and scribbled something down before passing it to her guard. He took the bound pages out of the room and down the hall. Prudence wondered what it was for. The Madame turned to Cain and took her spectacles off her nose. Her silvery white hair was pulled back tight behind her head in a neat braid.

"I'll have my men bring everything else onto shore by the morning and pass it on to your men."

Emily Durrant nodded. "Excellent. I'll have Mr. Wilton waiting with your men's wages." She noted something down in the book sitting open on her desk, before looking up at Cain. "I'm afraid that's not the only thing I've heard recently, Captain Morris." She frowned, all friendliness of the conversation gone in an instant. "They're here."

Captain Morris sighed and nodded his head. "I know. They arrived a few days ago." Prudence struggled to understand what they were talking about. Who was here? Why were they here? What was going on? Madame Durrant looked at Cain thoughtfully.

"How long do you think you'll have?" Prudence noticed Cain's face get tight and he huffed out a breath.

"I don't know. A couple of weeks if we're lucky. If we can hide out somewhere. Less maybe, if we can't."

Prudence glanced at the other crew members, who looked just as confused as she did. Obviously, this was something that Cain was keeping close to his chest. Well, he'd have to tell them now. Prudence's gut was telling her that something wasn't right, something was coming, something dangerous and she needed to know what. She needed to be able to protect Eleanora if someone was coming for them. Captain Morris smiled at Madame Durrant before getting out of his chair and walking towards the door.

"It was lovely to see you, Emily. I'm sure we'll see you again before we leave."

Madame Durrant smiled at him. "Without a doubt, my boy."

The group were guided out of the room and back towards the beach where they found the rest of their crew waiting. Eleanora was with them, much to the surprise of Prudence. Captain Morris collected the money from Madame Durrant's guard in a cloth sack which he kept tucked underneath his arm as Prudence went to check on Eleanora.

"How come you've decided to show your face then?" Prudence had never expected Eleanora to come to a place like this, it was even worse than the crew in Eleanora's eyes. Eleanora scoffed at her friend.

"I was hardly given a choice. These barbarians dragged me out here on your captain's orders."

"Oh. I see." Prudence glanced back at Captain Morris who was in deep discussion with Mr. Norton. Their eyes caught and Prudence mouthed a 'thank you' at Cain. This was the most Eleanora had left the cabin in a while, apart from her brief adventure to shore. She needed to get out of that room, it was affecting her terribly. She needed to be out in the sun and eat a healthy amount of food. She had lost so much weight since they'd joined the crew.

Eleanora crossed her arms, clearly frustrated. "Why are we here? Aside from selling on stolen goods. That's done now isn't it, so can we leave?"

Prudence sighed and shook her head. "Elea, this isn't about you. We stay until the captain says so. It's his decision." Eleanora rolled her eyes at Prudence and walked away to find somewhere to sit. She may be irritated but at least the two were speaking.

"Looks like she's warming up to us a bit, eh?" Mr. Norton came up behind Prudence, his eyes on Eleanora as she perched on the edge of a rock with a disdainful look on her face. Prudence scoffed.

"She'd be happier living in a pig sty than with me right now."

"Oh, come now, don't be ridiculous. She's confused.

142

She's got it in her head that the life she used to have was better, safer. She'll sort herself out soon enough."

Having dealt with business for the day, the crew set about making camp on the shore along with the other tents. Sheets were erected all around until there was plenty of space for everyone to sleep. Prudence found Captain Morris by the fire, staring into the flames with a vacant expression on his face.

Jorge, the bearded, lanky prize master, strode into the middle of their camp. "Payday boys!" He held the bag of their earnings in one hand and papers in the other. "One at a time, sooner everyone gets paid, the sooner you can all whore it away and drink until yer blind."

The crew piled around Jorge and their wages, one by one disappearing off to fritter their coin on women, booze, food, and drugs as soon as it was handed to them. Prudence watched them for a moment, amused by their recklessness, before turning to Cain.

"I need to ask you... about what happened in there with the Madame."

Captain Morris nodded unfazed, barely lifting his head to acknowledge her arrival.

"Cain, why are they hunting us so ferociously? I've not asked before as I presumed that they were hunting us like they hunt all pirates. But this isn't plain piracy, is it? What did you do to make them do this?" Cain huffed and rubbed his head.

"I suppose you deserve to know now. Now that it involves all of us." Prudence glanced at him expectantly, her hand resting on his. "I have been looking for vengeance most of my adult life. It hasn't been easy and most of it is indeed not relevant now. I was finally able to avenge my sister after all these years. The king's coronation gave me an opportunity. I snuck into the palace through the sewers and waited until my chance came. While most of the castle was distracted in the main hall... I killed the king's new bride. I took his best friend from him as he took mine from me. I drowned her in a basin." Prudence's eyes were wide like a deer when it senses a hunter. Not knowing what to say, she sat there in silence.

Cain pulled something out of his pocket and handed it to her. A wanted poster. "I don't regret my choices, Prudence. Unjust was the life my sister led. What I did may have been cruel, but it was nothing in comparison to how they treated my sister. I will always stand by what I did." The two sat in silence next to one another late into the night, until eventually sleep caught up to them. When morning broke, the crew packed up their belongings and like every time before, Madame Durrant watched from her window, as *The Bloody Maiden* sailed away from Thaira and back into danger.

THE MONOTONOUS DAYS OF LIFE AT SEA WERE BROKEN UP BY the spontaneous party that had sprung to life on the deck of *The Bloody Maiden*. Mr. Reed's awful singing voice was drowned out by the laughter on deck as the crew drank, betted, and feasted on the lavish foods that they'd brought back from Thaira.

Eleanora was reluctant to join the crew initially, but

after a nudge from Gabe, she begrudgingly agreed. She was surprised to find that she was enjoying herself. It might have been the alcohol swimming in her system, but she soon found herself joking with the crew.

The drums pounded in Eleanora's ears as Mr. Lowell's fingers danced across his lute strings. The music thrummed around the deck, making the air feel alive and crackling. Her eyes fell upon Rupert and Shuu, their hands pounding against the drum skins in front of them as the other crew members danced.

It had begun to rain but Eleanora didn't mind. The sound of the rain hitting the deck merely added to the exciting atmosphere. She grinned as Gabe pulled her to her feet, his hand slipping round her waist as their feet skipped across the wooden boards in time with the music. His tanned olive face, so close to hers, shone bright against the lanterns dotted about the ship.

Eleanora's mane of hair began to spill out of its braid as she and Gabe spun around and around in a tight circle, the skirt of her dress flying out around her as they turned. They weaved between the other men who were drunk and clearly enjoying themselves. She heard Prudence cackle loudly behind her as Charlie jokingly bowed to Mr. Kenny, who curtsied in return, before joining hands and waltzing around the deck. Pru snorted and cried with laughter as the men beside her jeered at their crew mates. Gabe twirled Eleanora with a flourish.

"Come on Gabe, share a little. Let someone else have a turn!" yelled Mr. Reed, his brown hair soaked from the rain.

Gabe shook his head and laughed. "I think I'd rather not!"

Mr. Reed chuckled and offered his hand to a tipsy Prudence. "Care to keep me company, miss?"

"Unless I get a better offer," she winked at him and took his hand. Eleanora smiled. She had never seen Prudence so carefree before. Happy. A wash of guilt swept over her. She knew Prudence had hated her life on Llynne... but she'd never realised quite how much until it was all gone. She released Gabe's hand as they slowed to a standstill and sat down on a nearby barrel. She could feel the warmth from her flushed cheeks and the smile that radiated from her lips.

For a moment she'd forgotten how entirely she'd hated being stuck on this ship. She'd even forgotten how much she resented her beloved friend for it. She wasn't entirely sure whether the resentment came in spite of her care for Prudence, or because of it.

Prudence cackled as Mr. Reed lifted her and spun her round as Garrick tried in earnest to steal her hand from the master gunner. "Boys, boys there's enough of me to go around, please!"

"Excuse me, gentlemen..." Cain strode towards the little group. "Can I have this dance, lass?" The captain extended a hand to Prudence and flashed a smirk at his crew when she took it. He may have been joking with his crew mates, but there was no denying to Eleanora that behind his posturing, Cain was smitten with Prudence.

"Why o' course, sir. T'would be an honour." She curtsied low and Eleanora laughed.

"The crew are verra fond of yer friend over there.

She's fit right in with them." Gabe said to Elea and jerked his chin towards Prudence dancing with Cain and the crew laughing around them, despite the rain pouring down over their heads.

Eleanora followed his line of sight. Prudence had her arms stretched out above her head, her face to the sky, and her mouth open, tasting the rain. She'd never looked that carefree at The Wanderer's Inn. Elea sighed. "She really has, hasn't she..."

Gabe looked at her. "You sound disappointed."

"Not disappointed. Just... she was never this happy with our life, she hated it. I wasn't enough for her."

"I'm sure tha's not true. She's just one of them is all."

Elea nodded, unconvinced. "Maybe." She watched the pirate crew in front of her, joking and dancing. They seemed much less fearsome now than they usually did. Rupert handed Gabe the drum and took Thomas by the hands. He smiled and dragged him towards the middle of the deck to dance. "I never realised they were an item." Elea said, trying not to sound shocked.

"Rupe and Thomas? They've been together since long before I joined the crew."

She smiled sadly. Watching the two of them so happy together made visions of Nell flash before her eyes. Elea wondered what Nell would be doing in that moment, whether she was thinking of her, trying to work out what happened to her. She'd never got a chance to say goodbye. Thomas and Rupert were moving slowly together, despite the fast-paced music, as if they were the only two people in the world. It made her ache.

"Are you all right?" Gabe asked.

"I... I'm—"

Mr. Norton stepped into the middle of the group and gestured for quiet. "Pipe down you dogs! We've 'ad some fun but now there's business to attend to. We lost brave souls taking our last prize, brothers that we loved fiercely. Mr. Brady was a great bosun, but now we need to vote in a new boatswain. Lads, I suggest our Mr. Morgan here as he 'as been bosun's mate for some years now. What say ye?"

Mr. Norton clapped Garrick on the back and Prudence put her fingers to her lips and whistled loudly, making Garrick laugh and cast a wink at her. "Let's take a vote then, aye?" Mr. Norton said. "All for Mr. Morgan to be our new bosun?"

Eleanora watched as all of the crew members' hands were raised one by one. "Aye!" yelled someone from somewhere in the group.

Mr. Norton lifted his drink in the air. "To Garrick, yer new bosun, treat 'im well lads... and lass." He gestured to Prudence as a chorus of cheers erupted from *The Bloody Maiden's* crew. Drinks were poured and passed around, or just drunk straight from the bottle, and Mr. Lowell began to play his lute once more.

Captain Morris let go of Prudence's hand and shook Garrick's hand vigorously. "Horace suggested the best man for the job, I've no doubt you'll do well."

"Aye, thank ye, Cap'n, I'll do my best to keep these ruffians in shape for ye." Eleanora smiled as Pru joined them to congratulate her new boatswain and he pulled her into a bear hug. The rain had begun to lessen, but having been sat still for so long, she began to feel a chill about her and wrapped her arms around herself for warmth. Completely unaware of the late hour, she felt herself yawning and by the third yawn, she'd decided it was probably best to retire.

She crossed the main deck, past Prudence and her new family, to the steps that led to the upper deck and their cabin. As she moved up the steps, Gabe appeared by her side again. "Yer going? There's still plenty of liquor to be drunk and dances. I'd prefer to have a lady to dance with." He flashed a tipsy grin at her.

"Yes, I think so. It's cold and I fear I'm still an outsider 'ere so it's probably better that I call it a night." She leant forward and kissed his cheek. "G'night... Master Gabriel," she murmured, borrowing the name that the crew so affectionately used for him.

He caught her hand in his rough calloused fingers and ran a thumb over her knuckles. "Goodnight, Miss Elea." Her cheeks flushed hot and she cringed knowing that Gabe could see the bright pink blossom across her face.

Back inside the cosy cabin that Prudence had purchased for the two of them, she removed the outer skirts of her dress and untied her auburn locks from their braids. The glow of the candles that were dotted about the room flickered, casting shadows on the walls that looked like monsters. A knock at the door made her jump.

Eleanora wrapped her blue shawl around her shoulders and unhooked the latch. A wave of noise came rushing to her from the party below, no longer muffled by the closed door. Gabe stood before her, dark brown curls misted with rain drops, shuffling from one foot to the other as he fiddled with the coins in his hand.

"I, I thought you'd maybe... want some company?" he asked.

Eleanora paused before stepping aside and letting him in. "I'd like that." She grabbed her dress skirts from the bed and threw them in the corner. "Please," she gestured for him to sit down and poured two drinks for them.

A moment of awkwardness that felt like it spanned a century stretched between them until Gabe sucked in a breath. "So... what was yer life like on that island before ye joined us? Nice?"

Eleanora sat down beside him and let out a heavy breath. "It maybe was'n' what some people woulda liked." Despite the muted raucous coming from out on deck, Elea heard Prudence's distinct cackle of laughter. "But I liked it. It was an easy life and fun, I had a lot o' friends."

Gabe smiled. "That doesna surprise me at all. Did ye have anyone?" he blushed, "Forgive me, I should not 'av asked... that was rude o' me."

"No, no it's all right. I did. But now I'm 'ere and she's... there." She could see from his face that he had more questions. It was understandable, it didn't make much sense to her either. Gabe merely put a hand on hers and squeezed.

"I'm sorry."

She squeezed back. "Thank ye." Eleanora stared at his hand on hers. Her fair, slim fingers laced between his olive toned sailor's hands. They were warm and despite being much bigger than her own, his hand fit together with hers perfectly. "Ye've made it less lonely being 'ere. Thank ye for keeping me company."

"'Tis nothin'. I like talking to ye, yer... verra easy to talk to." He smiled at her and Eleanora was suddenly aware of how close their faces were; how dark and rich the brown of his eyes was. They held little flecks of gold, like crystals deep within a mine. She shifted slightly as his lips brushed against hers, gentle and teasing. She closed her eyes just as they parted once more.

Gabe put the coins that he'd brought into her hand and closed her fingers around them. "Is this enough?" Eleanora nodded briefly and put them to the side, barely glancing at them before kissing him again as her hands found their way to the feather soft curls that started at his neck. They kissed one another hungrily, full of desperation and yearning, as the sounds outside the little cabin faded into nothingness.

7

CONFRONTATIONS

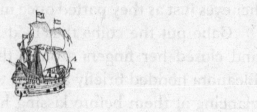

Prudence smiled at the trinkets that lay over the bed, scattered around so that she might admire all of them at once. They were beautiful. Rings and necklaces, brooches and earrings, all jumbled together. She had even managed to sneak a few books from the ship whilst the men carried over the barrels and boxes of spices, sugar, and cotton. Cain would love them.

She had never seen books like these before but they looked fascinating. They were obviously something that the sailors kept aboard to distract them from missing their home life. They looked like well-thumbed copies, she had clearly found some favourites amongst the mess that had been made during the raid. It was a pity to see so much of the ship and its contents get destroyed. She even felt a small ounce of sadness for the men that had died.

Though that didn't make her regret her part in the massacre. They worked for the Crown, people like them had taken and stolen from poor people like her, all of her life. And now they hunt her. All for what? For wanting to be free, to live a life away from the watchful eyes of soldiers.

She fiddled with the treasures that lay on the bed, putting them up against her skin and seeing how they looked. She was enjoying herself so much that she barely noticed Eleanora enter the room.

"I see you're marvelling over the havoc you've wreaked." She plonked herself down on the chair by the table and raised her eyebrows at Prudence. Prudence rolled her eyes before looking at her.

"I'm fully aware that I lack your approval El, but I hardly feel I need it. In all honesty love, you're a whore. Ye bed men for money. How is that any better than my cutting them down for it? At least I have my dignity." Prudence sucked in a breath almost as quickly as she had finished her sentence. That was too much.

Eleanora's jaw dropped in surprise before her expression changed into a sour scowl. She sighed and rose from her seat. "Well, I can see that *this* place has had a great effect on you. If that's how you feel, perhaps I should get to work on the men downstairs." She spoke curtly and brushed past the bed, slamming the door as she went. Prudence sighed. She hadn't meant to say that at all. She hadn't meant to hurt Eleanora. She loved her. It was all going wrong with her friend. She didn't fit in here; she clearly wasn't happy here. It seemed to be killing her, slowly. Prudence was making Eleanora feel exactly how she had felt.

"I'll sort this Elea, I promise," she muttered to herself, "tomorrow I'll find you somewhere to stay on the island.

I'll find somewhere for you and we can make it better."
She didn't know what she would do about Cain. Prudence
loved this life, the dangerous risks and the thrill of fear, it
was exciting. But she couldn't leave Eleanora alone, they
were family. Perhaps she could visit Eleanora often,
maybe that would be ok.

If not, then perhaps it was a sign from fate that this
freedom was too good to be true. Perhaps Prudence was
never meant to escape her imprisonment from a vile little
tavern in the middle of nowhere. Maybe that's where fate
had decided she should be. At least if she stayed with
Eleanora then they could be together. Elea would be safe
from everything and Prudence would have her friend to
keep her company.

ELEANORA AWOKE TO THE CLATTER OF METAL ON THE BED.
Opening her eyes, she could see that Prudence stood over
her, the bed laden with weapons. A sleeping Gabe lay
beside her, his soft curls dangling over his forehead, just
touching his closed eyes. He stirred but did not wake.

"Pru, what is all this?" she yawned and stared at her
friend, confused.

"Get up." She pulled the sheet off her and eyed the
coins that lay on the side table, payment from the night
before. Flashes of memory ran through Eleanora's mind.
Drunken kisses that smelt of rum, gentle and sloppy.
Gabe's murmurs as his hands ran down her naked
stomach. The coins shoved carelessly on the side as they
both got lost in the taste of each other once more.

"You need to learn to protect yourself. It's dangerous out there, Elea, you tried to leave before and look what happened! You're lucky that's all that happened." She pushed a sword into Elea's hand and strode to the door. "I'll be waiting on deck. Don't take long."

Eleanora moved to speak but she was silenced by Prudence shutting the door. She looked at the sword in her hand and scoffed, tossing it onto the bed. There was no way she was going to fight Prudence, much less learn how to do it properly. She pulled on the dress that she had been wearing almost every day since they first arrived on the ship. Despite her many, many dresses back at The Wanderer's Inn, Prudence had grabbed a couple of items for Eleanora and that was it. She missed her clothes. She missed the girls. Everything was so different here.

"Where are ye going?" Gabe mumbled, his face still pressed into the pillow; the ache of too much liquor had arrived along with daylight.

"Pru's lost her mind. It's nothing, just go back to sleep." She smiled at him as his mumbling turned back to the soft breaths of someone deep asleep. She picked up the coins he had given her and pulled out a tattered box. Trying to be quiet, she lay the coins down beside the payments from other crew mates; a gold trinket, a pocket watch, and some pearls, and carefully shut the lid.

Eleanora pulled her fiery mane of hair back from her face and knotted it at her neck. Prudence wouldn't let this go, best to just get it over with. She squared her shoulders and stepped out of the cabin, completely dreading what was to come next.

"Prudence this is ridiculous. What happened was a

unique situation. Not to mention the fact that it was entirely *not my fault*. If anyone is to blame, it's you for getting involved with these men in the first place. Had you not, we wouldn't be here." She crossed her arms decidedly.

Prudence frowned at Eleanora. "Pick it up." She threw the sword in her hand on the deck at Eleanora's feet. "All I've done is try my best to take care of you. Ye were just a child when we met, do you recall? A frightened, shivering little snot of a girl with no one to look after you."

She scowled at Eleanora with a look that had previously only been reserved for the worst kind of people. Never before had Prudence looked at her with such disdain in her eyes. Never before had she felt it so keenly.

"Years I spent in that gods awful place, being pushed around and taken advantage of because I couldn't bear to leave ye. Couldn't bear the burden of leaving you alone with those vultures. I could 'av left a long time ago if I didn't feel so guilty about you. I could 'av disappeared off the face of the earth," she yelled.

Eleanora froze in stunned silence. She had known Prudence hated their life, of course she had. But now Prudence seemed to hate everything. Everything and everyone. Eleanora had never imagined that Prudence had blamed her for it all.

"If I'm such a burden on you Prudence, then why in the gods' names did you insist on dragging me along on your insolent adventure to a life of crime? I did not ask for this life! Not any more than I asked to be ye friend. I was most content where I was... before you destroyed everything. I had friends, a good income, a roof over my head, hell you even took me away from the girl I loved! You took me away from Nell!

You broke my fucking heart Prudence. Ripped it up and stepped on it like I meant nothing to you. It was you that was so unhappy, I never was. Why you constantly feel the need to drag me along is beyond me. We are not the same and I can never forgive you for what you've done." By then, Elea was shouting at such a volume that a number of the crew on deck had turned from their tasks and towards the women who were glaring at one another with darkened faces.

"Elea, I—I'm sor—I never—"

"Don't you dare. Don't you *dare* stand there and try to feed me some feeble apology. You knew what you did, even as you were doing it. You just didn't care. You've never cared about anything but yourself."

The wind whistled across the deck as the women faced each other. Prudence pulled the sword from her belt and pointed it at Eleanora. "Pick. It. Up," Prudence hissed.

Eleanora bent to the ground, hesitantly, and picked up the sword. Her hand shook slightly but she controlled herself. She didn't wish to fight Prudence, nor did she stand a chance of winning.

Prudence's sword swung at Eleanora, a high arc that came crashing down at her. Eleanora blocked it right at the last minute, the vibrations travelling up her arm and into her shoulder. She let out a breath. Prudence's eyes were staring into hers, nostrils flaring, and breathing ragged. She lunged once more, pushing Eleanora back towards the wall.

"If you don't learn to protect yerself, you'll die. You've been hidden away in that place, naïve to how the world works! It's dangerous and cold, people are only going to look out for themselves." She pulled a knife out of her boot and sliced through the air in demonstration. She flipped the blade in her palm and handed it to her friend. "It's especially dangerous for someone like you."

Eleanora snatched the blade. "Someone like me? You mean a prostitute." She gripped the knife so hard that her knuckles went white. "You've always had a problem with it, haven't you? Always stood there so judgemental, as if you were better than everyone else. It's why none of the girls could stand you. I never sided with them, I always tried to defend you—for what?! I should have listened to them. You only ever do anything for yourself!"

"Myself?! Myself?! Everything that I ever did was for you! I dealt with their crap, got pushed around, got taken advantage of, all for you! You were like my sister! I couldn't leave you to those monsters, they'd have eaten you alive, Elea."

Eleanora hurled the blade at Prudence's feet. It landed with a clang on the deck. Prudence just stared at it. "I am not a child anymore," spat Eleanora, "so stop treating me like one." She turned on her heel and left Prudence standing there, alone and seething.

LATER, CAIN ENTERED HIS CABIN TO FIND PRUDENCE SAT ON the rug staring at the bookcase in front of her. His initial surprise was quashed by the look on her face.

"That sure was something back there."

"What of it?" she snarled, slightly harsher than she had originally intended. She bit her lip and looked at him. "Sorry."

"Are you all right?" Cain shut the door behind him and crouched on the balls of his feet in front of her.

Prudence shook her head. "No, I don't think I am. I don't know where it all went so wrong with her. I suppose it was back at the tavern... I never should have brought her here; it was a big mistake. She never wanted to leave. Not like I did. She was happy, ya know? She had friends, she liked her life. Even if it didn't make any sense to me." Cain had never seen such a mournful face before.

"You may not have made her happy by bringing her here, but one thing's for sure lass, she wouldn't have been better off staying there. And..." he shifted so that she was looking directly at him, "underneath all that anger she's got, she does love you. I can see it, bright as any star. You mean the world to her."

Prudence sighed and put her face in her hands. "Oh, I've made a right mess of things, haven't I? I don't want her to hate me. I don't. I love her. I just want her to be happy. I've ruined everything. She'll never forgive me now," she muttered.

"She's just angry, lass. She'll cool down after a while and then you can talk to her. She'll forgive you, lass, don't fret." He patted her shoulder and headed to his desk. The chair creaked under his weight. Perhaps he should use some of his share from *The Demelza* to buy a new chair.

"She won't," Prudence sniffed, "she's done with me. How can I even blame her after what I did to her?" she scoffed. "She's only still here 'cause she's got nowhere else to go."

Cain sighed. The girls' argument had been building since they first boarded *The Maiden*. It was getting tiresome. "Look lass, either she'll talk to you or she won't, no good fretting over it. Won't change things. What're you staring at that thing for, you want to borrow one?" He glanced at her still looking at the bookcase.

"Wouldn't be much point, Captain."

"Take one, there may not be much time for reading though mind you—"

"—No, what I mean is Captain, there'd be no point... because I can't read."

He looked up from his desk and caught her eye. Her long black hair fell down over her shoulders and chest, a few strands covering her left eye. She still sat cross-legged on the floor of his cabin, looking up at him with big blue eyes.

"Oh... guess you're right, not much point then, is there?" He shifted his gaze to the wall and back.

"Captain, I—"

"What? What is it?" He watched her shuffle on the floor, uncomfortable under his fixed gaze. She looked smaller in that moment. Vulnerable. "Tell me. Come on, lass."

Prudence fidgeted, her fingers twisting nervously with the hem of her neckline. "Captain... would ye teach me to read?" She tucked a strand of ear behind her hair and rose to her feet. Cain didn't realise that he'd been standing there staring blankly at her until she said, "I'm sorry, Captain, that was ridiculous. I shouldn't have asked, I'll... I'll be going now."

The captain smiled briefly. "No... it wasn't. I'd be happy to, lass. Although I'm not sure how good a teacher I'll be." He'd never seen Prudence look so uncomfortable before. She was serene amid chaos, even gleeful. But giving herself up for even just a moment left her as awkward and yearning as a child.

Prudence smiled nervously at him. "Thank ye, Captain. Truly. And I'd appreciate it if this were kept just between us?"

He nodded. The crew had not warmed to Prudence as their newest member as quickly as they would have a man. Women didn't usually make for piracy. Some of the men were highly superstitious, but they had begrudgingly become to accept her. Discovering this though, would be cause for more taunting. Not all of them could read of course, but getting lessons from their captain was out of the question.

"Course lass, not to worry. Your secret's safe with me." He winked at her and pulled out a fresh sheet of parchment. Along the top he scrawled letters in black ink. "The officer that taught me to read started off like this, learning the alphabet. So, I s'pose we'll start here."

Prudence took the seat that he offered her at the desk and he caught a waft of apples as she brushed past him. She ran her fingers over the freshly dried ink feeling the bumps of each shape. "My da could read y'know? Read real well for a fisherman, never got round to teaching me though. Didn't get the chance."

Cain sat beside her. "When did he pass?" he asked.

"He died when I was ten. He was a kind man but he had a way wi' drink and one day we was out on the boat catching a haul... he fell overboard. I couldn'a lift him back in, I was so small and the waves came in rough as anything."

"I'm sorry, that's awful."

"Me mother stopped looking at me after that. She finally had enough and kicked me out when I was twelve. I found a job at the tavern months later and was there ever since... well 'til you came along."

Cain's hand found hers and squeezed sympathetically. "Sorry to hear that lass. Seems we both had horrid mothers."

Prudence looked at him inquisitively but he didn't bother to elaborate.

Cain cleared his throat. "So, these are all the letters in the Aelish language. It's rather simple compared to some languages, thankfully it's not as hard to learn as Sovarian," he chuckled, "that boggles the minds of even the most intellectual people." He started at the first letter, reciting the name of each as he went. Prudence listened intently and copied the sounds that Cain used, her eyes strained as if trying to commit each sound and symbol to memory.

They went over the sheet of letters multiple times that afternoon; the men were busy enjoying the pleasures that Thaira had to offer, without any thought of consequence, and Eleanora stayed holed up in the girls' cabin refusing to speak to Prudence.

Cain had Prudence practise tracing the letters underneath those that he had written, occasionally asking her to tell him what they were called. Surprisingly, she seemed to soak up the information like a cloth with water. Clearly no matter the subject, Prudence had a knack for learning—from sword fighting to reading.

Once Prudence had almost memorised the letters individually, Cain pulled a handful of leather-bound books onto his lap. "Novels are probably not the best place to start with words, so I thought these log books might be easier. They're not as wordy as the stories, just simple sentences reporting the day to day." He handed one to Prudence who opened it cautiously.

"Are you sure? I mean... do we not need to work with the letters for a bit longer?" She flicked through the pages of the log, her voice nervous but her face curious.

"I think you'll do just fine, lass. We'll start slow." He paused her mindless flicking through the log with a hand on a page marked: 'Day 12 at Sea'.

"Did you write this?" Prudence looked over the page before turning to the cover for any indication.

Cain checked the year printed on the spine. "Yes. This was the year after I became captain." He smiled to himself, relishing the memory. He had felt such a sense of pride at becoming captain. He had only turned to piracy two years prior, the youngest captain that *The Bloody Maiden* had ever seen. Hell, the youngest captain most sailors had ever seen. A captain at twenty-two was practically unheard of. But Captain Hennesy had died taking a prize and the men had voted in their new captain —a young Cain Morris.

The crew he had now was almost entirely new, aside from Mr. Norton and Ephraim. Although Ephraim had only been a cabin boy at that point, not the carpenter and surgeon he was now. He had gone through a number of crew members in the five years that he had been captain of *The Maiden*, but that feeling of pride at being voted in... that was something he'd only felt once. It was something that he wasn't sure he'd ever feel again.

Prudence ran her fingers over the words in the log, staring at them intently.

"Now remember what we practised, some letters together make a different sound than their name," Cain reminded her. "Don't rush it, check the letters as you go."

Her face scrunched up in concentration, her lips mouthing the letter sounds to herself. Cain sat back in his chair letting her work it out, watching the little hand on the clock tick round its little cage. After a few minutes, Prudence threw the book down on the desk, making Cain jump.

"I can't do it. This is too hard." On her face was a look normally reserved for grumpy children and Cain couldn't help but stifle a laugh as he looked at her.

"It's all right. These things take time, effort. It's not something you'll pick up in one go."

Prudence huffed and slammed the book shut. "I can't do this. I need a break. This is too hard, Cain."

Cain placed a comforting hand on her shoulder. "You know you can fix it, don't you?" They both knew that he was no longer referring to the reading.

Prudence rolled her eyes and slapped her knees as she stood. "I hate making apologies."

Cain chuckled and shooed her off to find Eleanora. She could do this. She just needed to work out what to say.

ELEANORA SLAMMED THE DOOR OF THE CABIN THAT Prudence had paid for, and sunk down into the old fragile cot in the corner of the room. Prudence had always been hot-headed and often rude, but she had never spoken to Eleanora like that before. Never with such venom.

Prudence had changed. She had always been a little rough around the edges, Eleanora knew that. Pru wasn't happy with life at the tavern. She hated most people and she'd never liked being told what to do... but she was different now. She had become even more stubborn and violent since joining the pirate crew. Eleanora loved her. She always would. But she couldn't help the resentment that resurfaced in her gut every time that she thought about Prudence dragging her here with no choice.

A knock at the door made her pause. It was probably Prudence. Eleanora *really* didn't want to speak to her at that moment. She wasn't ready to listen to her guilt and apologies. Because she would forgive her, of course she would. And she wasn't ready to forgive... yet.

"Go away, Pru!"

She could hear Prudence leaning against the door as it creaked under her weight.

"Come on El, I'm sorry. Please let me in!"

Eleanora glanced at the door, reassured when she saw the lock bolted across. She lay back on the cot and stared at the ceiling. She'd go away eventually. She'd give up and try to forget it ever happened. That's what she usually did when she messed up.

Eleanora sighed. She missed her home. She missed her room and her friends... most of whom were dead now thanks to Prudence's friends starting that fight. She missed Nell. It all got so out of hand so quickly. How could that happen?

"Go away, Prudence." She could feel her resolve fading. She hated fighting with her; they had been like sisters for so long now. But there was no excuse for what Prudence had done. She had stolen and killed people. She had whisked Eleanora away on a wild adventure that Elea wanted nothing to do with... she had taken her away from home. That could not be so easily forgiven. No matter how much her heart ached when they were at odds.

She could hear Prudence sigh through the thick door before the footsteps retreated. Eleanora hugged her knees to her chest on the little cot they had shared since first boarding *The Bloody Maiden*. Even the name was barbaric. Tears filled her eyes and despite herself, they overflowed. Eleanora sat on the cot and sobbed until there were no more tears left to cry, yet she still didn't feel done.

PRUDENCE, STILL FRUSTRATED FROM HER LESSON WITH CAIN the night before, emerged from her cabin to the sound of

Mr. Norton yelling commands to the crew. Mr. Lowell scampered up the rigging like a monkey up a tree and untied the canvas mainsail. His curly brown hair hung so low over his forehead that Prudence wondered how he could see. Gabe took to his station at the helm and the crew prepared to set sail.

It was time to say goodbye to Thaira—a wild place that, despite its strangeness, had made Prudence feel welcome. The rocky patch of shore where their old campfire still sat was now a mess of ash, the barren landscape that featured only Emily Durrant's faded pink manor—it was an entirely different world to the one that she had grown up in. An intoxicating, fascinating world that she wanted to explore more of. Her life had been too tame, too mindless, too... nothing. It had been a nothing life. Nothing worthwhile until Cain and his crew had come along. In that moment, as the sun rose slowly on the horizon, Prudence made a promise to herself that she would fix everything.

She was going to fix her relationship with Eleanora, she was going to make something of herself in this new life, and they were going to make a perfect life together. Somewhere where they could both be happy.

The shoreline of Thaira began to drift away from them as *The Bloody Maiden* set sail. Mr. Abbott shoved a pail and a mop into Prudence's hands. "Your turn to wash the deck, Miss Prudence. Norton's orders."

She rolled her eyes but took the pail and began reluctantly washing the deck clean. It would take them around three days to get back to Vaerny, and with no plans to attack another vessel, and Eleanora currently not speaking to her, it would be a boring, hard three days of ship chores until they docked once more. She took to her task, vigorously cleaning off every stain left on the wood, focusing solely on her task so that her mind didn't drift off towards Elea as it had been doing so often since their fight.

Aside from the odd shift where Cain stood at the helm steering the galleon through the frigid waters of the Western Tides, he had remained hidden away in his cabin for most of the first day at sea. Prudence felt embarrassed by how she had left their last interaction. She hated feeling incapable and the lesson had made her feel just that. Vulnerable. Inadequate.

But she did want to learn, in spite of the feelings that made her blush so fiercely that she wished to hide in a dark room until it went away. She hoped that the captain would still be willing to teach her.

The days always flew by at sea. Without a town of people around her, Prudence failed to notice the sun moving across the sky or the hungry feeling in her belly as she completed task after task. Before she knew it, Mr. Duarte had rung the dinner bell. She dropped the tackle that she had been checking and brushed her britches off, before heading down the ladder to dinner.

She had always liked George, but Mr. Duarte was most definitely a better cook. The dinner consisted of salted meats, bread, and bone soup. It wasn't her favourite food but it left her feeling full and content. There wasn't much choice during a voyage but it was only a short distance from Thaira to Vaerny and so Cain had bought a few crates of fruits and vegetables from Emily before departing.

Prudence finished her soup and helped herself to a pear. She bit into the soft flesh, the sweet taste hitting her tongue, a delicious rare treat.

Garrick laughed and threw a rag at her as the juice dribbled down her chin. "You're almost as messy as the rest of us! I can see we've had a good effect on you, blue eyes. You're practically a man now."

She rolled her eyes and threw the half-eaten pear at him. He ducked swiftly and it landed smack on the back of Ephraim's head. Prudence's hands flew to her mouth.

"Now look what you've done!" he laughed. "You've awoken the beast!" He cackled to himself as Ephraim tried to punch him, the whole table breaking out in mischief as food was thrown all over the room.

"Sorry, Ephraim!" Prudence squeaked as Garrick chased her around the long table, his hands full of hard tack. She squealed and skirted around the corner, crashing into Shuu as she ran, Garrick hot on her heels. His dark brows sunk low over his piercing blue eyes as he caught up to her and they both slammed into the body of Captain Morris. Garrick lurched backwards so fast that he tumbled over Thomas' feet, sending him sprawling across the floor.

"S—sorry, Captain. I apologise, I should never 'av been running around like that. It, it was an honest mistake, it'll not—"

"Stop blathering like a fool, Garrick," Cain said as he brushed the crumbs off his coat. "Well, I can see we've had some real fun down here. Who started all this?"

The rest of the crew glanced at each other before looking at Prudence and Garrick.

"Betrayal." Prudence hissed at the men who tried their best not to laugh when their captain handed her the pail and mop once more.

"You best be getting to work then, lass. You'll not want to be here all night, not with the men looking to get some rest soon." He smiled wickedly at her as he squashed a fresh pear on her head. "You might want to clean yourself up first though, lass." He licked the juice off his finger and leant close to her ear. "You're looking a little sticky."

Prudence's cheeks flushed scarlet as his breath touched her cheek. She opened her mouth to scold him but no words came. Cain's cocky smirk left her stammering as she moved around him to get back to her cabin. She scrambled up the ladder as fast as her feet could carry her as the rest of the crew guffawed behind her.

Prudence slammed the cabin door behind her, sat down in front of the basin full of water, and attempted to remove the juice from her hair.

"What on earth happened to you?" Eleanora sat on the cot, a plate of meat and bread in her hand as she stared inquisitively at Prudence.

"Nothing. It was nothing." She scrubbed at her hair with wet hands but it didn't make much difference.

"Oh. Then why do you look like a fox has just broken into your hen house?"

Prudence turned to look at Eleanora. "What?"

"Flustered. You look flustered, Pru. And your face is red as a tomato."

Prudence spun back around to the basin and touched her cheek briefly. "It's not even that sticky," she huffed to herself.

THE DAYS SPED BY AND PRUDENCE FOUND HERSELF SPENDING most evenings tucked away in a corner alone, practising her reading. As soon as the day ended, leaving only the night shift on deck, Prudence grabbed the log book that Cain had leant her and settled down at the stern. She opened the thick old pages of the log book and stared at the page.

She thumbed the page as she mouthed the letters to herself. Her reading had improved greatly since that first lesson with Cain, but her confidence, not so much. "Ow-uh-er, our. Hunt. T-ooh-k, took. A. t-oh-t-ahl, total. Of f-five days." Prudence had been enjoying reading about the adventures of *The Maiden* from before she had joined the crew. Cain had certainly led an interesting life and it was nice to get some insight into it.

We finally caught up to the merchant vessel just past Pirn's southern coast. She was a swift ship but her men were inexperienced. It did not take long before we had caught up to her and forced their surrender. I dare say it was a plentiful haul that shall provide us with wages to last at least a month. The men were happy with their prize and we left the crew on their vessel to be found by sailors. Their captain, of course, was dispatched, but it was definitely a quick, clean attack with no other deaths to report.

I feel I am finally coming into my own as Captain. The

men have warmed to me as their leader, no longer their mate. I have gained their respect—

"R- res, p-eh-ct. Respect..." she murmured the letters aloud, learning their sounds as they mingled together to create new ones.

—and I have high hopes that this means we shall now become a much fiercer, well-known, and feared crew. If I can implement changes to our routine, I aim to have more successful hunts in the near future. More fear means more hauls with less death. The less death, the less time it shall take us and we shall be on our way to becoming rich men very soon.

I know that the crew do not tend to think too far ahead, but no sailor wishes to spend their entire life chained to the sea, no matter how much they may love it. I hope to lead these men to greatness. To ensure that we are all wealthy, successful men. I do not wish to leave this life like my predecessor, I wish to leave this life with pockets full enough to create a life of comfort and a belly full of food. I am a free man now, and I plan to use that freedom in the best way that I can.

Prudence heard the sound of footsteps behind her and shut the book, her head whipping round to see who had heard her.

"You're getting rather good, you know. Picked it up much quicker than I ever did." Cain came and sat by her side. They sat together with their legs crossed like children. "I hated learning to read, I only did it 'cause it was something to keep me busy."

"Did you really fight a lindworm?"

Cain smiled. "Uh, yes. Kind of. The crew and I were hiding out in the north of Morden, up in the mountains and... well to put it briefly, we picked the wrong cave to shelter in."

Prudence chuckled slightly. "That doesn't sound good."

"Yes, so, the men had started unpacking our gear in the mouth of the cave. Gabe, Charlie, and I had been hunting for dinner. We brought back a couple of rabbits. The smell of them cooking must've woken the lindworm and next thing we knew it was trashing our camp. Thomas broke his foot, you know? He was off his feet for weeks; the damn thing had crushed the bones through his boot. Its giant blue-grey toes flattened into the dirt and curled around his foot. It was nasty."

Prudence winced and pulled a face. "Ouch. So, did you kill it?"

Cain shook his head. "It turned out that the cave was home to a mating pair—that one was just the male. When the female came back, we didn't stand a chance. She was twice his size, with far more teeth. We had to leave most of our supplies and someone had to carry Thomas. We ended up camping out a few miles west, had to get out of their territory."

She couldn't help but let out a laugh. "I'm sorry, but it is funny." She could picture the crew clamouring to get away from two massive lindworms. It couldn't have been easy to escape, not across mountainous terrain, and not with Thomas' broken foot. Lindworms had always scared Prudence as a child. Not that there were lindworms on Llynne, but just the idea of them coming into your village and hunting your livestock had sent shivers down her spine. She wondered if she'd ever see one. "I can't imagine doing somethin' like that, it sounds terrifying."

"You're not wrong," Cain laughed. "So, how's the reading going?"

Prudence glanced down at the book in her hands. "It's going well, I s'pose. Pisses me off when I get stuck though."

"I definitely know that." Cain choked back a snort as Prudence hit his arm. "Sorry lass, but it's true, you're not exactly patient. You're stubborn and hard-headed... like me." The corner of his mouth turned up at that, as if the thought made him happy.

"Yes, that's been made painfully clear to me, Cain." She caught his eye and smiled. They sat together like that, in content silence, just watching the waves below their feet and the stars above as the night passed them by.

example of mischief. Kiss'n lass. 'Tis the right choice, to save you from embarrassment."

"Fuck you!"

Prudence felt her sword against the upper hand, she defended the attack and pushed him but Cain was the better swordsman and he was holding no prisoners.

She glanced up at him between ragged breaths and noticed for the first time his eyes were green. The kind of green that the grass gets when it grows too lush, a wicked bright green. The colour of a forest after the rain, the sea green that the raging waves turn during a storm. They were beautiful. The two of them stood there panting, trying to get their breath back.

8

TRUE TEST

Prudence swung the sword around to clash with Cain's and advanced towards him, eyes blazing. They had been practising for hours, sweat glistened her brow, and her muscles held a deep ache. It felt good to finally hold a real sword. She could feel the power in her grip, the weight of the metal in her hand. It felt good. She was doing well and they both knew it.

"Do ye wish to give in, Captain? I would not want you to be defeated by a measly woman," she smirked.

Captain Morris was pushed further into the corner by Prudence, until no longer had an escape. "Never, lass," he grinned at her. "I'm not one to surrender, even to such a terrifying foe. And you are far from measly."

Prudence grinned wickedly and tried to knock the sword out of his hand, but Captain Morris kept a tight hold of the hilt and barged his way back towards the centre of the ship. His answering grin was the perfect example of mischief. "Give in, lass. 'Tis the right choice, to save you from embarrassment."

"Fuck you!"

Prudence felt herself losing the upper hand. She defended the advances as best she could but Cain was the better swordsman and he was holding no prisoners.

She glanced up at him between ragged breaths and noticed for the first time that his eyes were green. The kind of green that the grass turns when it grows too lush, a wicked bright green. The colour of a forest after the rain. The sea green that raging waves turn during a storm. They were beautiful. The two of them stood there panting, trying to get their breath back.

"Good that was uhm, that was good," Captain Morris nodded to himself, "I think we can call it a day." He stood upright and chucked the sword at Mr. Norton who caught its handle with ease and put it away. Captain Morris glanced at his two companions before excusing himself to his cabin and locking the door behind him.

It was getting late; the sun was setting over the horizon and the dark night was rolling in behind the clouds. Prudence and Mr. Norton headed down for some food, hoping to get there before it was all gone. She spent the evening down there, eating and drinking and laughing with the rest of the crew. Prudence let her troubles with Eleanora float out of her mind for a while, once again caught up in thoughts of treasure and swordfights.

BACK IN VAERNY'S PORT, THE CREW WERE GETTING ROWDY and Captain Morris thought it best to let the men vent their energy. Everyone piled into the two dinghies, except for Prudence and Eleanora. Prudence took Elea by the hand to stop her from walking away.

"Ye have to come with us. It's not safe for you to be completely alone at night. I know ye hate me right now, but all I wanna do is look after you." Eleanora scowled and sighed, her expression turning soft again.

"I don't hate you... I think you're an idiot." She swept past Prudence and got into the boat, avoiding sitting near the men as much as possible. Prudence smiled, it was the first nice thing Elea had said to her in days. Perhaps this time they could work towards getting better. Maybe Eleanora was finally getting used to the new Prudence. Prudence sat down next to her friend and felt for the first time in days, a glimmer of hope. They were heading in the right direction.

In the prosperous town of Veida, the crew dived into The Raven's Nest, laughing loudly and making a mess. Prudence and Eleanora followed closely behind and found themselves a seat at the bar, away from the hollers of the men. Prudence was relieved to have her friend here —even if she had come unwillingly. It was nice to be close to her again. There were more people than Prudence would ever have expected inside the tavern. Far busier than The Wanderer's Inn, The Raven's Nest was packed full of people—so much that they were having to sit on one another as well as on the tables.

Prudence chuckled at the sight, it was strange to see,

but surprisingly familiar and welcome. This was a scene she was comfortable with. The girls found a seat by the bar and ordered some drinks. Eleanora still seemed rather uncomfortable with Prudence, but she had started surveying the room like she used to. Prudence hoped that she wouldn't go back to whoring around. She might be abused again. Prudence knew that Eleanora didn't approve of her new life but she hoped that Elea would be smart enough to realise that it was getting them money— money that meant she didn't need to work for it.

Prudence passed Elea a drink and paid the woman behind the bar with some coins that she had got in Malaine. The woman took the pieces and continued to wash the bar. She seemed rather content here. Prudence found it strange to watch. The woman smiled, spoke to her regulars, and brought out big plates of food for people that actually looked edible. Everyone seemed fairly happy even with the odd drunken brawl.

"Excuse me ma'am, what's yer name?" Prudence wanted to know more about this woman, she needed to know if it was just her own life that had been a misery.

"Ester." The woman looked at her strangely. "Who are you?"

"Oh, I'm nobody... you in another life perhaps." Ester raised her eyebrows but went back to work. Eleanora sat back in her seat.

"So, why are we here, Prudence?"

"For a good time? I don't know Elea, does it really matter? We're here and we'll likely stay 'ere tonight. Enjoy it." Eleanora sighed and gulped down more of her drink.

"Well at least get me some food then. I'm starved.

Haven't eaten a decent thing in weeks." Prudence laughed. Neither of them had really eaten well before they'd gone with Cain either. George had been a terrible cook. She pulled out the last few coins in her pocket.

"Ester! Can we get something to eat over here?" Ester nodded and went into the back, where Prudence assumed the kitchen was. She could smell all sorts of delicious food coming from back there. It made a change to what she was used to. The crew cook wasn't great. He let the bread go stale and the meat was far too salty. On the odd occasion that they had fruit aboard, he never gave it out early enough and it soon went mouldy.

Ester soon brought out some big plates of fresh-looking food—there were even some vegetables there. Both Prudence and Eleanora were drooling at the sight of it, not caring who saw them. There was more food on each plate than they had ever eaten in one sitting before. The girls tucked in, ferociously eating it all before it could get cold. Prudence pushed a pile of coins over the table towards Ester and she counted the lot before stuffing it in her apron pocket.

"This is so good. Oh god, I've never eaten this much food in one go before." Prudence stuffed a spoonful of mashed potatoes into her mouth. Eleanora nodded with cheeks full of food.

"It's wonderful. I hope I can eat all of this." The girls ate until their stomachs hurt. It was bizarrely wonderful being in The Raven's Nest, it felt like the world outside didn't exist. Like Prudence had never killed Mrs. Langley, Eleanora didn't hate her, and it had all been a dream. It felt good being with Eleanora like this, seeing her smile and laugh as she watched people spill things and get into fights with their friends. For once she looked like a child again.

The girls talked for a long time, happy in their little bubble, oblivious to the rest of the world around them. It felt like they were family again. Prudence could feel Eleanora warming up to her once more, most likely because it was easy to forget what had happened whilst they were having fun. Prudence could feel a nagging in her stomach telling her that she knew it couldn't last, not once they left the tavern; things like that were too good to be permanent. She tried her best to ignore it though, to smile and talk like they used to. After a while, the conversation died down and both of the girls went back to their people-watching.

Ester was cleaning glasses with a rag behind the counter. Men tried to flirt with her from their stools, without much luck. Some of the crew were busy laughing and grinning at the harlots attempting to seduce the drunken oafs. Cain sat towards the back of the room with a girl clung on each arm, smiling at him as he drank. Occasionally he'd bother to talk back to them as they stroked his arms and kissed his cheeks. Prudence's face reddened and she turned to see Eleanora watching her curiously. Prudence huffed and downed her latest drink. It burned her throat.

Eleanora snorted. "You're jealous?" She glanced at the girls swarming the captain. "Seriously? Prudence is jealous of a bunch of whores?" She choked back a laugh but the humour continued to dance in her eyes. Eleanora found the whole experience rather ironic. Prudence glowered at her.

"I don't see why you're so amused. And I'm not jealous. I just think it's below him to be hanging around with whores. Besides, how could I be jealous? He drives me insane." Her ears were bright red and she was glaring with such intensity at Cain that Eleanora thought a hole might burn right through his skull.

"Oh please, he makes you mad?" she snorted, "I've never met two people more similar."

Prudence scowled. "No, we're not."

"Water in the rain, Prudence. You're two sides of the same coin. You push each other, you wind one another up, you're both irritating, and stubborn, and grumpy. You've certainly got the same wicked temper." Suddenly, Elea's laughter was hard to contain and it bubbled out of her. Prudence had marched through the room and out the door before Eleanora could blink.

"Stupid, mindless, idiotic man. Indulging in girls that worship him like a god. Who does he think he is? The king? Stupid men and their stupid egos." Prudence kicked at the stones on the ground as she stepped out the door and onto the street outside the tavern. The air was harsh against her skin and made goosebumps rise on her arms. There weren't many people outside and most of them were rushing to get somewhere—probably to their warm homes. Prudence watched them dash down the street with their coats pulled up around their necks, bracing themselves against the cold.

It wouldn't be too long before the frost started to come in from the north, rising up the beach like a sweeping fog of cold. Prudence was not a fan of winter; it was too cold and miserable. The summer was so much nicer. In the summer, the light leaves your skin feeling warm and your cheeks turn rosy, and the sea feels like the most enormous bath, warm enough to spend hours in without catching a chill. Everything went dark in the winter.

With her mind elsewhere, Prudence didn't notice the man hovering in a dark corner nearby, shrouded in shadow. He watched her for a while before calling to his friend.

"Lookie what we've found here, Gus. Found ourselves a nice dessert for after dinner. But o' course," he muttered, "dessert is the best part. Maybe we should skip to the third course." He lunged forward and gripped Prudence's shirt before she yanked it away. Buttons popped off with the strain, exposing most of her middle.

Stepping away from him, she growled, "Back off old man. You don't want to see the world from down there on your back now, do ya?" Prudence pulled the dagger out from her boot and pointed it at the old man. She turned to go back inside but her path was blocked by the bigger guy, Gus, staring down at her like she was a beetle underfoot, or worse still... like food. Prudence's hand shook slightly but she trained the blade on Gus. He was roughly twice the size of Prudence in every way, but it was his expression that chilled Prudence to the core.

Turning her back on him to find another way out,

Prudence found herself nose to nose with the old man. His sickening grin gleamed in the darkness and he had the kind of eyes that looked right through you. Prudence couldn't help the shiver that came over her, a wash of cold that made her recoil, physically and mentally.

"Leave me alone..." she murmured, feeling an overwhelming urge to throw up as they tried to touch her again. The old man reached out and grabbed Prudence by the hair, yanking her towards him. Instinctively, Prudence thrust the dagger outwards, stabbing the old man in the stomach. He yelped in pain and fell to the ground, clutching his gut. The blood soaked swiftly through his shirt. Gus grabbed Prudence by the shoulders and flung her so hard against the tavern wall that it winded her.

Gasping for breath, Prudence gripped the dagger even tighter than before and got ready to take another swing when she noticed a few soldiers patrolling down the street.

Ignoring the fire in her side, she screamed as loud as she could manage and felt relief sweep through her when they noticed her. The soldiers came rushing up and glanced at the old man, now bleeding out on the floor and at Prudence, winded in the corner.

"Please..." Prudence whispered, still trying to catch her breath, "please help me." The soldiers glanced at Gus and back at Prudence. One of them opened a pair of shackles.

"Oh, thank you. Thank ye so much." Prudence sighed and dropped the dagger on the floor.

"Miss, you're under arrest. You're going to have to come with us." Prudence was baffled.

"What? Why?"

"For assaulting that man and a soldier of Vaerny." Prudence only now noticed the soldier's coat around Gus' shoulders and felt the life drain out of her. The shackles clapped onto her wrists, biting into her skin, and rubbed horribly. The three soldiers that Prudence thought had come to her rescue dragged her behind them and lifted her onto a cart. Prudence tried her best to hold back the sobs that threatened to take over.

Two of the soldiers sat at the front of the cart, holding the horses' reins and talking together. The third sat opposite Prudence, watching her quietly. The soldier tried his best to speak to her but Prudence turned away at the sound of his voice, curling into herself. Pru could tell from the look on his face that this man didn't want to arrest her. He looked almost sorry for her. She could also tell by the way he looked sharply away when his friends were looking, that he wasn't going to defend her. Prudence rolled her eyes. Wilful ignorance filled her with more rage than outright bigotry.

AFTER AN AGONIZING FEW HOURS, THE CART HAD PULLED onto the gravel, outside what she could only presume was the island's jail. The soldiers came around the side and stood her up, leading Prudence down the steps that led underneath the ground.

"Where are ye taking me? Let go of me, I don't need a sodding hand goddamn it. I can walk myself." This was where they kept the prisoners, underground in the cold and damp, like rabid dogs. It occurred to Prudence that no one would hear her once she was so deep beneath all the stone and rock. Most likely, none of the previous prisoners made it back above ground to see the sun again. Except to be hung, of course.

The soldiers had taken away her shoes and clothes, leaving her in a moth-eaten tunic that itched terribly. It seemed they went to every extent possible to make her time there that much worse. They had been very interested in the log book that had been tucked in the large pocket of Prudence's coat. There were a lot of trade routes and passages scrawled across the pages. It seemed to Prudence to be just what the crew needed if they were going to attack any other merchants in these waters.

Prudence was blind to her surroundings as the soldiers shoved her down the dark corridor, deep into the dungeon. She could feel the cold rough stone scraping her skin as they shoved her forward. The corridor was lit by oil lamps that hung from hooks high above, giving the place a dim orange glow. Prudence could make out cobwebs in the corners and the odd empty cell as they walked. A rat scurried over her foot and made her shriek in disgust. There didn't seem to be anyone else around as the soldiers unbolted a door at the end of the long corridor and hauled her inside.

Prudence pulled against the shackles, but the men held them tight. "Where are the other prisoners? Why is there no one down here?"

"Shut it girl, or you'll be joining them at the gallows sooner than you'd like." The room smelt of piss and looked as if it had been used as a toilet for every prisoner that had been there. Urine and blood stained the lower half of the walls, and on the table in the centre, clumps of dried blood and flesh remained. Prudence recoiled at the smell of the room but the soldiers tightened their grip.

"Stand still you stupid bitch," snapped one soldier. He dragged her over to the wall where bolts and hooks hung down and attached her chains to them. Prudence gasped. The chains were tight and pinched her skin, keeping her arms in an uncomfortable position. The men made sure that her chains were secure before leaving the room and bolting the door loudly.

"And how the hell am I supposed to piss like this?" Prudence gestured to her restrained arms. "Got no way of bloody doing it from here."

But the soldiers were long gone and could not hear her anymore. It was cold in the dungeon, there was nothing to keep her warm even if she could move around. The chains kept her close to the wall with only about an arm's length of movement. The hooks were low down and forced Prudence into a crouch that became uncomfortable within minutes. The soldiers hadn't told Prudence how long she'd be there for. She had presumed it would be a simple hanging... that was until they asked about Cain and the log book. It seemed to be the only thing that they were interested in. Perhaps their desire to find Cain would keep her alive for a little longer.

She wondered who else had been in this room. It was larger than all of the cells that they had passed on the way and Prudence thought that it must be used for questioning—if the table covered in blood was anything to go by. Maybe that's what they were going to do to her. Torture her if she didn't answer their questions.

The thought scared her so much that she thought she might be sick. Prudence couldn't help but imagine them using a knife or a hammer and hurting her while she screamed. It seemed an awful way to spend her final days. Maybe she'd even die on the table. At least that would be away from the humiliating public.

BACK INSIDE THE RAVEN'S NEST, ELEANORA LOOKED UP from her spot on the bar. Prudence had been gone for a while now. She got up and walked outside but there seemed to be no one around, except for the odd homeless person. She cupped her hands to her mouth.

"Prudence! Pru, you out here?" Eleanora stopped someone as they walked past the tavern. "Excuse me! Have you seen a woman out here? About my height, black hair, light blue eyes?" The man shook his head.

"I'm sorry, miss. I haven't seen anyone out here." Eleanora thanked the man and watched him walk down the street and turn off into an alleyway.

"Where the bloody hell could she have gone? This is just like her wandering off on her own." She huffed and stormed back inside to the table where Cain and his crew were sitting. Eleanora scoffed at the captain, sat with a bunch of harlots on his lap, and pulled at his arm. Her expression was enough to make Captain Morris stop laughing and push the girls off his lap.

"What is it?"

"Pru's gone. Nowhere in sight. I've tried calling for her but she's not here." Captain Morris sighed, scratched his beard, and rose from his seat.

"She must be here somewhere, love. She can't have disappeared into thin air."

9

WAVERING HOPE

After what felt like hours, one of the soldiers came back with some water. He was the taller of the two and had cropped brown hair. His uniform was impeccable; there wasn't so much as a scrap of cloth out of place. He helped Prudence take a sip.

"Now, there's more of that for you if you can help us. Where is Captain Cain Morris? We know you were with him when his crew attacked *The Demelza*. His Majesty has had soldiers searching for him a lot longer than that, so, where is he?" He looked at Prudence expectantly. Prudence thought for a moment, before scowling.

"And why on earth would I help you? Ye've chained me up, ready to await death." She looked him up and down, waiting for him to leave. The soldier pursed his lips before slapping her.

"That was your first mistake. Don't make another." He stood abruptly and left the room, taking the water with him.

"Well, nice to meet ye too." Prudence rolled her eyes. With the large door shut, the room was left in darkness and the cold made it even worse. Prudence could hear a dripping noise from a distant corner, most likely from a hole in the roof. Prudence wondered what Eleanora and Cain were doing right now. They must have noticed her disappearance. At a guess, it had taken about two hours on horseback to get to Valentya. They must be getting worried, well... Elea at least.

Prudence had fallen asleep when the door bolt was slammed open again and in walked the two soldiers who had brought Prudence here. This time they had no water. The shorter, meaner-looking one of them lifted her up by the arm so that she was standing before them. Even though he wasn't as tall as his friend, her head barely reached his shoulder.

"Davy, give us a moment, will you?" The brown-haired one glanced at his partner. Prudence guessed that he was the one in charge then. The other one, Davy, huffed and turned on his heel.

"Just make sure to leave her in one piece, won't you, Gibson? Wouldn't want her dying on us quite yet." The man's smile made his words less than convincing. After Davy had left the room, Gibson leant closer to Prudence and pursed his lips. He was clearly thinking about what to say, though Prudence had no idea where this conversation would lead.

"I'm under strict orders here to uh, to make you talk. No matter what. And Davy out there would sure love to beat the words out of you. The kid seems to live for it. I, however, don't exactly revel in the idea of torturing a woman, so if you could please help everyone here, and tell me what you know about Cain Morris. It'd be better for everyone, especially you."

Prudence locked eyes with him. He seemed to be sincere in his words but Prudence wasn't a snitch, she wouldn't give anyone up. He did seem nicer than his scowling friend out in the corridor though.

Drip drip drip. The noise was getting incessant now. It hadn't eased up for one moment since they'd thrown her in there. Prudence couldn't remember how long ago that was now. A day? Maybe two?

She sighed and shook her head, causing the lieutenant to frown, his expression disappointed.

"I'll try and keep the questioning nice for as long as I can. But if you don't talk, I'll have no control over how *he* goes about interrogating." He jerked his thumb towards the door. Prudence nodded and sat back down on the hard floor.

"I know. I can take care o' myself, Lieutenant."

Gibson glanced at the chains around Prudence's wrists before leaving and bolted the heavy door behind him. Alone again, with nothing but an oil lamp on the far wall for comfort, Prudence plonked herself back down and placed her head in her hands. It seemed that there would be nothing more than this isolation for the remainder of Prudence's very short life. That and the beatings that would occur soon enough.

They came in every couple of hours or so, it was difficult to tell the exact time in Prudence's cell as the sunlight didn't reach that far down. She could no longer tell if it was night or day. Her body clock was convinced that she was trapped in a never-ending night, and Prudence constantly craved rest.

The soldiers would come alone sometimes, which made it all the worse for Prudence. The cadet, Davy, took sheer delight in beating her senseless, pounding his fist into her face until her eyes swelled up so much that she could no longer see. He made her bleed all over. Opening up wounds on her forearms and around her neck, across her cheeks, and down her bare torso. He had taken his sweet time tearing her tunic open before running the cold blade across her goosebump-covered skin.

He was an evil man. It was a kind of power trip for him, to see her lying there helpless, unable to defend herself. She knew he took a sick kind of pleasure in it.

The lieutenant was different though. He was kind despite his commanding position. His pleasant demeanour was worse than the beatings for Prudence, but still she refused to give up her crew, her friends.

Davy had Prudence by the wrists and had slammed his fist into her ribs for what felt like the hundredth time this visit. Prudence coughed and spat out a glob of blood that had pooled in her mouth. He smirked at her.

"Seems like you've got some balls, princess. You haven't given me a word of use since you got here. You're tougher than most of the men I've questioned."

Prudence coughed and stared at him defiantly. "There's nothing ye can do to me that'll make me tell ye anything. I am no coward. Ye've already lost." They would hang her, no doubt, but at least it was satisfying seeing his scrunched-up face, eyes blazing with an insatiable fury.

The cadet flashed a leery smile at her. "We'll see about

that, *princess*." His final punch landed square on her face, knocking Prudence to the floor instantly. The cadet bent down to her and whispered in her ear. "I haven't even begun doing what I want to do to you. I'm going to enjoy making you squeal."

Prudence managed to hold back her shiver of revulsion until he left the cell and bolted the door behind him.

CAIN PACED THE STREET FOR THE THIRD TIME THAT DAY, kicking up dust that coated his clothes and hands in dirt. Prudence had been gone for ten days. No one had seen her. No flicker of recognition crossed their face when he described her tresses of inky black hair, her icy blue eyes, or the steely resolve that showed permanently on her face.

He glanced down the road to where Eleanora's petite frame was outlined by the lowering sun, frantically handing out papers to every person who passed her. She'd drawn her friend's likeness over and over again to hand out in the hopes that someone would know what had happened to her.

Cain admired the commitment but he was unconvinced that it would come to much. No one he had met could care any less about a missing girl. A man walked past Cain and he grabbed him by the arm. "Excuse me, sir, apologies, but a young woman has gone missing. She's about this tall," he gestured to the height of his shoulder, "long black hair, fair skin—"

"—I've not seen any girl." The man shook off his grip and carried on down the road as Cain sighed. They had searched all of Veida in the days since the tavern. Cain had sent most of the crew back to *The Bloody Maiden* but still Garrick, Shuu, Charlie, Gabe, Mr. Abbott, Mr. Rundstrom, and Khari had remained. Between them they'd walked the entire town, searching taverns, brothels, side alleys, and ditches. They'd spoken to hundreds of people. All to no avail. Prudence was nowhere to be found.

It was hard to not feel entirely hopeless. Eleanora's optimism irritated Cain more than it kept him positive. Her blind faith in Pru magically reappearing before them, as if she'd just walked down a wrong road and found them mere moments later, was infuriating. Prudence wasn't in Veida, of that he felt certain. They would have found her by now if she was. He didn't know how much longer he could keep the search going with the knowledge that each passing day was a greater risk than the one before. Sooner or later, his ship was going to be discovered in Vearny's harbour.

Captain Morris meandered down the winding roads of Veida until the pounding in his head became too much and he stepped into the nearest tavern and grabbed a seat at the bar. It was a dingy little building, with low sloping ceilings, and walls that smelt of years of stale liquor and smoke.

"Get me a brandy," he nodded at the owner. The man grabbed a bottle and placed it in front of Cain with a tankard. Cain chucked a couple coins onto the bar in front of him and poured himself a large drink. He gulped it down and poured another as he ran a hand over his forehead. He'd barely slept since Prudence had gone. The headaches had started a few days ago.

A young man in a soldier's uniform appeared beside him and ordered two bottles of beer. Cain glanced briefly at him and angled away from him to obscure his face.

"Roberts!" Another soldier, presumably with the man beside Cain, yelled from his table. "I'm hungry, get us some food!"

Roberts nodded and spoke to the owner once more as the other soldier kicked back in his chair. A group of them had congregated at a table not far from Cain's seat, clearly already a little intoxicated, despite it only just turning midday. They laughed boisterously as one of the younger members of the group struggled to finish the drink that they'd made him chug.

"So how was it working in the city?" one of them chuckled. "As bad as you'd expected?"

"The shifts are a bitch. Lieutenant's a real stickler, not like Harris that's for sure. But there's a real pretty face tucked away in the big cells." A stubbled, dark-haired man grinned. "Real nice. Lieutenant keeps a pretty close eye most of the time but, oh, if you could see her."

Cain swallowed the last of his drink and kept his eyes on his empty glass as he listened to them. The soldier's friends grinned as they polished off yet another bottle. "How are her tits?"

The dark-haired man smirked and held his hands out in answer and they all laughed. "Oh, what I would do to her if I got half the chance. Got these big blue eyes that are just begging for it."

"Is she blonde? Got a thing for blondes."

"Nah, black hair, but mate you wouldn't turn this down."

Cain's head whipped up. Prudence. It couldn't be, could it? There were hundreds of women with black hair and blue eyes.

"What 'av they got her in there for? Pretty little thing like that's not normally what you'd find down there."

"She's been with some smuggler, pirate or something. Probably just a whore but Gov'nor seems awful keen to keep her there till she sings."

"He probably just wants to fuck her himself, dirty old bastard." The table erupted into laughter once more as the jokes became cruder. But Cain had heard enough. He threw another coin on the bar and strode out of the tavern as quickly as his feet would allow.

By the time he reached Eleanora, still canvassing the street, he was practically running. She frowned at him. "What? What is it?"

"Elea I... I found her. I've found her."

LIEUTENANT GIBSON CAME INTO THE CELL WITH A HUNK OF stale bread on a tray. He placed it at Prudence's feet. "Here. Can't have you wasting away."

"No. Would be a shame if I died o' hunger before you could hang me," Prudence scoffed.

The Lieutenant cast his eyes to the floor. "I hope you know my hands are tied here. I'm doing everything I can to keep you from being hurt."

196

Prudence looked mockingly over her broken, bruised, and filthy body. "Well thank ye. I don't know what I'd do if they tried to hurt me. Thank the gods you're here." She shuffled her hunched and aching body around so that she was facing the wall. "Just fuck off, will you? Your delusion that you're a good man because you personally don't want to beat me senseless, and threaten to 'have your way with me,' doesn't mean you actually are. You're a coward, Lieutenant. At least your partner cannot say that about himself." She kicked the tray with a bloody foot so that it skidded across the floor to the soldier's boots. "You can go now."

The Lieutenant didn't bother speaking again, but Prudence heard his heavy exhale and pictured him shaking his head as he collected the tray and locked her cell once more. There were no good men here, only monsters.

Cadet Davy was a terrifying creature who never looked more alive than when he was carving bits of Prudence away. He reminded her of a boy she knew as a child. He had loved nothing more than stamping on bugs when they lay in his path. Prudence had always hated that boy. What could make a bug deserving of being crushed underfoot, for no reason at all?

She cast back in her mind to the age of six, watching the boy and his friends from the front steps of her home as they poked the bits of pig carcass that his mother cast aside from making dinner. It churned Prudence's stomach to watch them with their big sticks, prodding it and skewering bits to wave in their friends' faces.

Sometimes, Prudence had imagined being a giant,

and stamping on the boy with her giant boots to see how he liked it. She'd like to stamp on the cadet just the same. But at least he didn't pretend that he was just doing his duty, not like the lieutenant.

Prudence heard the sound of heavy footsteps in the hallway beyond her cell door. "Did ye miss me so much that you're back already? That's fast, even for you, Lieutenant." She grinned to herself. Winding them up wasn't smart, but it did make her feel a whole lot better. She remembered the sight of Avery yelling from the gallows before he swung. He was free and unapologetically himself. Prudence had decided, in all the time alone with herself in this dank place, that she would be the same.

But it wasn't the lieutenant's head that bobbed through the door frame. Cadet Davy flashed a wicked grin at her as he gave way to an older man entering the cell. His hair was a vibrant white, not a fleck of grey to be seen. His moustache was neatly trimmed and his clothes were clearly the most luxurious ones on Vaerny.

His gaze made Prudence's blood run cold. There wasn't a hint of humanity in it. People, even the cruellest of them, always had something in their eyes. Davy's eyes came alive when he was torturing Prudence, but it was a flash that Prudence recognised at least. Gibson's eyes always held a hint of sadness about them, as if he was truly bound by duty to torture her. But this man... he had nothing.

His eyes were a bright blue, similar to Prudence's own. But that's where the similarities ended—it was akin to staring into a void. They may as well have been entirely black because Prudence didn't see one speck of humanity within them. He merely stood and watched Prudence for the longest time.

Eventually, the anticipation grew too much for Prudence's patience. "Are ye here for something? I mean it's not like I've got anything better to do, but if this is all yer here for then, are we done?"

Cadet Davy hid his smirk before turning to the older man. "As you can see, Governor, sir, she's practically feral and despite my best attempts... she won't talk. I've used every tool available."

The governor. This was the man in charge of it all on the island. The man who took orders directly from the person who wanted Cain dead. Prudence studied him cautiously. He didn't look dangerous, not physically at least. But that look... it made Prudence's bones sing with a nervous energy. She had always prided herself on having a reliable gut reaction to people and her gut told her that this man would make Davy look like a child.

The governor unclasped his fingers and cleared his throat. "Prudence. That's your name, isn't it ma'am? My name is Governor Atkey, but you would be wise not to refer to me directly in *your* position."

Prudence scowled. *Cunt.* She kept her face deliberately vague as he continued.

"I don't normally make trips to the dungeon. I'm a very busy man you see, and this is quite an inconvenience," he drawled, every word dripping with poison. "You have put my men in a difficult position. It seems that no matter what they try... you won't tell us what we want to know." He moved toward Prudence, getting his face intimidatingly close to hers. "I intend on capturing that treasonous bastard and earning favour from our king. *You* will not be standing in my way, little girl," he spat.

Prudence recoiled as far back into the wall as her shoulders would allow. She suddenly felt much less sure of herself than she had before. Governor Atkey rose and removed his coat, shoving it into Davy's outstretched arms. He rolled his shirt sleeves up to his elbows and wandered idly over to the table where the tools from Prudence's last session had been left.

They never bothered to clean up. The table was a mess of Prudence's blood, now hardened and flaking. There were puddles of vomit splashed on the edge and down the table leg. The smell had been awful to begin with, a stench that clung to the inside of her nostrils and filled her mouth with bile, but she had been inside that cell for so long now that it was as if she couldn't smell it at all.

The governor picked up a wicked blade with a serrated edge that blanched the tiny bit of colour that was left in Prudence's face. The blade was no longer the colour of metal, but a rusty copper colour that could only come from years of coating it in blood. Prudence tried to stop the images from flickering in her mind: a man screaming as the blade dragged across his chest; a woman gagged and bucking against her shackles as it raked across her arm, almost removing it entirely.

She swallowed the vomit that filled her mouth. Prudence thought she had experienced true terror... but nothing had ever been as terrifying as this.

The cadet was too handsy as he removed Prudence from her chains and dragged her to the table. The built-in shackles clamped down on her wrists, pinching the skin. The metal was badly rusted and rubbed against her already sore and wounded wrists.

Cadet Davy leant down so that his lips brushed against Prudence's cheekbone. "I can't wait to stand here and watch you squirm." His breath tickled Prudence's ear and she grimaced.

She pulled the most charming smile she could muster and said in her sweetest voice: "I can't wait till the day you choke to death on yer own blood."

Davy grinned and ran a finger down her neck. "Nothing I love more than when you get angry. You should be careful... women often get punished for much less." The feel of his skin so close to hers made her skin crawl. She stifled a growl at the cadet as the governor came into view, his eyes focused intently on her face.

"Cadet. I suggest you back away from the girl. She is after all a *lady*. We should treat her as such. Now, onto business... this will go much easier for you, miss, if we focus on truth. We can be truthful with one another, can't we?" His eyes flashed with anger when Prudence didn't reply. "Can't we?!"

Prudence gulped and nodded frantically, her heart threatening to burst from her chest like a bird trapped in a cage.

"So," the governor's face was a mask of nonchalance as he studied her, "we'll start simple. Where are you from?"

Prudence hesitated, her gaze flashing between

Governor Atkey and Cadet Davy. "Llynne," she croaked, her voice almost a whisper from the lack of water.

The governor leant in closer. "Pardon?"

Prudence cleared her throat and spoke louder. "Llynne, sir. I'm from Llynne."

He nodded as he fiddled with the blade in his hand. "And how old are you?"

"Twenty-two, sir."

He pursed his lips. "You've been of marrying age for a number of years now and yet you have not taken a husband? Instead, you're cavorting with criminals. Tell me, Prudence," her name came out as a sneer, "are you a whore?"

Prudence scowled but bit her tongue. "No, sir, I am not." His calm manner was more maddening than Davy had ever been. Prudence pictured the shackles breaking as she sprang from the table to wrestle that gods forsaken blade from his grip and turn it on the both of them.

He smirked. "My dear, no respectable young lady roams with filthy, murderous *pirates*." He spat the word and pressed the blade against Prudence's bare arm. Just enough to bring blood to the surface. He didn't drag it across her skin, not yet, but it burned against her flesh like fire. Tears formed in her eyes and she bit the inside of her cheek to keep from wincing. Hard enough to taste blood. He smiled at her and raised a hand to her cheek. "No need for tears." Governor Atkey wiped a drop away with the tip of his thumb as he pressed the blade in harder.

"Now..." the pressure of the blade lessened, "where is

the pirate that you have involved yourself with? The man known as Cain Morris?"

Prudence sucked in a breath, preparing for the worst. "I don't know." The governor's brow creased and he put the blade back to her skin.

"Now, now I thought we promised to be honest with one another. So, I'll ask again, where is he?" The governor dragged the blade across her arm and Prudence let out a wail.

"I don't know!" she sobbed, her breath coming in ragged gasps as the pain ignited in her arm. The jagged edge tore through her skin, making a bloody mess. The skin was ripped apart in a rough gash that spread from just above her elbow, right down to her wrist. Prudence stifled a sob and looked away from her ruined arm.

"Don't lie to me, Prudence."

"I don't know. I've been locked up, 'ow could I possibly know where they are? Even if I did... I wouldn't tell ye." Prudence's vision swam hazily but between the blur of tears, their faces came to mind. Eleanora. Mr. Norton. Garrick... Cain. She'd never betray Cain's trust. She owed him more than that.

The governor let out a low growl, the blade momentarily taken away from her bare arm. He glared at her with such malice that the breath caught in Prudence's throat. The governor nodded at the cadet and walked away from the blood-stained table. Davy's fist collided with Prudence's face once more and the world went black.

"Right, the barracks and jail are about five hundred yards east of 'ere. Guards are on patrol round the clock at the main gates, and from what I can see, there's more at the back entrance." Mr. Rundstrom informed the group and took a seat at their table. Cain had sent Mr. Abbott back to *The Maiden* to inform the rest of the crew that they were going to Valentya to find Prudence.

After arriving in the capital, they had set about finding somewhere to stay where they wouldn't stick out. Bartholomew's Recreational Apothecary, a run-down opium den with cracked walls, a boarded-up window, and a host of dodgy patrons, had seemed like the perfect place. Eleanora glanced once more at the proprietor and grimaced. She hoped they wouldn't have to stay too long.

"Just gimme five minutes with 'em Cap, they won't know what hit 'em." Garrick slammed his fist into his palm and grinned.

Shuu scoffed. "Calm it there, kid, I know ye like the girl but she's not worth killing yerself over."

Eleanora rolled her eyes at them. "I can't believe you're jokin' at a time like this! She could be hurt... and cold. She could be dead! She could be fucking dead." She let her head sink into her hands with a sob. Gabe's hand was on her shoulder in an instant, comforting her.

"We're gonna do everything we can to find her, love. I *promise* you," said Cain. She lifted her head to look at him. The determination in his eyes helped her quiet the sobs. Now wasn't the time for crying. They needed a plan.

"How on earth do you plan on finding her?" she asked the captain.

"We're going to need your help." He exhaled a puff of

tobacco smoke and leant back in his chair, his expression cunning.

Elea gulped. "Anything. What will ye have me do?"

Cain smiled and turned to Mr. Rundstrom once more. "I'm sure those soldiers would be most willing to help a young lady in distress."

"Aye, Captain, I'm sure they would."

A wave of nerves swept through Eleanora looking at their expressions but she straightened in her chair. It didn't matter what they asked of her, she'd do it, she'd do anything if it meant finding Pru.

An hour later, Eleanora found herself sporting a fake bruise made of a gaudy mix of rouge and soot on her jaw as she made her way to the barracks entrance. Cain had told her to pretend to be scared but pretending wasn't required. Her heart hammered against her ribcage as she watched the soldiers on guard. She clutched her shawl tighter, took a deep breath, and ran towards them.

"Sir! Sir, please ye have to help me. Please help me, oh gods." She sucked in a ragged breath and resisted the urge to grin as a tear dripped down her cheek.

"Are you all right, ma'am?"

"There's... the... I—"

"Did someone hit you, miss?" The second guard moved away from his post to see what all the fuss was about. Eleanora caught sight of Mr. Rundstrom in her periphery, climbing the wall. She reached out to the closest guard and grabbed his lapel.

"There's a man. A man attacked me just down there." She gestured wildly down the small lane and stepped to the side so that their backs were to Mr. Rundstrom as he slipped over the wall and into the barracks, unseen. The taller of the guards lifted her chin with a finger to assess her bruise. Eleanora froze. She could feel the blood pulsing through her veins as he looked at her with scrutiny.

"Could be worse. That should heal soon enough." He released her chin and stepped to move back to his post. She needed to buy time.

She placed a hand to her head and groaned. "Oh, Artos be, I feel as though I may faint." She swayed dramatically towards the soldiers and the taller caught her by the arm.

"Oh fuck. Brentwood, take her arm, let's get her inside to sit down." They opened the big wooden fortress-esque gates to the soldier barracks and led her towards what looked like the mess hall. She cast a quick look around.

The cobblestone courtyard stretched out before them. To her right stood stables full of cavalry horses that stable hands were tending to. Beyond that, Elea could see off-duty soldiers playing cards, doing chores, and smoking outside their sleeping quarters. She counted ten, not including the stable boys. And to the left, a big gated pathway that led towards the prison. Another two soldiers kept post over there. No doubt there were plenty more soldiers within the jail itself.

Cain had said to stall for fifteen minutes, by her guess it had been about eight. The two guards sat her down outside the mess hall and Brentwood fetched her a drink. "Yer too kind Mr...?" she looked up at the taller soldier.

"Matthews. It's Cadet Matthews."

"Well thank you, Cadet. I'm beginning to feel better

already." She smiled sweetly and put a gentle hand on his arm. "I've not met many soldiers, ye must be so brave, such a dangerous job."

He shifted, uncomfortable under her flirtatious gaze. "Thank you, ma'am. It's an honour to serve my governor and my king."

She caught sight of Mr. Rundstrom's ashy blond hair just as Cadet Brentwood reappeared from the hall. Eleanora spun to face him. "Have you gentlemen fought any real dangerous folk? I can't imagine how scary it must be!"

Brentwood gave an arrogant smirk. "Not scary at all, miss, we've hunted down our fair share o' dangerous men. You've just gotta put the fear of the noose in 'em. Lowlife scum the lot of them, but deep down they're all cowards."

Eleanora feigned awed intrigue as the men allowed their egos to bloat whilst they talked about themselves. Mr. Rundstrom took his chance to slip away unnoticed. He was almost through the towering gates when Cadet Matthews turned his head.

"Stop! By order of our majesty's governing body of the colonies, I demand that you stop! You're trespassing on the governor's property." He ran in the direction of the crew mate, pulling his pistol from its holster. Eleanora leapt up and dashed across the courtyard along with the other cadet. They were screwed.

Mr. Rundstrom took one look at her and slouched. He stuck a finger up at her. "Tha's the dumb whore who kicked me," he yelled with a fake slurry voice. His expression took on that of a drunkard and he swayed on his feet.

"I did no such thing! You attacked me, ye slovenly bastard!" She turned to the soldiers. "Sirs, that's the man that hit me, please ye've gotta do something!"

Mr. Rundstrom yelled once again, gesturing wildly about the barracks as he tried to look more and more drunk. Cadet Matthews spun on his heels, looking between them, his pistol still aimed at Mr. Rundstrom. "I don't know what the fuck is going on but you best get out of here before I arrest you both!" He gestured to the gates with his pistol, his face covered in a dark glower.

They both hurried through the gates as quickly as they could without breaking into a run. Once they were clear of the barracks and soldiers, Elea grabbed Mr. Rundstrom's sleeve. "How did ye know that would work?"

He shrugged. "I didn't... but we had to try somethin'." She released her grip on his sleeve as he continued down the street in the direction of the opium den. Eleanora remained where she was, momentarily frozen with a bubbling mixture of exhilaration and worry.

PRUDENCE WHIMPERED AS CADET DAVY CRUSHED HIS BOOT into her hand, twisting and grinding his heel down until she heard the crunch of bone. He removed his boot and she lifted her hand. The skin was grazed and bloody and two of her fingers were bent at odd angles that made her stomach turn.

The cadet crouched down beside her. "We don't have to do this, you know? If you just tell me where your precious captain is then we can find something nicer to do, hmm?"

She pressed her lips tightly together. The thought of what he might do to her next made tears spring from her eyes, but she wouldn't tell him anything. She'd sooner die. Prudence cradled her broken hand gently. Davy had been with her for over an hour. She'd heard the guards change over at the end of their shift not so long ago, but Davy had remained.

"Not going to talk? That's fine, we have more games to play anyway." He ran a finger down her cheek and lifted her chin. "It's rude to not look people in the eye, *princess*. Lesser men would slap that behaviour right out of you." He gripped her chin tightly, digging his fingers into her jaw. "I'm going to get you to talk... one way or another."

She glanced at him then. An obstinate resolve had taken over and she spat in his face. The glob of saliva and blood landed on his cheek, just below his right eye. He stared at her for a moment before wiping it from his face with his sleeve.

Pain exploded in her cheek as the full force of Davy's backhand knocked her to the floor. He rose, towering above her cold, weak form as she curled up on the stone floor of the dungeon and slammed his steel-tipped boot into her stomach. She coughed. The blinding pain made her vision blurry for a moment and she retched, but nothing came out.

The cadet landed another swift kick to her abdomen before straightening his uniform and running a hand through his hair. "Well, I think I fancy a drink. What do you think? Rum? Or perhaps some whiskey?" He looked at her on the floor and gave a leery smile as she held her aching stomach. "You've never looked more beautiful. I'll be back for *you* later."

He left her lying on the blood and urine-stained floor, sobbing, with her arms wrapped around her bruised torso, and bolted the thick cell door behind him. Prudence tried to sit up but her head swam again and she lay back down. She just needed to rest. Just for a moment. She would get up in a minute. Despite the rank smell, the cool stone was soothing to her swollen face and she couldn't help but shut her eyes.

The sound of muffled voices calling her name made her look around. She couldn't quite make out the voices so far away in the dark. In fact, she couldn't see anything besides the oil lamp glowing on the far wall. It lit up the doorway in a warm orange glow that felt comforting to Prudence. The door... the door to the cell stood open, she realised with a start. The faint light of the lamp lit up a stretch of pathway out of the door, out of her cell.

She pulled herself up. Teeth gritted together, prepared for the onslaught of pain that never came. Tentatively, she stepped forward. Surely someone was coming, someone would walk through the door and close it and quash her chance at freedom. Someone would come. She listened intently, but she heard nothing, save for the distant voices calling her name. They called as if her name were a melodious tune. Beckoning her to them.

She took another step, and another, inching her way towards the open door. She paused and looked down the hallway. There was no one. No guards. No friends to save her. The oil lamp stretched out its light like a beacon leading her on her way to freedom.

She put one foot over the threshold of her cell and heard the voices once more. She took another step and finally stepped out of the cell. The hallway was never ending and yet before she knew it, she was running. Her feet pounded the stone beneath her, despite the cries of her poor sore soles. Her breathing came hard and fast as she ran. Though the end of the path was still so far from her grasp.

Her heart was definitely going to explode inside her chest; it was beating so fast, but she pushed on. She needed to get out. She had to. The voices kept calling, louder now but still muffled.

Prudence heard a loud pop in the darkness and something hit her chest. She paused. A burning sensation radiated out from her chest and she looked down. A small circle of red on her tunic began to spread, blossoming like a vibrant rose against the pale cloth.

The voices were yelling now and it sounded like someone screamed. She fell to the floor, her head bouncing against the stone slabs, her eyes frantically searching for the source of the voices, but it was too dark.

The light from the oil lamp in her cell began to diminish. Its reach crept slowly back down the length of the hallway, away from her, back towards the damp, cold prison cell as she lay there. Blood soaked across her chest, her hair splayed out around her head, and she lay there listening to the voices yelling.

One voice began to sound clearer, louder than the rest. A man's voice. "Pru. Prudence, just hold on." Her vision began to fail as the light disappeared altogether. She finally recognised the voice as everything went black.

DARKNESS FELL SWIFTLY THAT NIGHT, BRINGING WITH IT A chill that was sure to cause a frost come dawn. As the taverns and shops closed their doors, the little rescue group congregated down an alley just a few feet from the prison entrance.

"Now... thanks to our Mr. Rundstrom, we know that there are two guards on the main gates, two at the pathway to the prison, and two at the supply entrance. We won't know how many are inside until we're there but by my count there are about fifty soldiers currently off duty. So, we must assume that there are going to be a fair few inside." Cain's voice was husky and quiet as his crew crowded around him to listen to the plan.

"Elea." She turned to look at him. Her hair was covered by the shawl that she so frequently kept with her, and she wore a thick coat to fight off the cold. "You're going to need to remove those," he said. "I need you back by the supply entrance. Once we've got Prudence, we'll need to get out quick. I need you to distract the guards so Garrick and Charlie can take them out. Gabe, you go with them, take care of her."

They all nodded and Eleanora bundled her coat and shawl into a pile which she tucked into a dark corner. She undid the top buttons of her dress and shook out her long wavy hair. "No problem," she looked at Gabe, "let's go."

"Shuu, Khari, you're with me inside. We take out

anyone we come across; we can't have them raising the alarm. I don't care if you knock them out or kill them—but no guns. This needs to be done quietly." The men nodded at him and holstered their pistols, their hands going to their blades. "Mr. Rundstrom, I want you keeping an eye out front, you know what to do if anything goes wrong."

The group parted ways, quickly losing sight of each other in the darkness. This was their one chance and Cain didn't intend on failing. He, along with Shuu and Khari, were as silent and invisible as ghosts as they scaled the far wall of the barracks, keeping an eye on the courtyard.

They dropped down to the other side one by one, keeping to the shadows as much as they could. The guards at the main entrance kept their focus on the town square before them, unaware that the pirates were so close to them. The men slipped across the edge of the courtyard with ease.

Within seconds, Shuu had dispatched both guards at the prison gate and left them slouched in the corner. Cain grabbed the gate keys from one guard's uniform and unlocked the big wooden door. The first hallway was wide and well-lit but quiet. They could hear guards shuffling further into the prison.

"Right," Cain whispered, "the soldier in Veida had mentioned she was being kept on the lower floor. We need to get in and out as quickly as possible. Shuu, I want you to find that supply entrance, it should be in that direction." Cain pointed to his left.

"Aye, Captain."

"Khari, come with me." They crept down the hallway until they came to the stairs leading down to the lower half of the prison. Cain flinched at the vile smell that rose to meet them. A guard stood post at the bottom of the stairs. Cain clamped a hand over the guard's mouth and drew his blade across the man's throat. He crumpled in a soundless heap.

They looked through cell bars to see men hunched over, starving, beaten, and freezing in their own filth. They barely stirred at the sight of Cain and Khari peering through the tiny windows of their cells, most likely unaware that they weren't soldiers. His heart clenched tightly at the thought of Prudence being in the same state. He couldn't help but imagine what they had done to her down here in the dark. Alone, cold, in pain... probably never thinking anyone would come to help her.

"Captain!" Khari called in a hushed tone and gestured to him. Cain ran to where Khari was stood and peered through the cell window. Prudence.

DEVIL'S KISS

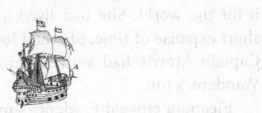

Prudence fell against the wall, her body limp from the wounds, her mind wading through an expanse of black that threatened to swallow her whole. She woke a few minutes later.

Prudence knew that she wouldn't have much longer—it was clear they were getting nothing from her, and the governor would be eager to send her for the noose soon. His reputation for hanging pirates was fearsome and merciless. The fact that she hadn't swung on the first dawn was simply because of Cain. Prudence wouldn't say a word. She'd never sell a friend out, especially Cain, she was loyal. But she was sure to meet the hangman's noose by the next sunrise.

Perhaps it was meant to be this way, to live a short life of adventure and excitement, and go out in a blaze of glory. It seemed slightly kinder than to live for so long that you grew old alone. She didn't want a life of nothingness where you had to watch your friends age and die. Prudence had wanted danger and the spark that makes you feel alive. She had gotten that. And she was grateful.

Tomorrow she would show them that they may kill her, but Prudence would not die a sad death. She would be a hero. They may take her life but she wouldn't change it for the world. She had lived a thousand lives in this short expanse of time. She had loved every minute since Captain Morris had walked through the door of The Wanderer's Inn.

Eleanora crossed Prudence's mind, and she could not help but sob a little, the poor girl had been through so much and now Prudence wouldn't even be there to look after her. Would she stay with Cain and his crew? Or would she leave them and struggle to find somewhere safe to live?

The cell that Prudence was being kept in was cold and grimy. Prudence wondered if this was where she was to spend the last few hours of her life; sat among the rats and urine stains. Prudence's stomach rumbled. She didn't know if it was time for dinner yet, or even what part of the day it was. She had lost all sense of time after being stuck in the dark for days. She hadn't seen any other prisoners, but there had to be others being kept in this dungeon. She couldn't be the only one... but perhaps she was the only one being kept alive to torture.

Maybe the hangman's noose would be better. At least it would be a swift death. Prudence's bruises ached and the cuts stung on her skin. They had beaten her to a pulp. She lay against the wall, trapped in chains, as she drifted in and out of nightmare-ridden consciousness.

The dungeon door slammed open and Cain hurled into the room with Khari hot on his heels. She winced at the noise, no doubt the guards would have heard that. Cain's eyes searched frantically round the room until his gaze fell on Prudence, hunched over in the corner of the room. Her hands and feet were fixed to the wall with chains, her body black and blue from beatings, and her face was a bloody mess. With what felt like a huge effort, Prudence leant against the wall to hold herself upright. Her vision blurred as Cain rushed towards her.

Before she could even speak, Cain crushed his lips to hers, stealing what little breath she had left. Her surprise gave way to relief and comfort despite the haze clouding her mind. The tension between them finally exploded with his lips against hers. She crushed her lips against Cain's, her fingers gripping his lapels tightly, drowning in the taste of him. Cain pulled away first and pushed her bloody and matted hair out of her face, making her wince as his fingers brushed the bruises around her eyes.

"I'm sorry, I'm so sorry," he murmured again and again, his eyes darting all over her injuries. Prudence looked away from him, his hands still touching her face. She couldn't look him in the eye.

"Captain, we've got to go!" Khari was by his side in a moment helping him break the locks that kept Prudence clasped to the wall. "Good to see ye, *keine*, even if ye are a little worse for wear."

Prudence smiled at him weakly as Cain slipped an arm over her shoulders and behind her knees, lifting her up as if she weighed as little as a feather. She probably did, she was so weak from lack of food. Khari grabbed the captain's sword from its scabbard with his empty hand and led the way out of the dingy cell. "They'll find the dead soldiers soon, we've gotta hurry."

Her head lolled against Cain's shoulder as the two men dashed for the gates leading out onto the street. It was hard. The pain in her sides doubled as Cain held her and ran, overwhelming her with a wash of nausea and pain.

Eleanora stood guard at the end of the alley with Gabe, Charlie, and Garrick. She gave Prudence a tight hug when she appeared, cradled in Cain's arms. Prudence pulled back, moaning in pain; her ribs burned like they were on fire.

Eleanora frowned. "Sorry, Pru," she grabbed her friend's hand and gave it what she hoped was a comforting squeeze.

"It's good to see ya, blue eyes." Garrick gave her a wink and covered her with a coat. She was grateful for the warmth as the night air seeped through her tunic and bit at her wounded skin.

The group snuck through the alleyways and stuck to the shadows, trying their best to avoid any soldiers on the way back to their ship. Mr. Abbott and Mr. Rundstrom scouted ahead and Shuu brought up the rear with his tri-star blades. Soldiers swarmed the main streets and houses, searching for the prisoner and her aides as bells rang out to announce their escape. Seeing no way out without capture, the crew headed away from the centre of town and away from the soldiers.

"Charlie! Take Mr. Abbott, Garrick, and Mr. Rundstrom in that direction. Distract the guards, set fires, start looting, whatever. Just get them following you," Cain barked, "buy us a couple hours. We'll rendezvous at *The Maiden* as soon as we're able."

Charlie nodded and gripped his pistol. "Aye, Captain. May Anu watch over ye all."

"And you, lad."

Prudence uttered a quiet thank you to the men as they passed her and disappeared into the dark. Within moments she could hear whoops and hollers as they fired off shots. A thin stream of smoke began to rise up above the lantern-lit street. If they died for her sake, she'd never forgive herself.

Soldiers kicked in doors and ransacked rooms within every street. People were pulled from their beds and their belongings thrown on the floor.

"Find them!" hollered a guard, shoving a woman towards a stone wall. Her head bounced off the brick with an audible crack. "Any person found guilty of harbouring these criminals will be sentenced to the gallows!" He searched the woman's house before letting her return to bed, furious at the guards and their insolence.

The governor would be extremely displeased to see his only lead to Cain Morris escape into the night with the criminal himself. There was no telling what repercussions there might be for the soldiers if the two could not be found. The governor was not a forgiving man. Prudence shuddered at such intimate knowledge of him, the memory of his nails digging into her skin as he smiled tauntingly was fresh in her mind.

Countless families were thrown out of the houses and left to shiver in the street while the soldiers trashed their homes. It would no doubt breed more contempt for the governor amongst the town, but that thought had not crossed the soldiers' minds as they searched high and low for the criminals. They would be brought to justice and hung at dawn if the soldiers had their way.

With the sound of soldiers at their backs, the wanted criminals and their little group carried on through the dark streets as quickly as they could manage, stopping to hide occasionally as they went.

The town seemed even more sinister in the dark. Just like when Prudence first arrived in irons, she once again felt that cold shiver of impending doom rush through her like a draft. Prudence couldn't see a way that would allow them to escape this unharmed—if at all.

The ground soon ran out of tiled roads and became hard, barren dirt again. With that landscape came less houses and more wildlife. It was clear that this is where Valentya kept most of their sizeable livestock. Huge farm buildings could be seen across the countryside with orange lights glowing from their windows and animals grazing outside.

It occurred to Prudence right then that this would be a nice place to live. There was plenty of open space for animals and crops, and that would mean hardly ever making the long trip into town. Whoever lived here could live in their own little bubble. They would never have to interact with the outside world at all if they did not want to.

The homes at the edge of Valentya were scattered across the moorland. There were hardly any people to notice the little group dashing away from the light at the centre of town. As the shouts of soldiers faded and the group hurried on, the city began to thin out and returned once again to an unruly heath.

AFTER AN HOUR OR TWO, THE GROUP MANAGED TO FIND AN abandoned farmhouse on the edge of Valentya. Its broken windows and collapsed roof made it clear that no one had lived there for a long while. There were definitely worse places to hole up in.

Cain and Gabe helped Prudence, limping and sore, into a dusty bedroom that had clearly not been used for many months. Sheets covered the furnishings and everything was grimy and dusty. They bent down to sit her on the bed and Gabe straightened first. "I'll fetch Elea. She's trying to find some food. And ye need to put something in that stomach of yers, you're so scrawny."

Prudence smiled at him. "Thank ye Gabe, truly." She squeezed his hand appreciatively. "Not just for this."

He flushed and nodded, backing out of the room in search of the redhead that he was so fond of.

"I've got something for you." Cain's fingers wrapped around the cold iron in his pocket. "You dropped this in the street when they uh... when we lost you."

Prudence cradled the knife in her uninjured hand and half smiled at him, careful not to stretch her bruised face. "Thank ye, Cain."

He nodded. "I'm going to get some stuff to sort your ribs." He promptly left the room in search of water. Prudence looked awful: her face was bruised and swollen;

her hair was matted with dry blood and dirt; and her body was beaten, covered in gaping wounds that filled Cain with an intense rage. He kicked at a chair on his way out of the cottage. He wished it'd been him. It pained him more than anything.

The well at the bottom of the yard still worked, albeit not brilliantly as it was slowly falling apart. Cain lowered a bucket down and brought up a pail of ice-cold water. He made his way back to the house, filled a basin up and tore an old sheet into strips. That would have to do for her ribs for now; they couldn't risk going in search of proper supplies.

He climbed the stairs and opened the bedroom door. A *crack* resonated as Prudence's hand collided with his cheek. Her gaze, a steely glare that looked right through him. Cain glowered back at her, eyes ablaze.

"What was that?" he grabbed her still stinging hand as she winced.

"That was for spending the night with those whores, then kissing me!"

She was jealous? Cain scoffed. Of course she was.

"Sit down, lass," he mumbled, letting go of her hand and soaking a rag in the basin. Cain dabbed at the dry blood on her face and arms, all the while not meeting her eye. The silence was deafening. Prudence winced and groaned at his touch, every inch of her adorned with cuts and bruises. He could feel her eyes on him as he attempted to fix her. He felt another wave of guilt wash over him. He stared fixedly at Prudence's ribs, focusing on the task at hand.

Prudence touched his cheek gently, lifting his chin to

look at her. All the anger had drained from her face. She looked at him with soft eyes. "You are not to blame for this," she smiled gently, wincing as the cuts on her face stretched. The connection between them burned in that moment and was interrupted far too quickly by the entrance of Eleanora. She coughed uncomfortably at the sight of Prudence sitting on the bed, with Cain kneeling at her feet.

"I've... uh, managed to find some salted meats in the pantry, would you like somethin' to eat, Pru? Are ye hungry?"

Prudence shook her head slightly. "No. Thank ye," she spoke quietly, almost like it pained her to breathe. Eleanora watched Prudence's every move like a hawk, examining every wince and grimace. Cain understood how she felt. Excusing herself and scurrying back towards the door, Eleanora left.

Prudence held up her borrowed shirt as Cain wrapped the sheet bandages around her middle. The yellow and purple bruising was a mottled canvas of pain. Images of Prudence bound and beaten plagued him, filling him with a bitter mix of fury and shame. He sighed and stood, placing the basin and cloth gently on the bedside table.

"I should... go," glancing once more at Prudence, her eyes swollen and her face and body scarred, he opened the door. "Get some rest. I don't know how long we'll be here."

Prudence rolled her eyes and lay down. Cain flinched at the twinge of anger that flashed through him. This was her fault. Had she not run out of that tavern, they would not be here, she would not be injured and everything would be as it was before. A groan escaped Pru's lips as she leant on her broken ribs.

He puffed a pillow for her, causing a cloud of dust to float up as he observed the room. The room was covered in sheets that had turned brown over time, and the dust and dirt that came in from the windows had turned the house into a disgusting place. With no one there to tend to it, the house was falling apart. Even the paintwork crumbled from the walls.

Brushing some of the paint flecks off her head, Prudence glanced out of the window to her left, it was small and covered in cobwebs. Cain followed her gaze and could just about make out a workshop to the right of the building. The door hung open, probably damaged from a storm. Inside, he could see many tools cluttering the bench and bits and bobs scattering the floor.

Perhaps the man who used to live here had been a carpenter?Past the workshop and out towards the fields there was a stable block and a barn in major disrepair.

Sleep did not come easy for Prudence that night. The sun set over the hills and darkness fell over the rugged landscape. The only light coming from the house now, was the warm glow of candles in their holders. Rising from the broken bed, Prudence crept out of the room as quietly as she could manage.

Eleanora slept soundly in the rocking chair in the corner, her mouth parted ever so slightly. Prudence placed a blanket over her and sighed. She had told Elea to sleep in the next room but she wouldn't hear of it. She wanted to be right there where she could keep an eye on her injured friend. It left Prudence with a mix of warmth and guilt considering what she had put Eleanora through.

She could hear Khari snoring down the hall, huge grumbling eruptions that somehow didn't wake Shuu or Gabe from their slumber nearby. Staggering down the stairs with little light to guide her, Prudence found her way to the living room. The nearest table held many enticing drinks that could numb her pain and restlessness. She poured herself a drink, then another, and when that did not sate her, she grabbed the bottle.

"Not able to sleep?" A voice from behind made Prudence jump.

Cain sat in one of the big chairs, drink in hand, watching her carefully. She hadn't realised that he was in there. Prudence mumbled a sheepish '*no*' and plonked down in the chair opposite him. He chuckled.

"You sound like Florence after she'd been sneaking drinks," he laughed, instantly looking down at his drink and frowning.

"Who's that?" she hiccupped and leaned forward, curious. Cain shut his eyes and sighed before looking at her.

"She *was* my little sister. She's gone now." The atmosphere grew cold as Prudence stared at him, embarrassed. He looked tired, exhausted even. A complicated man with a more painful life than she could have imagined.

"I'm sorry." Prudence didn't know what to say. What was there to say to someone who had lost someone so dear to them? Prudence took his hand and squeezed sympathetically.

"Tell me... what she was like?" It was a bizarre feeling to see a man, so strong, battle-worn, and commanding as he was, look so solemn, so vulnerable.

"Much like your friend upstairs, except she actually liked me." He chuckled half-heartedly. Prudence giggled and nodded. It was clear to everyone—Eleanora despised Cain. Maybe it was his life choices... maybe it was because of Prudence, who knew? Realising her hand was still locked with Cain's, Prudence moved to pull her hand away, only to have Cain grip it tighter. Prudence glanced at their interlocked hands and a warmth flushed her cheeks. She sighed heavily.

"Eleanora thinks we're no good for each other."

Cain looked down at her and smirked. "She thinks I'm a bad influence on you," he winked, "but it seems plain to me that you're the bad influence. You've wrapped your hand tight around my heart, lass, and I am at your mercy."

With one hand on her neck, Cain pulled her closer, their lips colliding once again. They were a fumbling tangle of limbs as they sank to the floor, lips locked, fingers untying laces, and breath short and panting. Prudence winced at the weight of Cain on top of her and he froze.

"Are you all right lass? Did I hurt you?" He pulled away to assess her, eyes full of concern.

She kissed him. "I'm just a little sore, Cain, it's fine."

They stared at one another for a time. "Don't stop." Prudence shuddered as Cain's lips found her collarbone, his rough beard tickling her skin. He smelt of liquor and tobacco and she breathed it in. It was intoxicating. She slipped her arms out of her shirt and tossed it to the side. They had never been this close before but it felt good. Right. As if the outside world might stop just so long as they were entwined.

The heady mix of whiskey pulsing through her veins and the feel of Cain's hands on her left Prudence feeling lightheaded. She felt like she could drown in him if she just drank deep enough. She never wanted to leave this embrace; his arms wrapped tightly around her waist as her hands gripped his broad shoulders. A groan escaped her lips and they froze, listening for sounds of people waking above their heads. They heard one of the men shift slightly but then silence.

Cain caught Prudence's eye and she giggled. He watched her quietly with a lopsided grin on his face.

"What are ye looking at me like that for?" she smiled.

"I love you, deep in my soul. I am yours. In whatever way you will allow me to be," his voice was thick with whiskey and emotion.

Prudence bit her lip to suppress the grin breaking out across her face and put on a mask of sheer innocence. "I'm sorry, *Captain*, I didn't quite hear that. Say it again?"

Cain chuckled and kissed her roughly. "I love you." He peppered kisses down her jawline and neck. "And I am yours, entirely." They sank into one another once more. Void of all thought except for each other's smell, touch, and taste, they made love into the long hours of early morning. The pair barely parted long enough for murmurs of 'I love you' as they lost track of time on the moth-eaten rug of the abandoned farmhouse.

PRUDENCE WOKE, BLINKING AT THE EARLY MORNING LIGHT trying to break through the trees around the farmhouse. The house remained silent as she rose and took in her surroundings. Still in the living room, drinks left untouched on the tables and a sleeping Cain, passed out naked beside her on the floor. Eyebrows knitting together in concentration, Prudence found it hard to remember the events of the night before, save for hazy flashes of intimacy.

Her cheeks flushed with every memory. There had been drinking, she remembered that extremely well. Florence, Cain had mentioned someone called Florence. She couldn't quite recall who she was though. Her body, still heavily bruised and beaten, felt like fire as she moved. A pain exploded in her ribs and back, and red seeped through the cloth against her side—the blood must've been soaking through the material for some time. Lifting the material away from her skin, Prudence could see that the gash in her side had torn and was now an even bigger hole in her flesh.

"Damn." Prudence threw on her britches and a shirt that she quickly realised belonged to Cain, and grabbed some fresh strips of cloth, before tiptoeing out of the room and out into the fresh morning air. The well was a few yards from the house, she would have to do her best with some water and cloth to fix this infernal bleeding. Prudence shivered. It was a shame they had taken away her warm clothes in the prison, she would have to get some more when they returned to *The Bloody Maiden*.

A thick fog lay over the landscape, enclosing the farm in a little world of its own, as Prudence made her way to the well. Hopefully they were far enough away that soldiers wouldn't find them. They had been careful leaving Valentya. Prudence didn't think anyone had seen them.

The well was quite old and had lost a few bricks over the years but luckily there was water for them to use. Prudence pulled the bucket up and washed her arms, shoulders, and face. The water was freezing but refreshing. It had been so long since she had washed properly. She winced as she pressed the cloth against her side but she needed to clean away some of the blood before she could bandage it. The iciness of the water helped soothe the angry wound, slightly.

She wound a long piece of fabric around her middle and tucked the end in. It wasn't the best dressing. Perhaps Eleanora could do a better job later. She drank deeply from a fresh bucket before filling it again to bring inside. The house was silent.

Prudence put the bucket down on the kitchen table and had a look through the cupboards. They were pretty bare. The crate of dried meat that Eleanora had found the night before sat on the worktop, but it looked fairly unappetising. The house looked like it had been empty for weeks. There was nothing perishable and there didn't seem to be much else in the pantry besides rats so

Prudence headed outside to see if anything had been growing.

Out back there were even more acres of land. There was a barn to the left of the house that looked like it had seen better days—the roof had some big holes in it and the door had fallen from its hinges. Prudence noticed a cat by the edge of the barn and watched as it slinked through one of the holes in the wall. Not wanting to scare it, she followed slowly and made sure to tread lightly. Prudence pulled the barn door open and cringed as it made a loud creak.

It wobbled and threatened to fall over but Prudence held it up. Inside the barn was dusty and dark, though a few spots of light filtered through the cracks. Prudence watched as the dust specks danced in the golden light. The animal must have slipped away to some hidden corner because Prudence couldn't find it. In amongst the dust, she spotted old farm tools that were clogging up the space at the back, while the left-hand side was piled high with bales of hay for horses; a supply for when winter stopped the grass from growing.

Behind the barn it was possible to see the shires grazing. Their manger was empty and there was stagnant water in the enormous trough, but at least the grass was still coming through in the paddock. The horses looked emaciated and tired; their ribs were stuck out, making them look old and bony. Prudence murmured to them softly:

"What are ye doing here, hmm? Did people leave ya here?" The horses hardly reacted when she reached out and touched them. After some searching, she managed to find some oats in a sack in a corner of one of the stables. It looked like the people who had lived here had filled their buckets of feed and water and then left them. The poor animals had been left alone for far too long.

"Is that better? Ye'll feel better now, I'll make sure yer all right." She grabbed a rope and tied the horses to a post and left to get them some fresh water from the well. It was amazing that they had survived this long. It can't have been that long ago that they ran out of water. She returned with two buckets of water in her hands to find Eleanora stroking the horses.

"Hey," Prudence smiled at her friend. She was glad that they were friends again. "Did ye sleep?" she asked.

"I should ask you the same," Elea smiled. Prudence flushed scarlet remembering the night before.

"You shouldn't be carryin' those in your condition, let me help ye." Elea took a bucket from Pru with a huff. "Fancy finding these here, huh? What luck! They could come in handy, you know." Prudence and Eleanora put the buckets down and the horses drank straight away.

"I think with a good bit o' food they'll be good as new."

Eleanora nodded and watched the horses. "Why would someone leave them here? They would have died eventually if we hadn't turned up."

"Perhaps they had been chased out. I don't know..." They watched silently while the horses finished off the oats that Prudence had given them.

"We're not going to be leaving here for a while, are we?" Eleanora glanced at Prudence with a hint of sadness in her eyes. Prudence sighed.

"No. I don't think so. Not for a few days at least. There are too many soldiers looking for us. Anyway... even if we got out of Valentya, they'd have soldiers in the other towns by now." Eleanora nodded vaguely, her mind clearly elsewhere.

"I'd better go find us as much food as possible then. It's winter so all the crops will be dying, if there's any left at all by now." She sauntered off with a determined face, prepared to battle any obstacles. It would be a shame to have escaped hundreds of soldiers only for them to starve soon after.

The horses finished their meal and had started on the grass at their feet, despite it being extremely short and rather brown. They seemed to be perking up somewhat but they still had a long way to go. Perhaps if Prudence could get them looking less thin, then they could take the horses with them when they left? It would be far easier to get back to *The Maiden* on horseback than on foot.

She remained outside for a while, watching contentedly as the horses grazed, her mind in a faraway place. Later, in the cramped living room of the house, Prudence tried to find a comfortable place to sit, but almost everywhere was heaped with junk. Books and boxes were piled up everywhere; whoever had left, had left in a hurry.

The open window let in a gentle breeze and Prudence jumped out of her skin at the sound of something leaping through and into the room. It was a scraggly grey-haired kitten that looked like it had been caught out in the rain one too many times.

It was sweet—in a rough and ratty kind of way. The

kitten walked right in and sat down on a worn old chair, like it had sat in that spot a hundred times before. It must have belonged to the owners of the house.

"Hey kitty, you get left here too, huh?" The cat stared at Prudence for a second before turning promptly away from her, uninterested, and licked his paws.

Prudence plonked down on the moth-eaten chair in the corner and picked up the book laid on the desk beside her. It was thicker than the ones she had practised with on the ship. It felt like an age had passed since then. She remembered it of course: running her fingers along the inked pages; Cain helping her decipher the letters; the frustration of it all.

She sank deeper into the old chair, her feet tucked under herself, and tried to recall her reading lessons as best as she could. Prudence felt the sensation of eyes watching her and she looked down to see the kitten at her feet and began to read to him in a low murmuring voice. The ragged kitten leapt up and rubbed its flea-ridden head against her legs.

"That's a good book, is it?" A laugh sounded from the doorway and Prudence turned to see Cain watching her too.

"Looks like I was right, you did go insane in that cell. Talking to cats." He grinned and perched on the arm of the chair nearest the door. Prudence rolled her eyes.

"Hush you. At least he's a good listener." She stuck her tongue out and couldn't help but laugh. This was the most relaxed she had felt in a long time. For now, Prudence wasn't having to worry about Elea, or Cain, or herself. There wasn't any danger here. Cain chuckled and glanced around the room.

"I guess whoever lived here was rather messy, eh?"

Prudence frowned. "I'm not so sure. All these boxes made it look like they were trying to leave but didn't get chance to take all of their things. Do ye... do ye think they managed to get away? I mean what if they tried to leave but soldiers cut them down before they got the chance? By the looks of this place they had no money, which means they wouldn't have been able to pay the governor. They must've been driven out on the streets or executed..."

Cain sighed, considering her words. He nodded. "That would make sense. What with the animals left to die and all, the governor would have no use for cart horses. And the people who lived here would've used them to leave if they could."

Prudence pursed her lips. It wasn't fair. She couldn't help but imagine these people rushing to pack their things and leave before the soldiers came knocking at the door, asking for more money that they didn't have. They would have grabbed what they needed and quickly fed the animals. They would've been almost ready to go, they just needed *more time* when they heard the dreaded knock and knew that there was nothing they could do except make a run for it. All that for nothing... all that only to get hunted down and dealt with on behalf of Governor Atkey. The governor couldn't possibly have people living on his island who didn't obey his rules.

None of this was fair.

They had to get off this wretched island before they

were dealt with in the same way. At least they should be safe on this farm for a few days. The soldiers wouldn't come looking in a place like this. Not when they knew where *The Maiden* was. They'd be staking out the port, waiting for them to arrive.

They needed to form a plan, get some supplies, feed the horses and take them with them. They weren't the fastest horses in the world but they couldn't travel all that way on foot.

Cain seemed to be thinking the same thing as Prudence because he muttered: "We'll be out of here in a few days. As soon as we can. Just gotta get you healed a bit first." Prudence cast a look down at her battered body. She had almost forgotten it had happened at all. Those few days felt like a distant nightmare now, a hazy, blurry dream where all she could remember was the barrage of agony from Davy, the hunger she felt in her stomach as it clawed at her; and the awful stench of urine from where she had been forced to stand in a puddle of her own piss and shit.

THE DAY PASSED FAIRLY SWIFTLY AND THE COLD EVENING descended on them like a thief in the night. Sudden and intense. Eleanora busied about with a cloth, cleaning all of the surfaces in the kitchen and putting away the crockery in an attempt to keep herself from fretting about Prudence. She cleaned and cleaned until the worktops were as clean as they would ever get. She heard a chuckle as Prudence entered the tiny kitchen.

"I can't believe in a time like this yer busy cleaning, in a house that's been abandoned for who knows how long."

"Well we can't live in this pigsty, can we? If we've gotta be stuck here for days then I want to be actually able to touch the worktops." She swiped at a fly buzzing around the window before turning to Prudence.

"I suppose ye have a point, *mother*." Prudence winked at Eleanora. "Used to be me looking after you, how times have changed."

"Well, I'm not a child anymore." Eleanora rolled her eyes. She felt a flash of that age-old annoyance and bit her lip. Once again, she was torn between her love for her oldest friend and feeling completely overwhelmed by her. Prudence's delusion that Eleanora needed all of her care and attention used to endear her, but lately it infuriated her. She was sick of Prudence's smothering attention and wondered for a short, horrifying moment what her life would be like if she'd never saved Pru from drowning that day on the beach.

After walking down many winding and narrow hallways, Eleanora found her way to the back door and opened it out into the sharp air. There was no doubt that winter would be on them soon, a harrowing season of freezing air and pouring rain, followed by torrential storms that ruined roofing and damaged houses.

Around the back of the house, there were wooden boxes filled with soil that the owners had used for growing crops. It was a small farm that produced mainly for itself but there were a few garden beds with enough extra to sell some produce at market, but only a small amount. Elea was so caught up in thinking about the task at hand, that she jumped out of her skin when a hand touched her back.

"Do ye need any help?" Gabe smiled questioningly at her, his brown eyes almost hidden by the brown curls. He held out a wicker basket for her to take. "I thought you'd be needin' that if yer gonna find anything for dinner. Not that there seems to be much."

Eleanora took it gratefully. "Thank ye, Gabe. Think it might be a bit of a meagre meal, don't you?" She pursed her lips at the sight of the beds looking so bare.

They went to work in comfortable silence together, searching for whatever Eleanora might be able to use. It was slow work with few rewards but Eleanora found that Gabe was quite skilled at foraging and managed to scrounge up a decent amount of bullaces, rosehips, and sloes. They were digging around in the furthest bed with dirt up to their elbows when Prudence joined them.

"Find anything?" Prudence knelt down to help but Elea refused to let her.

"Yeah, not too bad. Found a couple of potatoes that must've been missed at harvest and there are plenty of leeks and turnips growing in that bed over there. Luckily, whoever lived here planted winter vegetables while they were still here." It seemed like they wouldn't starve after all then. And they had plenty of water in the well out front. As long as no one found them here, they could hide out for as long as they liked.

"That's really good then. I don't think anyone will come looking this way, Malaine is north of Valentya and we're on the west side of the town here."

"They should'n but we'd still best be on high alert. By

now both your face and Cain's will be plastered over all the posters in Valentya. We can't trust anyone, they'll all be looking to get a reward for yer capture." Gabe's sombre words left the atmosphere harsh and cold. It was all too easy to forget why they were there and his train of thought left the women silent and on edge.

Eleanora mumbled and carried on pulling up vegetables to make something for dinner. After some time, she turned to Prudence, eager to bring the conversation back to a lighter subject. "Do you ever think, at some point in our lives, we might have a place like this? Somewhere we can both live the rest of our days, a garden to grow food to eat, a couple of animals, and no need to go out into the rest of the world again? I mean potentially Cain as well if—"

Prudence smiled at her.

"We could have chickens, Pru. Fresh eggs in the morning. Some horses for us to ride into town. We could decorate it any way we wanted." Once the heat had died down and they weren't being hunted anymore, maybe they could find a little cottage in the middle of nowhere and make a home for themselves, something neither Prudence nor Eleanora had had in a long time.

It was a nice dream, something that they could work towards. Deep down she wondered if they would ever be in that place, where they weren't being looked for. So long as Prudence insisted on staying with Cain, Elea didn't think that could happen. Gabe helped Eleanora find as many of the vegetables as they could from what was left, and soon they had enough food for a few days at least.

Eleanora took the basket of food inside as Gabe

helped Khari chop up some wood for the fire and Prudence collected a bucket of water from the well. Once inside, they washed the vegetables, peeled them, and cut them up. Eleanora put them in a large soup pot that she found in one of the dusty cupboards and cooked them over the fire.

They ate better than anyone could have expected. The soup was surprisingly delicious and most welcome to their starving stomachs. None of them had eaten since they had rescued Prudence from prison, apart from a handful of those awful salted meats. Even after two helpings each there was still enough for the next day, and Eleanora managed to find some ingredients to make biscuits, which she vowed to do first thing in the morning. Prudence and Cain swiftly left the room to sleep and Elea fell asleep soon after. The house had settled into a comfortable silence, save for the occasional jeer as Gabe lost yet more money to Khari and Shuu in a betting version of whist.

11

DESPERATE SPRINT

A couple of weeks had passed since they first found the farmhouse. Prudence's wounds had begun to heal nicely. Her stomach gashes were beginning to seal up, and the fire that blazed in her sides when she walked had dulled to a small yet constant ache.

Eleanora had busied about making sure that they all ate as much food as she could find before they made the journey back to the ship. The horses had been getting better over the last few days as they built up their strength and drank plenty of water. With some luck they'd be able to use the horses to travel on through Veida and up to Malaine.

Cain spent most of his time wandering the furthest fields during the day, and drinking and reading well into the night. He had been restless and growing more agitated as the days went on. He wanted to leave as soon as possible. Staying in the one place was driving him crazy; he felt like a rabid dog when cornered. He had told

Prudence of his desires to stop running and live a quiet life, uninterrupted by civilization, but Prudence knew that this wasn't exactly what he'd had in mind.

She found him outside, watching the horses grooming each other in the field. "Did you sleep?"

"I'll sleep when I'm home." Cain hadn't slept properly since the first night at the farmhouse and Prudence was growing concerned about his mental state. His eyes were constantly glazed over, he hardly spoke, and he definitely didn't eat enough.

"Eleanora's just packing up some food and once Shuu, Gabe, and Khari are back with more horses then we'll be gone, all right?"

"All right."

She knew there was something that he wasn't saying but she didn't probe him.

"You're going to ride with Elea, you're not healed enough to ride by yourself for such a long journey." Prudence nodded reluctantly. It was infuriating being impeded like this. Prudence loved to ride and now she was practically incapable. Prudence despised asking for help. It was humiliating.

"I'll be fine," she huffed.

Cain looked sideways at her. "I know. I'm sorry lass, I'm just worried about you. You didn't see your face when we found you. But if you can think of any other way for us to get back to my ship... we have to get away *now*. Or we're all dead."

Prudence scowled at Cain and strode past him into the field where the horses were. They looked a lot better now that they had had a few days with plenty of food to fill their stomachs. You couldn't see their ribs as much as before and they seemed rather content. Prudence just hoped that they were up for the trip across the island. She doubted whether they had ever gone so far or as quickly before. It was going to be a hard journey for them.

Prudence wandered through the house one last time before they planned to leave. She had managed to find some men's clothes that weren't too big on her in one of the bedrooms. They didn't fit perfectly and they had holes in some places, but they were a considerably better fit than the clothes the crew brought with them. At least she wouldn't freeze before they arrived at *The Maiden*. With enough luck, they'd be moving too fast to feel the cold creep up on them as the night got dark.

Prudence caught sight of herself in the mirror. Her black hair made her face look even paler in this light, so pale that you could almost see through her skin and into the blood vessels beneath it. She could have been a ghost. For a moment she caught sight of what Cain must have seen... hollow, vacant, lifeless, but in a blink, it was gone.

Once she had walked around the house for the last time, Prudence found herself in the living room once again with its books and boxes piled high. In the short time that they had been here, Prudence had grown to love this room with all its quirky nooks and crannies. She had found a worn and broken wooden doll in a back corner, covered from head to toe in soot. She had spent a few hours that night cleaning the doll and fixing her eye back on. She left her looking pristine once again on the end of the bed upstairs, ready and waiting for a child to come and find her. She had named her Elea, of course, and sat her proudly on the sheets as protector of the farmhouse.

Prudence could remember having a doll like that as a child. She had loved it dearly and taken it everywhere with her. After her father died, Prudence's mother felt that she was too old for toys and games and had thrown her away. Prudence could still remember crying for an entire week.

PRUDENCE SAT IN THE WINTER SUNSHINE AS THE RAGGED farm kitten played with the loose lace of her boot. She smiled and breathed in the cold air deeply, letting it fill her lungs with life. The sun bathed her face in a warmth that helped to clear the cobwebs from her mind. Everyone had been preparing to leave, so focused on getting away unnoticed, but Prudence couldn't shake the gnawing in her gut that something bad was going to happen.

"Pru!" A sharp whistle rang in Prudence's ears and she turned to see Shuu waving to get her attention. "Tell the little miss we're ready to git! I'll alert the captain." He sat astride a coloured quarter horse with Gabe and Khari bringing up the rear. She nodded and stood.

Eleanora was still in the kitchen when Prudence came in. She had packed them a sack full of food that would hopefully last them a couple of days, until they were out of Valentya. Once they were far enough away, they could find more food. Until then, they needed to lay low and stay hidden. They couldn't afford to buy food with soldiers scouring all over the place.

They would have to be careful. One wrong move would put them all back in the prison that they had rescued Prudence from. Prudence couldn't let that happen now. They had come too far to get caught at the last minute and die by the noose come dawn. She could feel it in her heart that they were meant for better things, for something extraordinary. They would be famed throughout history once they were dead. And death was not ready for them yet.

"Are you ready to go, Elea?" Prudence helped Eleanora take the bag outside and put it with the other few things they were taking with them. There were two canisters full of water; a couple of coats and blankets, rolled up into neat rolls for when the night got too cold; and lastly, a sack of oats for the horses.

"I think so. I keep going over the list in my head and I don't think I'm forgetting anything, s'just a weird feeling, taking so little with us. We hardly own anything. We're vagabonds, Prudence. Once again we're back where we were when we were children."

Prudence chuckled. "I think we're doing considerably better than we were back then. We have a family now." Her eyes wandered over their little group until they latched onto the sight of Cain stroking the bigger of the two horses, the one he'd named Gypsy, after a childhood pet. Eleanora coughed and brought Prudence back to the present.

"Let's get out of here, Pru." Eleanora winked at her best friend and skipped over to where the horses were standing ready. Prudence placed a hand on her bruised side and sighed. It was all nearly over.

The girls helped Cain tie the bags onto the backs of the horse's saddles before he helped Prudence onto the smaller of the horses behind Eleanora—the one that Elea had sarcastically named Captain in an attempt to wind up Cain—which had obviously worked. Pru's body howled in agony but she kept the noise down to a whimper. It was hard to do anything without hurting herself and she didn't want them to be worried. It would only slow them down if they thought that Prudence needed more rest.

The horses whickered to each other and flung their heads in the air as they moved off, keen to get away from the place where they had been abandoned. They were going on an adventure. Shuu rode out ahead of the group, his long knives strapped to his back and whistling happily to himself.

They rode along in silence for the first few hours of the day. Nobody had anything to say and for now it seemed nice to enjoy the peace. There might not be another opportunity for silence if there were soldiers stationed in all of the hamlets on the way. Prudence rested her head on Cain's back, nodding in and out of sleep, only half-aware of her surroundings.

THE ROAD THAT RAN FROM THE EDGE OF VALENTYA AND down into Veida was long and dusty. There was no need for cobbles since the road was barely used. The only people that frequented the road were merchants travelling to different towns to sell their goods—and most of them had carts and horses.

There hadn't been a single person in sight for miles and so the group decided to have a break. They pulled the horses to a stop so they could share out the water. A rest while it remained quiet was the most that they dared hope for. None of them knew when they would get the chance again. Gabe watered the horses as the rest of the group stretched their legs and passed out some of the rationed food.

"Malaine is only about an hour's ride past Veida. So, once we get there, we'll move as quickly as possible. I don't know what to expect so we'll have to stick to back roads and try to go around the town as much as possible. Hopefully we'll get to port without seeing too many soldiers." Cain took a long swig of the water before putting it in the bag behind Prudence. She placed her arms around his middle before they started walking again.

It was actually rather amusing to Prudence to think that they were being hunted down to be killed, all while they sat on the back of horses, strolling down the road without a care in the world. It was a beautiful day. Cold but bright. Prudence imagined that they were going out for the day, perhaps to find a nice place for a picnic, instead of running from the noose.

The day went by fast as they resumed their journey, and before anyone had realised, night had fallen and the sun had been replaced by the moon. The giant ball of white light illuminated the six travellers and their horses with a haunting glow.

They carried on moving for a while before it became clear that they needed to stop. Eleanora's eyes were drifting shut every now and then, and it wouldn't be long before she fell off, completely asleep.

Prudence leant over Elea and grabbed hold of Captain's rein and pulled him up to a stop at a cluster of trees before shaking Eleanora awake.

"Come on. Get off. Time to sleep. You look like you haven't slept a wink in days. You've gotta rest, El."

Eleanora raised an eyebrow at Prudence. "I'm fine," she muttered, but hopped off the horse regardless and led him over to the grass at the edge of the road.

Prudence slid down from Captain with a sharp breath and held Gypsy while Cain got down. He got the bags from her rump and set them down on the ground, getting out some blankets and food for them to use in the night. The other two men hopped down from their mounts and tied up their horses before sinking down onto the long grass, eager to rest. As sailors, the men were not used to riding for long periods of time. Their legs ached fiercely and their backs felt sore.

The horses seemed relieved to be free of riders for a little while. They grazed eagerly and groomed one another, nipping at the hairs on each other's backs. The group of fugitives fell asleep very quickly after that. No one bothered to eat the food that Cain had got out. It would get eaten tomorrow when they got moving again.

Prudence woke after an hour or so and saw the moon high in the sky. She looked at the quiet landscape around them and mused to herself... they could be the only people in the world; it was so quiet. Eleanora and Cain slept soundly, both of them snoring with their mouths slightly open. Gabe and Khari had passed out by the horses, pistols to hand and their heads lolling back at awkward angles. Shuu slept at their feet with his hat balanced on his face. Prudence didn't understand how their minds could be at rest at a time like this. They needed to stay on guard. The second that they let their guard down, someone was going to get hurt.

The night was silent apart from the occasional *hoot* of an owl or the scampering of a rodent. Prudence looked blindly around her, trying to make out the shapes in the darkness. Her head whipped up at the snap of a branch.

Prudence scanned the area, her hand going instinctively to the knife at her belt. There was something or someone out there. How she wished to be an owl in that moment so that her eyes might spot something that her human eyes could not. Red eyes. Her gaze caught a pair of gleaming red eyes in the distance.

Its black body slinked out of the darkness in the direction of their camp. Prudence recognised its shaggy mess of fur and pointed ears instantly. A yell hound. She tightened her grip on the knife and held her breath. It watched her, unblinking.

"What are you here for?" she whispered, too afraid to speak louder. This was the second time she had seen it, that had to mean something. Yell hounds didn't just appear for nothing. Not according to the stories. Was it her? Was it informing her of an impending doom, ending in death? She had escaped so much that she didn't know whether to laugh or cry at the idea of her death first being predicted all those months ago, back on Llynne. So, she had done it all for nothing.

The yell hound watched their camp silently for some time. Eventually as Prudence felt her eyelids getting heavy, it left. She watched it slink back into the night as smoothly as it had appeared. The night was serene once more.

Leaning against the fallen tree next to the horses, she sat and watched her friends sleep. Thoughts drifted into her mind and tried to consume her. The first time that she had seen the yell hound back on Llynne was near her father's grave. There were many times that she had escaped death since then. Sirens, storms, soldiers... and as though her brain wanted to cling onto such dark thoughts, every time Prudence shut her eyes, she was back in the dungeon again.

It was hard staying awake sitting where she was and she definitely wanted to stay awake right now. The whole world had gone dark and the only sound that she could hear was the soft breathing of her friends. Before long, she began to sing to herself, quietly, in an attempt to stay awake.

"A maiden fair without a care, a maiden filled with glee, a sailor's kiss, a life of bliss. If only she'd agree...

> A maiden fair, so unaware
> Of what her life would be
> Plans all foiled, romance spoiled
> She'd no choice but to flee
>
> At sea! At sea!

She longed for life at sea

A maiden fair she says a prayer
For innocence lost at sea
She faced the dawn, her friends all gone
Alone, and lost at sea

Unaware of the time, it soon became morning and the sun rose over the horizon, shining bright in Prudence's face. It tinted the world with a beautiful orange glow that soon woke the rest of their motley crew. Eleanora stretched and smiled at Prudence, looking considerably better than she had the night before. The bags had gone from under her eyes and her cheeks had regained their usual rosy pink colour.

"Good morning." Elea yawned and pulled the blanket from around her waist. It had gotten tangled in the night and left her wrapped up like a present. "How long have you been awake, Pru? I told you, you needed to sleep. You still do." She folded the yarn blanket in her hands before shoving it inside the cloth sack. Prudence leant forward from her perch by the fallen tree and stretched.

"Well, someone needed to keep watch. I'll sleep when I'm dead."

Cain laughed and grinned at Prudence. It was that self-destruction inside them that they had in common. He looked extremely relaxed, spread out on the ground with his arms underneath his head and his feet crossed. It looked like he didn't have a care in the world.

Prudence kicked the foot closest to her. "Come on, lazy. We've gotta get moving. It's still two days until we get to Malaine, we need to get on." She could feel the warmth of his gaze as she bent over, packing up their supplies from the ground. The gentle curve and dip of her lower back held his gaze for just a moment too long; long enough for Eleanora to notice and thwack him round the head with her boot. A snort erupted from the back of his throat as he moved to get up. Prudence bit back a grin.

"On we continue, I suppose. What do you reckon our likelihood is of reaching Malaine before the soldiers catch up to us?"

"You might try and sound somewhat more positive, Cain. I should like to see a couple more sunrises before I die, if you don't mind." Prudence raised an eyebrow at him as she tied their belongings to the horses.

"The both of ye are positively morbid. Jokin' about death as if it were a game, when on our very tails, are men who'll certainly kill us if they find us. Either of you continue like this and I shall 'av mind to leave ye for 'em."

Prudence and Cain met each other's gaze and tried, unsuccessfully, to keep a straight face. Eleanora's distaste for their humour made it all the more amusing. Given their current state, they had to laugh when they could. Neither of them had had much cause to see the enjoyment in life prior to this, and now such fatal consequences hung over their heads.

"Hate to break up this little moment *keine*, but we really should get moving if we're going to get back to the ship in one piece," said Khari as he threw a roll of blankets at her.

Prudence nodded. "I know, I know. Come on, let's go." She tied the roll to Captain's saddle and caught sight of

Gabe helping Eleanora pack up the rest of their things. She smiled. Anyone with eyes could see that the young sailing master was completely smitten with her dear friend.

She often found his deep brown eyes locked on Elea, no matter what she was doing. Prudence didn't even think Gabe was aware of how often he stared at her with a besotted smile on his face. Eleanora laughed at something he had said and shoved playfully at his arm. Prudence's smile dropped as she her argument with Elea came back to her... she didn't deserve the forgiveness she had been given. Elea might have been smiling at that moment, but Prudence had pulled her away from everything she'd loved. Her friends. Her home. Her life. Nell. If she could take it back... Prudence's gaze sought out Cain, who was deep in conversation with Shuu and Khari. If she could take it back, she didn't know what she would do.

She pulled a small vial of laudanum from her pack that they had found at the farmhouse and drank it all. Her wounds held a dull ache and she hoped the liquid would keep the pain at bay for a few hours. She could get more once they were back on *The Bloody Maiden*.

They mounted the horses, Prudence sat behind Eleanora on the smaller of the two, and moved further down the road, closer to Malaine. The day was mild for now, but looming dark clouds from the horizon threatened a turn in the weather. Prudence only hoped that it would stay at bay long enough for them to reach their destination.

THERE WAS NOWHERE TO SHELTER IN SIGHT WHEN THE RAIN started pelting down. The horses and their riders soon became sodden to the bone. Prudence could feel the hairs on her arm stand up against the cold but to no avail. The rain seeped through their clothes, chilling them down to their core until their fingers and toes could not be felt anymore.

"We have to get out of this weather before we all catch the grippe!" Cain called to the girls behind him, but he was barely heard over the boom of thunder across the sky. Although it was still some hours until nightfall, the sky had grown crowded with big, black clouds that blocked the sun from view.

Lightning flickered above their heads and concern flashed on their faces for an instant before it all went dark again. Cain's horse snorted at the brightness and stamped his feet impatiently.

"There's nowhere for us to go, Captain!" Shuu yelled through the din. The group hastened their speed through the rain in the hope of finding some shelter. The booms of thunder grew louder as they clattered down the dirt track. Malaine and its port, where *The Bloody Maiden* lay waiting, were still a day away and if shelter could not be found soon, they would have to rest out in the storm.

Prudence's wounds began to ache once again as the damp and cold set stiffly in her bones. The shivering increased until it rocked her body. It was becoming ever harder to keep her hold around Eleanora's waist. She grimaced as a sharp pain throbbed in her abdomen.

"I can't cope like this for much longer, Elea. We must find somewhere to shelter soon, or I fear these wounds will open up again from all this riding."

Eleanora nodded and moved her horse up beside the captain's. "We're never going to find a house or any kind of building in the middle of nowhere. There looks to be a patch of trees just a couple hundred yards away from the track up there. I think that's the best we're going to get for now. Pru needs to rest and the trees will provide some shelter, it shan't keep us completely dry but it'll have to do. We haven't got another choice!"

Cain glanced behind him into the dark and could vaguely make out a patch of firs that would hopefully give them a place to lay their head for a few hours. They'd get wet but it was out the way of the road and anyone who might be looking for them.

It was windy. And provided that kept up, the storm might move past them in the next hour or so and then they could be on their way again. Every hour that *The Maiden* sat in that harbour was an hour too long. The longer it stayed there, the more chance there was that she might be recognised—and they'd already been gone weeks. Another bolt of lightning flashed and the smell of wet earth filled Cain's nostrils.

The trees clustered together like a giant gorse bush in the middle of a barren moor. Their branches wound together to form a canopy overhead, providing much needed protection from the pouring rain. The horses were tied next to one another with just enough rope to reach the grass at their feet. The group secured themselves in the upper branches of two poplar trees.

The branches were thick and held their weight nicely and the gnarled trunk served as a backrest. The wind blew through the gaps in the leaves, the cold nipped at their faces, but it could not keep away the exhaustion that brought on sleep.

They awoke to complete and utter silence after the thunderous noise of the storm. The horses were sodden to the touch and shivered from being drenched. As the crew prepared the horses, their captain sat atop the tallest tree in the copse and watched the horizon through his spyglass.

Before long, he caught the glimmer of dust in the sunlight, rising from the ground. As Cain adjusted his spyglass to scan further back, the sight of pistols and men rode into view, astride slender beasts whose hooves clip-clopped down the track in the direction of the little group.

Leaping down branch by branch, he raced to the girls. "They're near. They'll be upon us in an hour if they see us."

"Oh gods, there must be another way." Cain could tell she was panicking as her voice took on a note of hysteria. "We could ride around, ride behind these trees and circle around to Malaine, couldn't we?"

Cain shook his head. "It won't work, Elea. It'll take us days away from Malaine, they'll hunt us down like dogs. We have to leave now if we're to have any chance of reaching *The Maiden* before those animals catch us and string us up like prize meat." Cain mounted his horse and handed the rein of the other to Prudence. "You are the faster ride are you not, even with your injuries?"

Prudence nodded, took the leather in hand, and got on the horse with a grunt, helping Elea up behind her.

Once clear of the trees, the five horses broke into a gallop, their hooves barely touching the floor as they flew across the ground towards the road. The soldiers saw them at once and kicked their horses, advancing down the hill towards them.

Prudence pushed the gelding on as she bent low over his neck, the reins tight in her grip. Their horses were slower than the soldiers' and they would need to take advantage of the distance between them. It would not last long. If they were going to survive this chase, then they'd need to think of something, fast.

"Elea, cut the bags behind you, let them go. They're slowing the horses down." Prudence handed her a knife from her pocket. The men followed suit and let their supplies fall to the ground. If they didn't get away then they wouldn't be needing them anyway.

They continued at that pace with the soldiers dipping in and out of sight for a minute, before coming back into view as they rounded a corner or rode along higher ground. A few shots were fired but they weren't close enough to make a hit.

"What's the plan then? How do we get rid of them?" Prudence glanced behind her to see six men still on their tail. A few of them had turned back, presumably to gather reinforcements.

"We'll reach the town in a few minutes. If we split up and head down the narrow, darker streets, perhaps we can stall them. Find a way through where they can't follow us to port. It's a small chance, but it's the only one we've got. If we lead them straight to the ship, it won't only be us three dead. We'll sentence everyone on board to death." Prudence locked eyes with Cain for a moment and nodded before splitting off and leading her horse down a side street and away from him.

The now cobbled streets only aided in making Prudence and Eleanora more noticeable as their shire *clattered* along the road. People glanced up and stared at them quizzically, not used to seeing a horse canter down the middle of the street. They rode down alleyways and into the darkest and most empty streets, until they had completely lost sight of the soldiers on their tail.

As they burst out of the other side of the mass of houses, the town seemed to stretch out and breathe. Everything was open and light. From here, Prudence and Eleanora could see port, and in front of them, Cain. The other men were rushing to join him. Prudence sighed with relief.

The unease that had been building since they parted ways made way for a flood of relief that swept through her like rapids on a river. It had only been minutes, but the idea of them being apart while they had death looming over their heads didn't feel good. They'd clicked the horses on towards port when a foot soldier emerged from a little alleyway. Prudence hadn't considered that there might be soldiers already in town waiting for them.

PRUDENCE HEARD THE SOLDIER'S PISTOL FIRE AND A SHOT rang out through the street. They were so close to port.

They couldn't get caught now! Soldiers advanced on them from every street in sight with guns at the ready, but the horses had given the group an advantage. The soldiers who had horses of their own were too far behind to do anything. The crew thundered down the road and the horses' hooves clattered on the cobbles. She could hear the foot soldiers shouting to each other, pushing on to go faster, to reach them. But the men on foot were no match for the horses.

It wouldn't be long before they got to the edge of Malaine and from there Prudence had no idea what they would do. They couldn't head straight for *The Maiden*—they wouldn't stand a chance trying to leave the port. They would have to find somewhere to hide out, a nearly impossible task.

Another shot blasted in their direction and Prudence heard a *thump* as it collided with flesh. She turned to see Eleanora's face struck with an expression of utter shock as she looked at her chest. The horse reared and threw the both of them off before bolting from the noise. Prudence's scream sent the other horses into a state, nostrils flaring and eyes bulging. They stamped their hooves hard on the ground and flung their heads around trying furiously to get out of their riders' grip.

Eleanora had landed in a funny position when she hit the ground. Her leg stuck out at an odd angle that made Prudence feel sick; the bone had snapped and ripped through the flesh of her shin. Prudence heard herself let out a roar of anguish and dropped to her side. She pushed down onto Elea's chest, trying desperately to put pressure on the wound and stop the bleeding, but the bleeding carried on. Eleanora gasped in a ragged breath, struggling for air.

Her eyes darted around wildly as she looked from Prudence to the street behind her, where more soldiers would come from. Her chest rose and fell as her breaths came out rough and forced.

The bullet must have punctured her lung.

She lay on the floor, ragged breaths coming short and sporadically. Blood soaked her chest and dripped down into her hair. Her face was growing more grey by the second and Prudence struggled to control the hysteric bawling that made her face wet and her nose run. She wiped the tears and snot away with the back of her hand as the light in Eleanora's eyes faded and they became dull. Her heart no longer beat underneath Prudence's hand and she finally stopped struggling for breath.

Gabe sank to his knees at her side, his hands reaching out to do something, anything. But he froze. There was nothing to be done, they both knew it. He let out a gasping sob and pulled his pistol with tears and anger filling his eyes. He fired shot after shot at the soldiers coming for them, but none met their mark.

"Captain! They're going to get us all killed. *Shit*." Shuu leapt off his horse and tugged at Gabe's shoulder, hoisting him up onto his feet. "We have to go! *Now!*"

Prudence pulled her friend's head into her lap and shook her violently, the sobs taking over her whole body. A warmth spread around the two of them and Prudence noticed then, the urine leaking over the ground. The smell of faeces was intolerable but she was unable to move herself away. She couldn't move away from her family, lying dead in the road.

Cain dropped from his horse, aware of the soldiers gaining on them, and reached out to Prudence. She ignored his hand and continued to rock Eleanora's dead body back and forth. He grabbed her from behind and pulled her away.

"No! You bastard! Let me go! I can't leave her. We can't leave her there! They'll get her. We can't leave her there!" Prudence kicked and screamed at him to let her go but he held on and threw her onto the horse's back before mounting himself and spurring it on as fast as he could, leaving Elea behind.

12

HAUNTING GUILT

Prudence kicked and hit Cain as he pulled her down from the horse. Her fists hit their mark over and over again as she screamed at him with tears cascading down her face, but his grip didn't change. There was now a gaping hole inside Prudence and it threatened to destroy her.

"Ye left her there. You, you... we left her there. Left her in the middle of the road, all broken and covered in mud. Ye bastard." Her sobs made the words come out sporadically. "You should have left me with her," she yelled. Angry and exhausted, Cain was filled with a sudden rage that he could not ignore.

"She's dead, Prudence! Dead. There was nothing we could do!" By now they were both screaming at one another. Prudence hit him again but Cain caught her wrist firmly, refusing to let go. "She died because she saved you. If you died now too, then it would have been for nothing."

Time barely seemed to register as he held her by the shoulders and stood there waiting for her to calm down. It seemed to take an eternity, but finally the struggling slowed, and her screaming turned to sobs. Eventually, there was only silence as Prudence and Cain stood facing one another, his hands gripping her shoulders and Prudence finally quiet.

She sunk into his shoulder, letting his broad chest and arms envelope her in a cocoon of safety. The hairs of his beard tickled her ear but she didn't move away as he shushed her and whispered calming words. His hands stroked her back softly in soothing motions as he listened to her breathing return to normal, and the occasional sniffle of tears that had overwhelmed her only moments before.

"It should have been me."

Cain pulled back to look at Prudence's face.

She stared, unblinking, at her feet. "I should have died. Not Elea. It should have been me. They were aiming for me, not her. She didn't even want to be here. I should've died."

Cain sighed loudly and rested his chin on Prudence's head, his arms wrapped around her. "You know that's not something she'd ever want. She loved you. She wanted you to be happy, Pru. I may not know her as well as you do, but I know for a fact that she doesn't blame you for any of this. Not truly."

Prudence sniffled against his chest. "But I—"

"—I know." Cain lifted her chin so she was looking him in the eye. "She knows too."

THEY FOUND THEMSELVES AT THE FAR END OF MALAINE, where the population began to thin out. More and more homes disappeared as they encroached onto Maenon territory. Whilst the witch community tended to enter Malaine for the market and their daily chores, their houses were kept well apart. Many of the townsfolk had a tendency to be scared by the community. Though their trinkets were often bought from the market as little luck charms, the real magicks made people nervous.

Prudence had fallen silent and still. She stared off into the distance without actually looking at anything in particular. It was almost as if switching off from the real world would help protect her from the intense grief that consumed her.

"Khari, take the horses. Keep an eye on him." Cain nodded at Gabe who was staring off into the distance, a mix of fury and agony on his face. "Shuu, let's go find somewhere to spend the night."

As long as they had to hide out, they would need a roof over their heads. They walked for a long time, searching the huts and cottages that were separate from the main village. After a while, Cain began to lose hope that they would find somewhere abandoned, and he was doubtful that anyone would give them shelter, but nonetheless they persisted. They knocked on every door they came to until Cain and Shuu had walked miles in search of somewhere for them to rest.

"Captain, we may have just found our bit of luck." Shuu pointed to a house up ahead. It was far away from the others and from the look of the clothes on the line outside, whoever lived there, lived alone. Cain opened the door and stepped inside, ducking his head under the low door frame. The floor creaked beneath his boots and the oil lamps on the walls flickered silently.

The captain glanced at the table and the loaf of bread that sat on the chopping board. Clearly, they weren't alone. As quietly as possible, Cain crept through the room to the closest door while Shuu swept the perimeter. He flung it open and stepped through to find a woman crouched behind the dresser. He clamped a hand over her mouth as she ran at him, lifting her up with his other arm and holding her still.

"I'm not going to hurt you. Shh, shh, shh... we just need to stay here a while. I'm sorry, we don't have much of a choice." He dragged her back through into the kitchen in search of something to tie her up with. Cain's grip loosened slightly as he searched through the drawers. She wriggled out of his grip, snatched the knife from the chopping board, and swung the blade towards him. At the last minute, Cain grabbed her wrist and twisted it sharply, making her cry out. He pushed the knife-wielding hand away from himself and back towards her, just enough so that the blade was away from him and so she wouldn't think about trying it again. He realised his mistake when he heard a squelch and watched her slump against the table.

"No no no no, shit. No, you can't die. You're not meant to die. I didn't mean to." He sighed and slammed his hand hard against the wood, angry at himself. "Fuck!" He stood there for a long time, staring straight ahead at nothing. It was all feeling rather fruitless at this point. How many people had died, and how far they had come, and all for what? They were trapped in a corner, no closer to home than they had been at the beginning. If home was even still there at all. Perhaps the soldiers had seized her and slaughtered the rest of the crew. He sighed and placed his head in his hands. He just needed to rest, just for a moment.

Shuu came through the front door. "Everything's clear outside Cap, think we'll be good here for now—oh shit. What happened?"

Cain sighed, avoiding his gaze. "Little accident."

Shuu nodded silently and put his pistol on the part of the table that wasn't covered in blood. "I see that. Well, come on, let's get this cleaned up. Don't want this here when the girl comes in, she's only just calmed down. Gabe's a fucking mess too, poor kid. Think she liked him too, who'd'av guessed?"

Cain listened to Shuu talk as they cleaned the blood up. He dumped her body out the back in a little shed that had been badly constructed. It was falling down and the roof had dipped on one side. Since it was likely to cave in soon enough anyway, it was the perfect place.

He laid her down as softly as he could, her hands placed gently over her stomach, eyes shut. If it weren't for the blood staining her clothes, she could have been sleeping. Once she had been dealt with, Cain returned to the patch of grass where he had left Prudence, Khari, and Gabe, whilst Shuu kept watch from the cottage. Prudence had remained in exactly the same place, still as a statue next to the gelding, whose only concern was the grass in his mouth.

"Pru... ehem, Prudence. I've found somewhere for us to hide out. Come on. We need to get out of the open." He untied the rope from around the horse's bridle and patted his rump. The shire trotted off to a longer patch of grass a hundred yards off, perfectly content with his new surroundings.

"You found somewhere empty?" Her words came out as a low drone of sound. No emotion at all. She spoke as if she were heavily drugged.

"Sure did, lass. Come on let's get you somewhere warm." Leading her by the shoulder, Cain managed to steer Prudence back to the hut without much trouble. Walking her through the house, he managed to get Prudence to the bedroom, sit her down on the bed, and put a blanket around her shivering figure. Her face was even paler than usual. The fight in her eyes, the fight that had shined out so bright and caught his affections, was dimmed so low that it may have gone altogether. He huffed slightly and his hands paused in mid-air. Suddenly, he didn't know what to do to help her.

"Um, I think I'll just uh... give you some space." Captain Morris left feeling defeated and useless, shutting the door softly behind him. Prudence was in a trance, but that would end once it had all sunk in. Captain Morris had experienced it himself and knew all too well that this was the calm before the storm.

Florence's image swam into view, making him cringe. It may have been years ago but the pain and guilt still remained, painful as ever. Florence had died and his beautiful sister had turned into a monster because he couldn't save her. And now the woman he loved was cursed to forever feel the same turmoil that he felt. His hands clenched into fists. He wanted so badly to help Pru but he knew all too well that there was nothing to be done.

Prudence and Eleanora were like soul mates, they completed each other. He didn't know how she might cope without her other half. The only thing that kept her alive, back when life wasn't worth living, was Eleanora. What would she do without her now? Even if she didn't blame herself for Elea's death, would she still want to live?

The men were huddled round the small kitchen table, stuffing their faces with the bread that had been left out. "She'll be all righ' Cap, just needs some time."

"Ooh I dunno..." Khari shook his head. "Tha' girl was her entire life. Ye shoulda seen her before. I seen her with that hag that paid 'em, she'd a ripped anyone to pieces that looked at that girl wrong. What's she got left now?"

Shuu glared at Khari. "She'll be fine. She's got all of us, hasn't she? Ye just gotta be patient Cap, she'll come back to ye."

Cain sighed and headed to the door. He didn't want to listen to what any of them had to say. This was all his fault. He spent an hour or two out in the open air, walking with no destination in mind. The wind on his face brought him smells of the salty ocean. It grounded him. He ventured back to the house and examined the surroundings for neighbours. Finding nothing, he collected some vegetables from the allotment out back and returned inside. The bedroom door was still closed and all he could hear was the same silence that filled the house.

The door closed behind Cain as he entered the bedroom. The lamps had all been extinguished, filling the room with lonely blackness. He had come to apologise, yelling at Prudence earlier had caused her even more pain. Moving towards the bed in the corner, Cain noticed that it was empty. She wasn't here. Almost everything in the room had been knocked over or smashed. The chair and vanity had been kicked over and one of the legs had been snapped. The vase on the chest had been shattered into little pieces with water and flowers spilled everywhere. Sighing, he headed for the door.

The wind had picked up again, whipping harshly against Cain's skin. Prudence sat right at the edge where the grass met the shore, toes in the sand. Prudence's hair blew violently in the wind as she stared far into the distance. Her knees were pulled up to her chest and arms wrapped round herself tight as she shivered from the cold. Prudence barely noticed Cain behind her.

"You should be inside, it's very cold." Cain tried his best to convince her to get up but she stayed put.

"There must be something I can do, Cain. I'm s'posed to look after her. I'm her family. I have to do somethin'." Prudence's chest heaved and her words caught in her throat. "If I don't do somethin' then, who will? She can't be dead... she can't be. She, she needs me... I'm supposed... I'm supposed to..." but her brain could no longer come up with the words to express the grief she was feeling and she sank to her knees as her body wracked with sobs.

Cain stood and watched helplessly as she cried. He could offer no comfort or solace in her pain. Instead of moving to her side, he turned and headed back into the hut. There was nothing out there that could help Prudence, the only aid he could offer was keeping the two of them alive, for now.

They had managed to create some distance between themselves and the soldiers, but they hadn't enough time to find somewhere to hide where there weren't any people. He hadn't meant to hurt that woman, only lock her in a room or something to keep her from giving them away. He couldn't help what had happened when she tried to bring a knife down across his face.

He didn't revel in killing—well, not the majority of the time—but it had become intrinsically entwined with his life from the moment that he was pushed out into the world by his mother. Death had followed him closely wherever he went. As a slave. As a brother. As a criminal.

He sighed and leant against the kitchen table. He could not work out how his life had ended up at this moment... born a poor farmer's boy in the beautiful countryside, sold to the fleet; watching as the bastards that tortured him murdered his baby sister; and then taking his revenge. But that was all over, why did he deserve more suffering? He was never able to stay put in one place, even for just a moment, just for a snippet of a quiet life.

A tear slipped from his eye at the thought of his sister before he shook his head and punched the wall. Outside, Prudence remained motionless as if the life had been sucked right out of her.

"Just gotta wait them out. A few days and the soldiers will think we will have moved on from here, they might even be moving on now," he spoke to himself as he cleaned up. Thinking out loud helped him prepare for what was to come. He had to think of everything that might get in their way. He had to find a way to get them back on his ship and as far away from here as possible.

DAYS PASSED AND PRUDENCE FOUND HERSELF PACING THE floor at the foot of the bed, often. Unable to rest, her mind raced as she replayed Eleanora's death over and over again, torturing herself. Every time her eyes closed, she could see Elea sprawled on the floor, and every time Prudence was unable to help her. She muttered to herself in the darkness, talking of regret and pain, thinking of ways to make herself suffer like her dear Eleanora had.

Occasionally, she would have a change and move her pacing outside, but the rambling still continued. Her mind tortured her with voices of guilt. They toyed with her emotions, convincing her that she was a monster and taking her back to those horrid days of torture that nearly drove her insane. That there was no one to blame for what happened to Elea... no one except her.

On one of these occasions, Prudence found she had wandered deeper into Maenon territory and had come across some of their people chanting out on the grass. She stood and watched, momentarily transfixed as they held hands round the burning embers. Prudence glimpsed a head of silver hair and her eyes fell on a familiar face. She recognised her from before. Prudence stayed out of the way, not wanting to interfere, but all the while her mind was whirring with possibilities. Plans that may or may not end in her salvation.

Prudence sat on the grass and watched the Maenon children running around playing with sticks as their mothers hung new herbs around their doorways. The young girl was now playing with the children. Prudence recognised her silvery blonde hair from the market, when they had first arrived on the island. Without giving it much thought, her feet moved across the dusty ground and over to the group. The girl's head lifted and she saw Prudence.

"I know you... you came to market once," the girl stated.

"Ye sold me some jewellery. My name's Prudence." The girl nodded, remembering.

"Rhearn. This is my little brother, Joss, and my sisters, Deva, Helene, and Chandra. Say hello, children." The boy, Joss, puffed his chest out and grinned at Prudence.

"I'm going to be eight soon, don't you know!" Prudence chuckled despite herself. The child was amusing. His younger sisters clung to Rhearn's skirt and peeked out to get a glimpse of Prudence when they thought she wasn't looking.

"What brings you so far from town then, Miss Prudence?" Rhearn scooped Chandra up into her arms and stroked her hair. Prudence thought for a moment.

"I'm actually here to see if anyone could... help me. I —I lost someone very important to me. There must be someone here who can help me get her back." Rhearn raised an eye at the word 'lost' but chose to stay silent. She put Chandra down.

"You need to go back to the hut now little ones. Joss, make sure your sisters clean their hands and are ready for dinner when Mama gets home." Joss nodded and grabbed his younger sister's hand, herding the other two back towards their home. Rhearn took Prudence's hand and stared quietly at her face for a long time before saying anything.

"I don't know what you are feeling right now. It's not possible for me to, I've never lost anyone. But I can't imagine you mean lost in the literal sense, do you?" Prudence shook her head. "That's dark magick that is, miss. It can cause more harm than good. There *is* someone who can help you. But you need to consider, right now, if it's going to be worth the price." Prudence pulled her hand away from Rhearn.

"There isn't anything I wouldn't pay. I can't live without her."

Rhearn's forehead crinkled but she sighed and turned towards the community regardless. She had seen many people with a goal they were determined to reach, but none so desperate and wild-eyed as Prudence.

"My grandmother is the chief elder here. She is the only person I know that has the power to aid you in your task. But it's not going to be easy, miss. Blood magick is something that should not be trifled with. It's dangerous." Weaving through the huts and stone cottages that made up the Maenon community, Rhearn led Prudence to the largest of them, right in the centre.

It was circular and made of wooden stakes. The roof

was straw and the walls were adorned with crystals and herbs. They'd been hung as charms to ward off things that Prudence couldn't even begin to imagine. A shiver ran down her spine as she reached the door. No light came from underneath and there was an eerie silence that surrounded the hut. It was completely unaffected by the bustling village surrounding it. Rhearn opened the door for her and took a step back.

"It is here that I must leave you. My grandmother, Orenda, will listen to you. If she can help, she will. But I urge you one last time to reconsider, Prudence." She gripped Prudence's arms tightly and squeezed her so hard that it hurt, her eyes boring into Pru's. "Blood demands blood, that is the way it has always been. For a job this big, the cost will be large and I worry that you may be the one to suffer the price. Are you really willing to give up your life for someone who is already back amongst the earth?"

Prudence paused. "You've been very kind to me, Rhearn, but I can't expect ye to understand the risks that I am willing to take. This life has not been kind to me, but I expect it might be kinder to my friend." Rhearn smiled softly and squeezed Prudence's hand one final time before retreating back the way she came, presumably to find her siblings and await their mama's return.

Prudence turned back to the door before her and took a deep breath. She pushed it open and stepped into the darkness of the room. Inside, there were yet again numerous trinkets and charms hanging from the ceiling, so low that Prudence had to duck underneath them to pass. She saw a giant oak table in the far corner of the room as her eyes adjusted to the gloom.

"Um, excuse me... ma'am? I've uh, I've come to ask for yer help. Yer granddaughter, Rhearn, suggested ye may be able to assist me. I was hoping, for the right price of course, ye may be able to bring someone back to me." The woman in the corner lifted her head to watch Prudence as she ambled through the cluttered room towards her.

"Blood magick is it, then? You seem to be rather far from home young lady. 'Tis very dangerous games you mess with, are ye sure you know what you're asking?"

"Blood demands blood, yes I've been told. Please, I'll pay whatever I must." She produced a fistful of coins that she'd taken from the cottage and dumped them on the table, the pile spilling everywhere.

Orenda chuckled and pushed the charms she was making to the side. "Oh, dear child, you know nothing. Yes, blood demands blood, but even then you can never bring a corpse back as they were before. How long 'as she been dead?"

Prudence gulped. "A few days... maybe a week." Orenda nodded and pulled some jars down from the shelf above her head. She sprinkled something that looked like dirt into a mortar. Dried herbs and flowers that Prudence didn't recognise were added sparingly to the bowl as well. Orenda grabbed Prudence's arm from across the table, and using a knife the length of her forearm, sliced along the vein and held it tight as it poured into the bowl. Prudence drew in a sharp breath at the pain and clenched her teeth.

The old witch chanted in a guttural language that

Prudence didn't recognise. Orenda's voice was no longer her own, but a deep chanting growl. She ground the bowl's mixture together into a thick paste and smeared it across her forehead with a thumb before doing the same to an apprehensive Prudence. The smell was enough to make her retch but Prudence held still. She needed this to work.

Orenda lit a stick of herbs from the fire burning in the hearth and dropped it into the mortar with everything else. A bead of sweat dripped down her forehead. Prudence looked at the chief elder, and suddenly, she felt fear. A raw, burning sensation began in the fingertips of Prudence's right hand and she stared at them in horror.

"What's happening?!" she asked, her voice rising in fear. The only part of her fingers that she could feel was the burning and bubbling of her skin. The pain crept further up her hand and to her wrist until she lost the ability to move her hand altogether. Welts began to form on her arm and her skin became an ashen grey as the veins swelled. They were no longer blue but a thick, oozing black.

"Do you know what happens to bodies once they're dead? There's no blood going round, their organs and skin start to rot. Right now, your friend's body is bloating and leaking blood and foam from every orifice. Do you really wish to see her like that? Do you think she would like to live like that? Her skin a sick green from the lack of life?" Prudence bit her lip but the tears started to fall regardless. She had not yet considered what might be happening to Eleanora. Had anyone buried her? Had they left her there in the street for the dogs to fight over? She gasped as the pain grew sharper and spread higher up her arm. It looked rotten.

"That is, if your friend's body is still together..." Orenda seemed to read Prudence's mind. "By the look on your face, I'd guess there wasn't a nice funeral."

"I—I can't just leave her like that though! She needs me. It wasn't her they meant to get; it was me. How can I just leave her like that when she was never meant to die! It was meant to be me!" Prudence couldn't hold herself up any longer and sank to the floor, clutching her arm in pain. She let out an ear-piercing scream as the pain reached new heights. Tears streamed down her face in equal measures of grief and agony.

Cain slammed the door of the hut open with Rhearn and Khari following close behind. Orenda's head snapped up, her glaring eyes locked on Cain as he swept everything off her table and pointed his pistol directly at her face. He glanced briefly at Prudence writhing on the floor, but his focus was on the old woman.

"Do you not think she has suffered enough without you filling her with false hope?! That girl will never come back, not properly, and you know that as well as I do. No need to torture the girl more than she's doing so herself," he hissed at her.

Khari sunk to his knees beside Prudence and helped her sit up, careful not to touch her arm. "Oh *keine*, what have ye done to yerself?"

"I just... I—I just wanted her back." She managed to force the words out in gasping breaths between sobs. Her arm burned like fire, the welts were open and weeping, the skin a repulsive grey-green colour. The sight made her

276

stomach turn. Was this what Elea's body looked like? She whimpered.

"Come on. Let's get you up." Khari put his arms around her shoulders and lifted her.

Orenda straightened, her gaze unwavering. "She came to me boy, 'tis not my fault, nor my concern that she didna know better. The girl knew what she was getting into when she sat down. Ye cannot blame me for the results, no matter how much they are not what ye wish." She jutted her chin out and cast her eyes to the door. "I suggest ye leave. Keep a watchful eye, Captain, the gods don't rightly like strangers, especially those that interrupt rituals."

Cain scowled at her but holstered his pistol before helping Khari half-carry Prudence from the dark hut.

"Lud, God of the watchful moon and tides, hear me," the elder began, "Barinthus, Father of the sands and sea beds, I beseech thee. These foul mortals have dishonoured You and our ways." Prudence cringed as Orenda's next words reached her ears. "Bring forth mighty judgement upon their heads so that they might *drown* in their regrets. Let their world come crashing down around them with a *hail of fire and death*." Orenda spoke with an unholy power that seemed to radiate from the air around her.

As Khari scoffed in disbelief, a shiver ran down Prudence's spine. The men helped her walk as they put the hut behind them. Prudence wanted as much distance between them and the witch's words as they could get.

The pain dulled as they got further away, but the damage had already been done. Prudence's right arm was rough and scarred like tree bark, a decayed shade of grey-green.

BACK AT THE HOUSE, CAIN FLUNG A BLANKET AROUND Prudence's shaking shoulders and perched next to her. Her face was tear-stained and dirty. He grabbed whatever cloths he could find in the kitchen and filled a pail with water. He returned to the room and attempted to soothe the boils that had formed around her knuckles, but it didn't do much. Prudence just stared blankly at her ruined arm, no recognition on her face, just the wallowing sadness of grief.

"Khari!" Cain yelled.

The tall smuggler poked his head round the door. "Aye?"

"You know something about healing, don't you? I heard you talking about it when Rupert took that shot on the merchant vessel."

"Aye, I do. My mother was our tribe healer when I was a young'un. I know my way round plants... enough at least." He strode into the room and crouched down in front of Prudence. "Let's take a look."

Cain grimaced at the sight of the gaping wounds across her ruined forearm. It looked like death. How Prudence wasn't in more pain, he didn't know. Khari took the cloth from Cain and pressed the damp fabric to her grey arm. Khari glanced at her face with his eyebrows knitted together.

"How does that feel?"

"I can't feel anything," Prudence mumbled.

It was as if her forearm were no longer there. She stared at it for a long moment but it was as if her brain would not realise it was her own arm that was lying there ruined. The cloth washed her arm clean of blood and pus, leaving only it's grey exterior. Rough and ragged.

Cain touched it gently with a finger and flinched. The feeling of the rough jagged skin made his head swim and his stomach churn. It didn't feel natural. Prudence tried to force her fingers to move, but there was nothing. Not even a little twitch of movement.

Khari pulled Cain aside and spoke in hushed tones. "It don't look good that she can't feel anythin'. I'm not sure if she'll be able to move it neither." Cain's face fell. "But I can help those wounds a little. I'll head out and find the plants I need, it's too late in the year for agrimony but there might still be some lady's mantle about. We'll sort it as best we can, just have to wait and see then."

Cain sighed and glanced at Prudence. "All right. Go. I'll keep an eye on her."

Khari nodded and left in search of something to help her arm. Cain sat down beside Prudence and wrapped an arm around her shoulders. "You didn't fail her, you know." When Prudence didn't respond he pressed on. "I never told you what happened to my sister, did I?"

She shook her head. Cain carefully wrapped her arm in cloth as he spoke.

"My parents were farmers on Aelin, that's where I was born, it's... it's where I'm from. We did all right for a while but years of drought made us poorer and my mother couldn't buy food to feed us. She sold us as slaves to the royal fleet when I was ten." Prudence's eyes flicked to his face. He felt the pain contort his features as he spoke.

"They beat us, regularly. Florence more than myself; they took pleasure in abusing her. I dread to think how much worse they would have treated her had I not been there. I tried to keep them away from her as best I could," he sighed, "One day, they were hitting my sister and whipping her. She was ill, she couldn't keep up with her chores like they wanted and I snapped. I don't know what came over me, but I snatched the whip away from him and I hit him.

"I hit him again and again, I didn't stop hitting until he stopped breathing. They threw me below deck and didn't feed me for days. But not before they made me watch them bind my sister's ankles and throw her overboard. They forced me to watch her drown and sink to the bottom of the ocean."

"Oh Cain, I don't know what to say..." Prudence's eyes filled with tears and she reached her hand out to comfort him, but he brushed her off.

"They turned her into one of those monsters to spite me. They laughed as water filled her lungs. They didn't know what she would turn into, I don't think. I don't think it was intentional to make her into one of those things, especially not when the crew then got ravaged by the very same beasts a few days later—some of them died. I heard it all from below deck in my cell. I remember banging on the metal and bloodying my hands, I was so desperate to get to them." He paused to glance at Prudence once more.

"It is not your fault what happened to her. You didn't force her to be here. Neither you nor I forced her to help me rescue you. She was here because she loved you. She was here because she wanted to be with you. No one can blame you for that."

Prudence sighed and laid her head on Cain's shoulder. "But I did force her," she whispered softly. He watched a tear bead on her cheek and hang there for a moment. Cain lifted his hand and wiped the tear away with a thumb.

"You'll be fine lass, just fine." His arm slipped over her shoulders and he pulled her into him. Prudence's head fit perfectly against his chest. Her hair brushed against his cheek as she turned around, her fingers tangling in his blond locks as she looked up at him. He felt her warm breath against his face as her nose pressed against his neck.

She slipped her shoulder out of her sleeve. The cold air hit her skin, making goose bumps rise on her arm. The warmth of Pru's body was warm and just as inviting to Cain as his was to her. She pulled his shirt over his head and ran her hands over his chest, running her fingers over the raised pink skin of his scars; a constant reminder of his painful childhood. Prudence ran her fingers over a large gash at his side. The skin was pulled taut, the angry colour of healing that would never go back to normal.

Cain's arm tightened around her and she looked up at him. His lips found her cheek, his rough beard tickling her lips, and she squirmed. Cain shifted until he was facing her, his hand gripping the back of her neck. He tipped her head back so that they were staring at one another and pressed his lips against hers. In that moment, after everything that they had been through, everything they had grieved for, it could all be ignored through something as simple as comfort. Comfort could erase the pain, even just for a little while.

They reached and grasped for one another, trying to entwine themselves so deeply that they became one. It was solid and real as they pressed against one another in a fervour. Trying to drown in the moment so that they might never resurface.

There was no need for words. No need for Prudence to do anything but sink into the comfort of Cain, the weight of him on top of her. Her breath as it came out in harsh gasps as his fingers explored the delicious curve of her back, her neck, and finally entangled themselves deep in her knotted black hair.

They moved together in a dream-like state, only half conscious of themselves until they pulled apart, physically exhausted but emotionally content, for now.

Prudence drifted off into a peaceful sleep as Cain played with her hair. As her head rested on his chest, the sound of her heartbeat lured him into a deep, satisfied slumber.

13

TILL IT KILLS US BOTH

Prudence woke in the bedroom of the house that they were occupying. There was an empty space in the bed where Cain had been only hours before. She wiped the dried, salty tears from her face and let her feet touch the wooden floor. She pulled the blanket from the bed, wrapped it around her shoulders, and was heading in search of Cain when Khari stopped her in her tracks.

"Hold on a minute *keine*, Captain asked me to do what I can for tha' arm o' yours, so let's take a look." He took her arm and unwound the makeshift bandage that Cain had wrapped it in.

"Oof, yer a brave lass tha's for sure." Shuu left his knives on the table and moved closer to take a look, recoiling instantly. "Must hurt something fucking fierce."

Prudence shook her head. "I can't feel it at all, actually."

"Looks no different than it did yesterday, ye still can't move it at all?" Khari asked. Prudence shook her head.

"Witch nonsense. Don't trust it, never 'av, s'not natural," Shuu grunted. He shivered dramatically and went back to sharpening his blades.

"Now, couldn't find much mantle but I found some black lovage root," Khari produced a mortar of plant root that looked like paste, and spread it across the shirt bandage. "This'll 'elp those weepin' sores on yer arm, hopefully." He wound the bandage around her rotten arm once more.

"Thank ye, ye didn't have to do that." Prudence smiled at him.

He grinned and gave her a wink. "Yea I did, I owed ya."

Prudence left the house, her arm hanging limp and useless by her side. She found Cain soon enough, grooming the horses that they'd ridden from Valentya. He groomed the bay gelding quietly, brushing the clump of straw in his grasp from the horse's neck down to his rump. He was so lost in thought that he didn't even notice Prudence behind him.

"Morning."

Cain swivelled around to look at her. "Finally, awake! How are you feeling? Not going to hit me again I hope." He chuckled but the sombre look in his eye didn't shift. "I'm sorry about..."

"Don't be." Prudence pulled the blanket tighter around her and stepped closer to the horse, patting the gelding's side. "I was wrong. I shouldn't have gone to her for help. It was a stupid mistake. I think I just had this moment where I thought I could fix it, fix her, and bring her back to me. But that can't ever happen."

Cain sighed and stood so that he was facing Prudence. "You did everything you could for her, Pru."

"I know." He put the straw down and pulled over a bucket of water.

"We'll have to leave here soon, you know? Won't be long before they've had time to check the whole island. We need to get back to *The Maiden* and leave here once and for all. We can't come back."

Prudence nodded silently. Quite frankly, she hadn't given any thought to the soldiers or Governor Atkey since Eleanora had died. It was all she could to stay alive, she couldn't think about anything more on top of that and her grief. The fight in her seemed to have dimmed to a dull spark. She had never been so without purpose before.

She'd never known a life where she wasn't trying to escape something, but those yearnings had all seemed worth it with Elea by her side. What was the point now? Her best friend in the whole world was dead. With no idea what would happen to her, Prudence was still running for her life, literally, and she was back to being the same girl that she had been on Llynne. The girl with nothing much left to live for.

"I'll be ready to go in a few moments." She turned and made her way back into the house to collect the few items that she had left: the shawl she had bought Eleanora for her birthday; the only thing that she had of Elea's, just by the sheer coincidence that she hadn't been wearing it the day she died; and the knife that had seemed to stay with her ever since that fight long, long ago in The Wanderer's Inn, the night that Cain came in and saved her.

How sad to have had an entire life and only a handful

of knickknacks to show for it. Prudence shoved the shawl and knife into the pocket of her britches, pulled her shoes on, and left the house. She was ready to leave this place of sorrow forever.

Outside the hut, Prudence knelt down in the white sand and felt her chest slump forward. The shawl she had bought for Eleanora's sixteenth birthday was clutched in her fist again. A tear glistened on her cheek and she wiped it away with her palm, sniffing harshly.

The wind was bitingly cold but she barely felt it. She could hardly feel anything besides the pressure of grief weighing down on her chest. "I'm sorry," she whispered, "I'm so, so sorry. You should be here, not me. I can't ever take that back," she sobbed.

Prudence collected the biggest stones that she could find and began to pile them up into a tower. It was tedious collecting them one by one with just her one good hand. "You deserved so much better than me, Elea. I don't know what I'm goin' to do without ye... you always coped so much better with this shit than I did. I don't know how I'm going to survive this. I'm not sure I want to. I don't know how to live without ye, Elea."

She yelled out as the anguish in her chest overwhelmed her. She balanced the on top of one another, almost in the form of a triangle. Prudence stifled her sobs and tied the blue shawl around the rock pile, a wash of vibrant colour against the bland landscape. It was a stark reminder of Eleanora's bright soul that was now gone from the world. And the world was so much more grey without her in it.

"Da, I hope you're looking after her. I need you to look

after her while I'm not there to do it." She placed her hands on the rock pile and silently said a Caeli prayer for her fallen sister. So, this was how Cain had felt losing his sister. There was a void inside Prudence's soul that could never be filled. Would it feel like this forever? She imagined it probably would. This was something she wouldn't come back from.

CAIN AND GABE PACKED THE GROUP'S BELONGINGS INTO THE horses' saddle bags. The gelding that Cain had named Gypsy was now burdened with the last remaining food stores they had, plus a couple of garments and weapons that they'd found when they first came across the hut.

Khari checked Prudence's arm over in the kitchen as they prepared to leave. "The root seems to have helped the sores some, so tha's good."

"I'm never goin' to be able to use my arm again, am I?" Prudence asked.

Khari sighed. "I don't think so *keine*, jus' looking at it, it should be agony for ye."

She frowned.

"But ye never know. I've never seen anything like this before, who's to say it'll last." He feigned a cheerful smile but it was unconvincing. "Best strap it up for now though, yer not gonna be able to use it and it's jus' gonna get in the way while we ride." He applied a new bandage and used a leather strap from one of the horses' tack to fasten the dead arm to her torso. He pulled it tight and did up the buckle. "There. That should keep it immobile, don't want it flopping around."

"I hate being so useless." Prudence scowled.

"*Haei*, yer not useless ye just need a bit 'o help for now. Stop feelin' sorry for yerself and just get on w' it."

Despite the initial shock at his words, they were the best words he could have said. She had spent so long feeling sorry. Sorry for herself, sorry for Cain, sorry for Elea. There wasn't anything she could do to change it. But she could at least try to survive, to thrive. For herself. For Cain. For Eleanora...

All they needed to do was make their way back to port and find their crew before the soldiers found them. Khari ushered the newly determined Prudence, and Shuu—who was still sharpening his knives—out of the little house and towards the horses.

Cain and Gabe were already mounted, waiting. Prudence put her good hand up on the saddle behind Cain and froze. "I don't think I can do this." She glanced up at him.

"It's all right, lass. Here, give me your hand. One of you, give her a leg up, will you?" He called to Khari and Shuu.

Shuu nodded and strode over. She lifted her left leg up and as Cain lifted her by her left arm, Shuu helped her leap and scramble onto the horse's back behind the captain. She flushed with embarrassment. "Thank ye." She shifted in her seat and wrapped her good arm around Cain's waist as they moved off.

The road, or more accurately, the dusty track that led from the Maenon community and back into Malaine, was narrow and long. It had plenty of coverage on either side from the trees that hung over, providing shade as well as a place to hide if they needed one. They remained hopeful that they would make the trip without crossing paths with anyone. They were more concerned with getting through Malaine and the harbour without being noticed.

The track that led away from the Maenon community was rocky and nowhere near as worn as most other paths. The community rarely travelled outside their own peoples and for the most part, the general population of Vaerny left the Maenon alone. Even the governor's reach didn't extend to their camp. Cain must've chosen it to be their hideout for that very reason.

Prudence watched the final leaves flutter down from the tops of the trees. The beauty that came from death in autumn had faded into a bleak and dreary winter. Prudence's mind wandered back to the Great Feast, it had been so long since she had made an offering. Shutting her eyes tight, she swore to herself that she would make up for it come the next Sumbel. No matter where they were, or how little they had, she would make a feast fit for Artos and Herne; offerings at their seats and altars in their name. She would beg the gods for a prosperous next year. It occurred to her in that moment that she had never seen Cain worship in any way. She cleared her throat.

"Cain..."

"Prudence..."

"Do ye believe in the afterlife? Something more than this life? Something... better?"

"I don't know, Pru. I've gone back and forth over the years."

"Do you observe the sabbats?"

Cain turned to glance at her, his green eyes shadowed by his heavy brows. "I'm not particularly good at keeping up, to be frank."

She squirmed. "Are you... I mean do you..." she huffed, "are you a religious man?"

Cain laughed. "Why? Does it matter to you?"

Prudence's face scrunched up; she didn't really know the answer to that.

"I was raised Terramian, but the crew come from all over. Most of them follow a religion of the west, some Caelian, some Terramian, some Solistic."

"I was raised with the faith o' my tribe, yer beliefs have never made much sense to me," scoffed Khari.

"What do ye mean?" asked Prudence.

"All these gods. The earth was made by The Mother, it's ruled by her and her daughters. They gave birth to the birds, the trees, the wind, us—everything. That is what I was taught."

"That sounds beautiful."

"Women are the source of all life," he shrugged, "why yer people choose to worship so many men, I'll never know."

Prudence laughed. "Sounds like your people had it right, my friend. So, what do some of the crew worship then? And you, what do ye worship, Cain?" Prudence asked.

"Well, Jorge comes from the Eastern Shores, Ivan from the Northern Border; Darius from the South—although I've actually never seen him worship anything other than booze and women," he chuckled.

"I was raised w'out religion but became a practising Caeli as a young teen." Gabe interjected. They all turned to look at the young sailing master. It was the first he had spoken since Eleanora had died. Prudence smiled faintly at him. She had been so consumed with her own grief that she'd forgotten all about his pain.

"I guess if I'm being totally honest, I don't worship anyone."

"You mean you don't have faith, Cain?" Prudence couldn't comprehend not believing in a deity, not when all around them there was mystery and magic.

"Maybe some of the gods are real. Perhaps even all of them, but that doesn't mean I spend my time praying to them and leaving offerings. They've never done anything for me. I don't owe them anything. I've spent most of my life a slave to something or other. First it was my parents, then my master, now I am slave to a life of running, never settling anywhere for long. I am not a slave to some divinity, though. Besides, one day we may discover that it was all for naught and there are no gods, and if that day comes, I will be glad that I did not waste my time."

Prudence, despite her efforts, could not doubt his logic. Truth be told, Artos and Herne, Gods of the Sky, had not done much to aid her in life. Still, it provided her with comfort more than anything else. It was a comfort to observe the passing of spring with Sumbel. It was a chance for her departed father to come visit her at the Great Feast, and she always put out a chair for him.

When Prudence was feeling deeply alone, she took solace in writing to her father and burning it so that Herne might fly the message to the netherworld for her father to read. She didn't need a response in order to feel like she was no longer alone. She knew he would read it.

"Thank ye."

"For what?"

"Tellin' me, I guess."

He smiled. "You're welcome." Prudence sat behind Cain in the saddle in quiet contemplation. She thought about Cain and his life of sorrow and heartbreak, and in some ways, she could understand his reluctance towards religion. But she couldn't get the image of a teenage Cain out of her head, praying to the goddess, Anu, to smite those that had tortured his sister. It pained Prudence to think of what he must have felt.

It had ripped a piece of Prudence away when Eleanora died, a piece that she might never get back, but she knew in her heart that Elea was at peace in the netherworld; she hoped beyond reason that perhaps her father had found her upon arrival and taken her under his wing, to be her companion where Prudence could not. But Cain... Cain's sister was not dead. She had not died as the water crushed her chest, she was still down there; morphed into a creature of darkness and evil. Perhaps Florence was the reason that Cain had renounced his faith.

After a number of hours, they stopped off. Two people sharing a saddle was uncomfortable and Prudence was relieved to stretch her legs for a moment, freeing up her aching spine from its hunched position. Gypsy seemed to relish the feeling of an unburdened back as well, as his head dropped to the floor and he began grazing.

Cain, however, pulled one of the bags from the back of

the saddle and dumped it against a tree on the side of the path. He began clearing sticks from the ground at their feet to make room for the group to sit. Prudence wriggled and stretched her toes inside her shoes, groaning with satisfaction before helping Cain. Gabe and Shuu stretched their aching joints in turn as Khari held their horses for a moment.

"How long are we going to rest for?" Prudence glanced at Cain. She was eager to keep going and get to the ship as fast as they could, for fear of the soldiers catching up. But Cain didn't seem too hurried.

"We'll stop to eat, but I don't think there's time to rest now. We need to get through Malaine. That's going to be our biggest problem," she reasoned.

"I'm not goin' anywhere till I've had somethin' to eat, *keine*," Khari chuckled.

Gabe pulled a hunk of bread from his pack and threw it at a sprawled-out Khari. He tossed a piece to Shuu, who caught it without looking.

"Thanks, lad."

Cain grabbed a stick and sketched out a few crude lines in the dirt. The shape vaguely looked like the town ahead of them. "Now, you see, we have to get down these main streets." He gestured to his makeshift map. "Thankfully, we're coming from this side of town so we can miss out the market completely—as it's midday, most people will either be there, or be working. If we play it right and stick to the shadows, we should be able to sneak through the main bit of town unnoticed. I can't begin to assume how many soldiers there'll be. I imagine they've searched the rest of Vaerny by now so there will be some

293

there, of course. It could be twenty... it could be a hundred soldiers trawling the streets."

Prudence sighed. If there were lots of soldiers around Malaine, she wasn't so sure they'd manage to get through without someone recognising them. Their faces would be plastered on wanted sheets all over Vaerny by now. Prudence remembered seeing a sketch of Cain with a price on his head in the back of the wagon when the soldiers captured her in Veida. Her heart clenched at the thought of that happening again. She could still feel the cold steel of manacles around her wrists that kept her pinned against the damp, mouldy wall of that cell. She rubbed at her rotten wrist absentmindedly. She looked at Cain.

"There's no point in puttin' it off. Regardless of how many soldiers there are, we won't know until we get there. Let's eat and get going, Cain, I want to be gone from here. I can't stay any longer." He nodded and chucked a stale loaf of bread at her which she caught and ripped into it hungrily. They'd find *The Maiden* and be gone from here soon, with the wind in their sail, taking them somewhere far away that held no misery for them. They could go anywhere in the world. They could leave the Western Tides, there was nothing stopping them now.

THE REST OF THE TRACK WAS RIDDEN IN SILENCE. AS THEY neared the town, feelings of angst could almost be felt in the air. Cain's jaw seemed permanently clenched as soon as the first few houses came into view. Gabe once again fell into miserable silence; he'd not spoken much to anyone since Elea had been shot. Shuu and Khari had been chatting away to one another the entire ride, but even they became quiet as they reached the town. It wasn't the time for talking. Cain pulled his horse up and turned to Prudence.

"You're going to need this." He pulled two cloaks from the bag and handed one to her. He covered himself with the other, hood pulled up over his head, and face in shadow. Prudence followed suit and they moved onward. The men pulled their own coats closer.

She could feel the hairs on the back of her neck stand up as the nerves crawled down her throat and into her gut. At any moment, someone could see Cain's face, or hers, and it would all be over for them. Just one sheet pinned up showing their faces with that reward underneath and crowds would clamour to get their hands on them for that money.

Prudence felt short of breath as they passed the first house. She couldn't imagine how terrified she would feel once they were in the middle of the town with houses and people surrounding them in every direction.

Time stood still as they moved on, passing faces in the street and feeling like every person that they passed had their eyes on them. But after what felt like an eternity, the port came into view and Prudence let out a sigh of relief. They weren't safe yet, but their freedom was in sight. They were so close now, truly. The track down to the docks was stony and the horses picked their way around the biggest stones, wary of moving any quicker than a slow walk.

Stalls lined the wooden walkway leading down to the ships that were anchored just off shore. Dinghies were tied to the planks, ready to transport people and their belongings to their ships. Cain hobbled Gypsy on a patch of grass by the nearest boat as the others waited a short distance away.

"How much for a ride?" He asked the sailor curtly. The man stuck his hand up, two fingers raised, and Cain reached for the pouch tied to his belt. Just as Cain was about to pay the man, a little boy with ochre skin, big bright eyes, and tightly cropped hair ran up to Prudence and tugged at her skirts.

"S'cuse me, miss. You're lookin' fer yer friends, right?" He smirked at her briefly and leaned in close. "Yer crew o' *The Maiden*, aren't ya?" Prudence frowned and glanced at Cain before crouching in front of the kid.

"An' what would make ye think that?"

"I seen 'em. Old man in a cap gave me some coins to pass on a message." Prudence smiled, old man in a cap? That was Mr. Norton without a doubt.

"All right, what do ye know?"

"The name's Taj. I was o'er there playing with ma friends the other day when that old man came up and offered me these coins." He produced a fistful of silver coins from his pocket. "Said to keep an eye out for a group o' people dressed like youse and tell ya that they were leaving the harbour to hide from the soldiers while they waited for ya."

"An' did ye happen to see another little group, four men—two older, one o' the younger ones had short, dark hair?" Prudence felt guilt seep in then. She'd barely spared a thought to Garrick and the rest of the men who'd risked their lives by helping to rescue her in all the chaos. How her heart ached with worry for them all now.

"Oh yes, ma'am, they were 'ere a few days ago, they left on the ship with the rest of yer crew."

Prudence sighed with relief and called Cain over.

"Tell him what you told me."

"Yer quarter master paid me to tell you that there was too much heat in the harbour, so he's moved her away to a little cove round the island. It's only a little ways thataway," he flung his hand over his shoulder in the direction they'd gone. "Shan't take yer more than an hour on horseback." Taj's grubby face grinned up at them, his hand outstretched, expecting payment. Prudence handed him a couple of coins, smiling at him. She liked the little boy, he was sweet in a cheeky way. It was refreshing and a nice change from their dire circumstances of late.

"It'd be a damn sight quicker if ye showed us the way... I can pay ye a few more coins to make it worth your time," said Cain. Taj nodded and turned on his heel in the direction he had pointed. An ungroomed and flea-ridden mule stood tied to a post a few hundred yards away. Taj took the rope and swung his leg over its back. Prudence gripped Cain's arm as he lifted her up behind him onto Gypsy, and the group followed Taj on his donkey down the track.

Despite the rough track that wound its way around the edge of the island, they made good time getting to the cove. Prudence felt the pressure of the oncoming army lessen as they moved away from the town and into the rough heathland. The soldiers and violence that they had been running from seemed far away and it gave her hope. Hope that they would succeed.

There was no doubt in the eyes of the law that Cain and his crew deserved to be imprisoned and hanged, but Prudence could only see the man in front of her and she knew that he deserved to escape and be free. She also knew that they could share that freedom together, away from the heartache that they had both suffered.

Taj hopped off his mule and walked to the top of a narrow track that led to the shore. A row boat was waiting for them. He held out his hand for the gelding's rope as Cain and Prudence dismounted. Cain breathed in deeply. *The Bloody Maiden* was in sight, right in front of them. She was so close that they could almost smell her, feel the rough edges of her bow, hear the wind roaring in their ears as she cut through the water, swift and sure. Cain was home.

"I don't suppose, sir... that yer in need of a cabin boy? Me mam died in the autumn and it's not easy being a beggar." Taj squirmed where he stood and looked up at Cain, who seemed gigantic in comparison.

"I could be... you've been very helpful thus far. But it's not an easy life kid."

"I'm no' afraid of working hard sir, I promise." Prudence smiled softly at him, her eyes turned to Cain, pleading. They couldn't leave him here alone.

Shuu ruffled the boy's short hair and grinned. "Come on, Cap, we could do with a powder monkey on board."

"All right then, but you've gotta earn it, ok?"

Taj nodded and grinned a gappy smile at them both. Cain's pace was fast as he moved down the track, bits of gravel kicking up under his feet as his steps got quicker and quicker, until he was almost running. Prudence followed close behind with Taj, and the men pushed the dinghy into the water as the wind picked up and the surface moved like a restless child.

The ocean fought back as the oars cut into the surface pulling with all its might. Prudence could see the men on deck. Mr. Norton stood at the helm and flashed a crooked smile at her. After a few minutes of rowing, they were almost at the ship, almost home and safe. Prudence glanced at Cain but he was looking off in the opposite direction, his eyes squinting at something in the distance.

"What is it?" she asked as Khari dropped an oar.

"Look."

Prudence used her hands to shield her eyes from the sun. At the very edge of the cliff that formed their secret little cove, Prudence could just make out a dark shape. Her eyes tried to adjust and as it moved closer, Prudence could see the rigging.

"Bollocks. We're done for."

Cain gripped the oar. "Not necessarily." He yelled across to Mr. Norton, "Weigh anchor! Make way!" Prudence stared at him.

"You don't really think we can outrun them, do you?"

His face was solemn. "Or die trying."

FROM THE DINGHY, PRUDENCE COULD SEE THE MEN RUNNING around on deck. Mr. Norton yelled commands and looked worried, a look that truly unnerved her. Cain gripped the oar tighter in his grasp and pulled with as much might as he could muster. *The Maiden*'s anchor cranked up her side and she started to move away from them.

Cain and Khari rowed as fast as they could, gaining speed on the larger vessel. The dinghy's front bashed into the side of the ship and Cain threw their sole pack up and over onto the deck before pushing Prudence towards the net to climb.

A sound like Artos himself had come down to smite them almost launched Prudence off the net as *The Bloody Maiden* lurched wildly to the right. She struggled to hold on with only one working arm. The governor's ship had opened fire on the pirate crew as they tried to flee. Prudence managed to get a foot over the side and scrambled onto the deck, making way for the men and their small companion.

"Can't we go any faster?!" The governor's ship had the advantage of being mobile before they were and it wouldn't take long for the space between them to disappear. The rest of her little group made it onto the ship. Pru breathed a momentary sigh of relief. Cain barged past his men, eyes fixed on the helm, and promptly took over. The ship began to make progress but Prudence stared over the side. She dreaded going back to that cold dark cell.

Another roar exploded in her ears, so close that she ducked. Splinters of wood flew over her head, and beyond the sound of ringing, Prudence heard a scream come from somewhere. She rushed to the helm beside Cain and Mr. Norton, the terror evident on her face.

"We're not going to make it, Cain."

"Yes, we are." He gritted his teeth and clenched the wheel, his knuckles popping up turning a fine shade of ivory under the pressure.

"*Cain.*"

"Do not proceed to tell me something that you do not know, Prudence." He spat the words out in the flurry of anger, but Prudence could hear the fear behind them. The sea grew rougher as they made their way out of the cove, the governor's ship following close behind.

"What are we gonna do Cap'n?! This is madness!" cried Mr. Norton.

Cain ignored him. "Raise all the canvas another five degrees, Mr. Lowell!"

"Aye, Captain!" Mr. Lowell yelled at the rest of the crew and they dashed to raise the canvas higher. "We need at least three more knots if we're to outrun her, Captain!"

"Raise the gallants!" Cain gestured to Gabe to take over the wheel as he ran to help Mr. Lowell. It didn't take long for the wind in the canvas to increase their speed. Cain rejoined Mr. Norton, Gabe, and Prudence at the helm, pacing the deck as he kept checking the distance between them and the fleet with his spyglass.

They moved as swiftly as possible, cutting through the water like a blade. The gap between *The Bloody Maiden* and the governor's ship wasn't much, but it was enough for now. It felt as if the chase had been going on for hours. The distance closed and then widened, always changing but never enough to make a difference to either side.

But their likelihood of survival seemed slim. The fleet was upon them, no matter how far they ran, they would follow. Prudence couldn't see a way out of this, other than dying. Worried, she gripped Cain's arm with her good hand. She hadn't moved from his side since they rejoined the crew. She wasn't going anywhere now.

"Marry me." Cain pulled one of the rings from his finger—it was all he had to hand as the waves crashed against the hull, and cannons fired from the rear, blasting holes in the deck of the closest ship behind them. "Marry me, Prudence."

Prudence stared at him, wide-eyed. She didn't know whether to laugh or cry. "Are you deranged!?" She cast him a look of wild incredulity. The fact that he was proposing at all was surprising. Cain struck Prudence as the type of man who would always want the option of freedom. They locked eyes and she was filled with a sudden rush of warmth. It was madness. But she loved him and wanted nothing more than to marry him right there in that moment. An ear-piercing scream interrupted them as one of the crew was shot off the rigging and fell into the unyielding sea.

"Ye can't propose to a woman simply because we face almost certain death, Cain."

Cain grasped her hand and looked hard into her eyes, though his voice was low and his gaze soft. "I said marry me, damn it woman. Do what you're told for once in your life."

She nodded and grinned as he slipped the ring onto her finger, grabbing her by the waist as the devil danced in his eyes. "The captain I first met would've seen commitment of any kind as worse than the gallows,"

Prudence teased. Cain ducked as a cannon ball shot through the back of the ship and rushed past them.

"It appears you've tamed me."

"How long before you get sick and tired of it?" Prudence wanted to be with this complicated man, but his mood changed like the tides. Cain let out a dry laugh and grinned.

"How long? Till it kills us both."

14

ULTIMATE END

"M r. Norton!" Cain yelled, "would ye do the honour of marrying us?" Prudence pulled back from Cain, looking confused. "Did ye not know Mr. Norton was a Caeli chaplain in a past life?" he grinned.

"Will you do me the honour of marrying me, right here, right now, Prudence?"

She kissed him urgently. "I will."

In a blur, Mr. Norton had whipped Prudence away into her cabin and threw a raggedy dress at her. "Yer can't go getting married in a man's clothes. It should be done proper." He turned away as Prudence threw her britches and shirt onto the bed in exchange for the faded white garment.

"Where did ye get this from?"

"Och, had it fer years. Raided a vessel off the coast of Pirn, a merchant of fine silks and cotton. He had chests of ladies' dresses in the hold. Sold most of 'em 'o course, but this one musta got forgotten about in the back o' the wardrobe. Seems like fate, no?"

Prudence slipped the soft fabric over her head and did up the buttons on her chest. It fit perfectly. She wasn't much of a believer in fate but there was no denying the lucky coincidence. The ship lurched violently to the left and she almost fell over. Finally, she pulled her hair loose from its braid at the back of her head as the sound of cannons hit the stern.

Cain stood before her at the helm of his ship. Chaos surrounded them as men yelled and cannon balls flew, destroying things before their very eyes, but they didn't see it. Mr. Norton cleared his throat and took their hands together.

"We haven't much time so perhaps the short version is best... Cain, if ye will."

Cain squeezed Prudence's fingers. "I'm a little rusty on the words, forgive me..."

> I take you my heart at the rising of the sun
> And the early morning dew.
> To protect and to share
> Through everything we face.
> Through all our lives together
> In all our lives, may we be reborn
> That we may meet and know
> And love again,
> And remember.

He slid the ring onto her fourth finger and let out a long breath. Mr. Norton smiled. "Prudence."

I take you my heart at the rising of the
    moon
And the setting of the stars.
To love and to honour
Through all that may come.
Through all our lives together
In all our lives, may we be reborn
That we may meet and know
And love again,
And remember.

Cain's grasp on Prudence's hand tightened as he pulled her close and their lips collided to the sound of a cannon destroying what was once Prudence and Eleanora's cabin. There was no time for happiness now. There would be time for that later... if they survived. In the time since they had reached the ship, they had travelled away from Vaerny and towards Thaira, but it would still be some time before they reached her shores and the aid of Madame Durrant.

The fleet gained speed on *The Bloody Maiden* as the wind took their side. It would not be long before they sunk her. *The Maiden* would drift to the bottom of the sea with her crew falling closely behind her. The Crown had hunted them for long enough. All they needed was to reach Thaira in time.

Maybe then they could have the extra help that they needed from the island's cannons. Madame Durrant would assist them, Prudence was sure. Cain was like a child to her and there was no way she'd let her beautiful town of thieves fall under control of the Crown. It was her whole life.

As they progressed, more of the fleet's ships joined the chase, *The Maiden* was now being hunted by five of the fastest ships in this corner of the Western Tides. There wasn't much hope to be had... if any.

"Cain, we must think of something, it can't end like this. Not now." He frowned and pursed his lips.

There seemed to be no way out, no clear solution in her mind. Her thoughts raced to his sister, Florence, down there in the cold, merciless ocean; of Eleanora crumpled and broken on a dirt track; of Cain's mother walking away as he was sold into slavery; of herself... singing that night in the tavern, unaware that her entire life would change... her bloody and injured body in the dark; of crying and screaming in her grief... they had both endured too much pain.

There must be something that they could do, something that would save them both from further heartbreak—they'd had enough to last a multitude of lifetimes. It was their time for some peace.

"Cain... what if—" Prudence gripped his arm but hesitated in her thought. He watched her expectantly. "What if we crashed *The Maiden*?" Cain's eyes baulked. "Just hear me out. Cain, they're never going to stop chasing her, or you. But... if they see the ship crash and think ye dead, they'll have to give up." Cain stayed silent for a moment, taking it all in. Another explosion, minor this time, grazed the side of the ship, drowning out their conversation. A grunt of pain behind them caught their attention. Mr. Norton leant heavily against the bannister, his hand clutching his shoulder. Red slowly soaked through the shirt, his hand clasped around the thick splinter of wood that impaled him. He laughed dryly.

"I always said ye'd be the death of me, Cain. I'm an old man, didn't have much left of this life left anyway... and it'd be an honour." Prudence stifled a sob as a tear slid down her cheek. "I'll steer her where ye want her to go lad, don't you worry none. Ye've got a wife to be lookin' after now, tha's more important." Cain clenched his teeth and enveloped Mr. Norton in a tight embrace. His voice was hoarse.

"I don't know what I ever did to deserve a friend such as you, Horace." He sniffed and Prudence could see the tears in his eyes when he blinked. "Forget Thaira then, sail for the closest bit of rock ye can see, friend. There should be an outcrop of rock a few leagues ahead if I remember the map right." He clasped Mr. Norton's hand in his and shared an unspoken farewell.

Cain took Prudence's hand and pulled her towards his cabin. Inside the door, on a small hook, hidden behind layers of clothes, was a locket. Cain slipped it on and tucked it under his shirt before grabbing a couple of items and shoving them into a canvas sack.

"It was Florence's, it broke when they bound her. I kept it... as a reminder." She took his hand and squeezed gently. It didn't need an explanation.

Outside the cabin, the crew were doing their best to keep the ship in one piece and afloat but in their eyes, they knew it to be a dying cause. Prudence felt a pang of guilt at seeing them.

"Shouldn't we tell the crew what we're planning?"

"No, the fleet would see people jumping overboard, they would know..." Prudence could see how much it hurt him to say the words, to sacrifice the men that had been his family for so many years. But self-preservation and a selfish desire to save one another took hold, making their choice for them. It would be a sacrifice that they would have to live with. Prudence made a silent prayer to Artos and Herne that the men may be delivered safely to land, that they may not be harmed, but in her heart, she felt it to be a futile request. Men were going to die and it would be her fault.

THE TIME DREW NEARER AS THE BARREN, ROCKY SPIT OF land that held Vaerny's worn, old lighthouse, Talah, came into view. Prudence and Cain hovered by the side, steeling themselves for the moment they would have to jump and abandon everyone to their fate. Prudence was unsure what would come after, only that for now, all they could do was abandon ship and hope for the best.

She watched the men around her as they did their best to keep *The Bloody Maiden* going. They were fearful but determined. Charlie was doing his best to reinforce the wood where she had split near the bow; Rupert and Thomas were working side by side, their eyes every so often drifting to each other; Jorge, fiercely loyal to his ship and crew, was yelling orders to the crew, a rough, passionate scream coming from his lips; and finally, Mr. Lowell, high in the rigging, so sure-footed despite the danger. It pained her heart.

It was unclear how they would get off this island, if it could indeed be called an island. Talah was small and grey, merely rock and sand. As they drew closer, Mr. Norton shared a grave look with Cain. His face was now ashen and the blood had stained most of his shirt. Prudence knew that he couldn't hold on for much longer. Her heart ached for him and she silently thanked him for his sacrifice.

The fleet continued to follow as if they were skirting around the edge of the rock to keep distance between them, little did the sailors know that they were heading straight for it. With a heavy sigh and one last look at the loyal crew around him, Cain slipped inconspicuously over the side of the ship, with Prudence right behind him. She strained to hold onto the net with her good arm. They stayed like that, waiting for the right moment. It would be a close call; they couldn't jump until they were facing the rock and out of sight of the fleet's sailors. If they timed it wrong or didn't swim quickly enough, they would be caught in the wreckage along with everyone else. Prudence took a deep breath and shut her eyes.

The Bloody Maiden steered straight towards a piece of rock that jutted sharply up and grew tall out of the water. The crunch of wood against rock pierced Prudence's ears and she heard the shouts of men from the deck. They panicked, trying everything that they could to steer away before it was too late.

"Are you ready?" Cain looked at her. "Mrs. Morris?" She smiled at her new name and nodded, taking his strong hand in hers. Cain watched the fleet behind them. "Jump... now!"

The bow groaned and bent before snapping in two. Under the rush of water in her ears, Prudence could still make out the screams and the gut-wrenching crack as the hull broke bit by bit, condemning anyone who was still inside. The first ship in the fleet had been following too close and couldn't steer away in time. Instead it ploughed into the back of *The Maiden* with a deafening smack as its men were thrown forward into a mess of broken wood and rock. Cain felt for Prudence's hand under the water and tugged gently.

"We have to go." With one last glance at the helm and Mr. Norton's face as he braced against the impact, Prudence swam as best she could against the might of the waves, towards land. Her head just dipped below the icy surface as her husband's hand slipped from her grasp.

THE
WAYWARD
DAMNED

COMING SOON

ACKNOWLEDGMENTS

The Bloody Maiden was a book five years in the making. It started with a mere spark of an idea in a lecture hall one windy autumn day when my professor talked of the beauty in the season, that what makes it all the more beautiful than other seasons was its relationship with death. Of things ending before they come back anew.

It was in this lecture hall with this inspirational teacher that the debate of the justification of murder gave that spark of an idea exactly what it needed—a focus, a concept that the story enveloped and allowed me to explore the darkest depths of morally grey characters, societal ideals around ethics, and the ever elusive 'good' bad guy that all readers love to cheer for.

I want to thank Seamus for his ever-stimulating lectures, his infuriating tactics of leaving me to stew angrily before letting me voice my opinions, his passion for literature and its exploration of the human condition, and his guidance during my years at university. I would not be the person I am today without his input, and this book would never have been written without him.

I would also like to thank the entire English department, especially Devon. Your wise words, your passion, your wacky, kind, badass character for all those years of support. I miss our lectures fiercely. You are one of my biggest inspirations and I'll cherish our time together for my entire life.

To my best friend, soulmate and alpha reader, Des, 'thank you' does not come close to expressing what I wish to say to you. You are my rock, my biggest cheerleader, Maiden's number one fan and there isn't a day that goes by where I'm not eternally grateful to have you in my life. That serendipitous day so long ago where I began speaking to a fellow writer about our stories, both of us in search of feedback - I think of it as destined to be. For how else can you explain such a strong, powerful relationship to have blossomed from such a casual meeting?

To Elora, my confidant, my safe place, my dearest friend - I owe you so much. I shall forever be indebted to the universe for bringing us together for I cannot, and do not wish, to imagine my life without you in it. Our unlikely meeting was no doubt fate, to find someone so much your twin and develop a bond so strong so quickly, there is no other explanation. You have supported me, laughed with me, cried with me and bolstered me every day since our first meeting. I adore you and cannot wait to see the success that I know awaits you. I don't know what I'd do without you both in my life, my found family, who mean so much.

To my editor and wonderful friend, Brittany, you are to sum it up in one word: elysian - beautiful and creative, divinely inspired, peaceful and *perfect*. TBM would not be what it is today without your incredible insight, assistance, support and brilliance. I could not have asked for a better editor, or friend.

I'd also like to thank Kristin for her absolutely breath-taking covers. You went above and beyond and managed to perfectly capture exactly what I wanted for Maiden's cover when I didn't even know myself - that to me is magic.

I'd also like to thank my brother and artist, James, for his beautiful illustrations that made the inside of *The Bloody Maiden* look so beautiful. I can't wait to see what we come up with for book two, I just know it's going to be awesome.

To my family - thank you for putting up with my whining and inherently mad conversations over the years, and for never once questioning that I would one day get to this stage - it made all the difference.

And finally, to everyone who has taken even the slightest interest in my writing - you've helped keep the passion alive even at times where it felt like it might be gone forever. I hope Maiden gives you value - regardless of whether that value is enjoyment, inspiration or simply gets you arguing over who is the real 'bad guy'.

If you work it out, let me know, I'm still undecided myself.